THE BAY OF LOVE
AND SORROWS

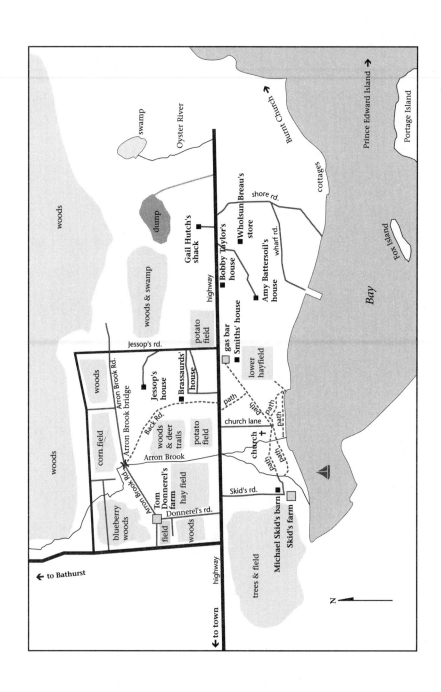

The Bay of Love
and Sorrows

DAVID ADAMS RICHARDS

M&S

Canadian Cataloguing in Publication Data

Richards, David Adams, 1950-
The bay of love and sorrows

ISBN 0-7710-7458-1

I. Title.

PS8585.I17B38 1998   C813´.54   C98-931298-4
PR9199.3.R53B38 1998

We acknowledge the financial support of the Government of Canada through the Book Publishing Industry Development Program for our publishing activities. We further acknowledge the support of the Canada Council of the Arts and the Ontario Arts Council for our publishing program.

The author wishes to thank his editor, Ellen Seligman

Typeset in Minion by M&S, Toronto

Printed and bound in Canada

McClelland & Stewart Inc.
The Canadian Publishers
481 University Avenue
Toronto, Ontario
M5G 2E9

1 2 3 4 5   02 01 00 99 98

For Alistair MacLeod
and, too, for our Lady of light

THE BAY OF LOVE
AND SORROWS

PART ONE

ONE

Karrie's father owned the gas bar just above Oyster River, a small gas bar, a hang-out for kids, with a penned-in mass of dark, worn tires in the back yard – tires worn by miles of travel to places going nowhere along the hard-bitten coast – and with the grass unkempt and bordered by a rundown fence. A circular drive led to their gas pumps and small store that sat dead in the heat on summer days.

Tommie Donnerel was a neighbour. He was busy renovating his house, building a new room for his brother and restoring the front porch. Sometimes he would come down to the gas bar for a moment. Or he would be seen at the dances at the community centre. Karrie liked him, but he never seemed to pay much attention to her.

He had the run of the farm now that his parents were dead, and people seemed to empathize with him, because his older brother was retarded.

Karrie liked to think of him as heroic, and to think that she was willing to invest in him because of his sterling qualities, which were apparent to everyone.

The trouble, if it could be said to be trouble, was that his best friend was Michael Skid. Michael was the person who helped him with the renovating of his house, the one with him after the death and during the funeral of his parents, who were killed in an accident at Arron Brook. Karrie had to weigh this as a serious problem, for, all in all, she wished to be liked and side with the right people on her road. And Michael Skid was well known as wild and unpredictable. Besides this, she didn't like the way he looked at her. And there was that fling he had had with Nora Battersoil. And what became of it no one knew. But Karrie's stepmother said he was awful, and that like most rich people from town he loved to argue about the world and used some kind of drugs.

So Karrie bided her time and waited. And just as she suspected, the summer following Tom's parents' death the two men had a falling-out of some kind. In fact, she heard they had almost had a fistfight. Michael went away, and Tom was left to finish the porch and the room alone.

For a long while, Tom seemed to be unmoved by Karrie or her reddish blonde hair. She had invited him over to the local graduation party at the church centre – as soon as she had heard about the falling-out between him and Michael – but he had not come.

She then sent him an invitation to come to her graduation, which took place a week later. Yet, in the cramped auditorium with so many sweaty people, the gowns of the graduates half-askew, and the outside June evening pale with gusts of heat, she couldn't see him.

She won the prize for Home Economics, but when she received it she felt that no one clapped for her like they did the others.

4

Then she went to the prom with a boy from her class, who wore an audacious white tuxedo and kept saying he knew where all the parties were. They ended up driving the roads in his father's car until after midnight, finally finding a party at a house of a boy neither of them knew. The boy, whose name was Lyle McNair, saying: "Come – get acquainted – please don't stand back, now."

They spent the evening sitting in the kitchen with Mr. and Mrs. McNair, who tried to make them feel welcome.

But after an hour Karrie insisted that she go home. She let her date kiss her once, smelling stale aftershave on his white chin. Going up to her bedroom she combed the perm out of her hair, and got into bed with a romance novel.

Sometimes that summer she would go to the first Mass on Sunday instead of the late Mass, because Tom was known to do so. After Mass one morning she stayed behind to light a candle, just to see if he would stay behind too. But he didn't. And she left the church by the back way and ran home down the narrow path.

Later, in July, she walked the highway when she knew he would be bringing hay up from the lower field. She would pretend to be surprised every time she saw him.

This, in fact, went on for a long while. She was very sad about this, and quite sensitive. And she would write in her diary: "How can he go out into the middle of the bay alone? I went out to the shore – but as always – he came in on the far side of the wharf and didn't even notice me – why is he so cruel?"

It was very strange, but all this made her feel somewhat special. She found her stepmother cruel to her too, and bossy. Especially once when Vincent, Tom's brother, came by the gas bar with a note written on his shirt that Tom had pinned there. There was a great deal of gaiety about this note, and everyone had joined in this gaiety except her. Her stepmother had laughed the loudest, looking around at everyone with her face beet-red and startled.

"Please send home by ten o'clock," the note read. Vincent started laughing also, without knowing why.

And then one night, Karrie invited Vincent into the house for a Coke. The house was very warm, had a miserable quality permeating it, which Karrie herself had understood from early youth. It was not that the house, with its pink shutters and long wainscotting, was a violent house. It was the absence of affection.

Karrie wandered about, as if sleepwalking, got Vincent a Coke and a dish of ice cream, and watched him eat at the kitchen table. It was her stepmother, Dora's, quart of strawberry ice cream, and Dora watched her to see how much she was going to take.

"Do you like that, Vincent?" Karrie said.

He looked up at her, wiped his mouth, and said, "I gotta come home by ten."

"Would you like me to walk you home, Vincent?" she declared suddenly, as she rested her pretty head on her hand in a bored way. There was a fly walking up the wall behind him, and watching it made her eyes brilliant and bright.

"Let him find his own way," her stepmother said, in characteristic meanness that Karrie was so familiar with. She looked over at Dora, who was only eleven years older than herself, and said nothing.

Karrie put on a kerchief and lipstick, and she and Vincent started on their way. It was well after ten.

They could hear the waves crashing far beyond them and, beyond the dark immovable trees, they heard the roar of Arron Brook, which always stayed high, and which Vincent was told never to go near.

Thin clouds swept the night sky, like crooked hawks, and the moon shone on the old potato field to their right, behind some forlorn hedges. Wrappers and cardboard lay in the ditches that once had many flowers. It made Karrie melancholy and sad to think of this road, and those broken trees, and her mother, who used to come in from work every night at quarter past five all winter long, and who died during a simple appendix operation.

As they approached the halfway mark of their journey Karrie ran out of things to ask Vincent about Tom, and things to say about herself, so she kept talking about the moon, and the clouds, and wasn't it a lovely night – and how many more nights would they have just like this?

They saw a man approaching them along the road. His body looked strong and fit, without ever taking pains to be.

"Tommie – Tommie," Vincent yelled, and ran up to him, patting him all over the chest and shoulders. "Tommie, Tommie."

"Thank God," Tom said. It was at this moment, and with a certain amount of emotion, that Karrie realized how protective Tom was of his brother.

"I brought him home for you," Karrie said, and emotion rang in her voice.

"Thank you," Tommie said. "Thank you, thank you. My God, I thought he had gone up Arron Brook."

"Thank you, thank you," Vincent said, turning around. "But she has to come and see my puppy."

"Oh, the puppy," Tommie said, smiling.

"It doesn't matter," Karrie said.

"Oh no – come on up to the house – come on – have a cup of tea – all right?" Tom said. "Please, I want you to – I wanted to invite you over before now."

"Okay," she said.

And off they went, the three of them together.

The puppy, named Maxwell, stayed in Vincent's part of the house, and Vincent had his own key to the door. He was proud when he was able to open this door, and prouder still that Maxwell ran to him before anyone and began to pee. Karrie did not like puppies very much but she pretended to for Vincent's sake. And she patted its matted fur with her painted fingernails, crouching down on her haunches.

Vincent was very pleased that Karrie could see his pictures of his mom and dad, and even more pleased when she said she liked the room, and found it "just right" for him.

She had a cup of tea. The wind was blowing, and the trees waved in the darkness. Far below them they could see the street-light over her house, which her father was proud of.

Each time Tom spoke she would nod and look away from him, and then bite at her lower lip, as if afraid that she was going to say something inappropriate. He seemed so strong and self-reliant at this moment that she felt he wouldn't look upon her as anything but a schoolgirl. And as she sat there she felt her legs shaking just slightly.

She finished her tea too quickly, she thought, and then thought she was too abrupt when she said she didn't want another.

"Do you want me to walk you home?" Tom said.

"Well, okay," she said, as if angry with something.

And they started down the road together.

"I didn't come to your graduation party, or your graduation either," he said.

"I know," she said. There was a peculiar emphasis on the word *know* that sounded, in the dark night, longing and sensuous.

"I wanted to – but I don't know what to do at them things – and then I wanted to tell you that in church – but you were busy lighting candles, I think to your mom's memory, and so I couldn't. And then – well, you ran out the back way, while I waited for you. I haven't been able to figure out when I was going to see you at the right time. A long time ago I tried to ask you for a dance – but I couldn't get up the nerve, I s'pose."

8

"You did –?" she asked. There was a tiny smile at the corner of her mouth, just visible, which because of the way she was walking, with her arms folded like a country girl, seemed indispensable to her character.

"I don't know 'nough to go up to no graduation," he said. "I shoulda answered ya – and then I thought ya might have been mad at me – or eventually I thought you had a boyfriend – Bobby Taylor is always over there at the store."

She burst out laughing and turned and hugged him. He could feel her warm body press into him, and he was somehow overwhelmed by her. Instinctively he felt he must hold her the right way or lose her to someone else.

"Bobby Taylor," she laughed. "He's already engaged!"

She looked up at him in a very strange way, as if asking a question, and then, without finding an answer, hugged him hard again.

TWO

Snow started falling by November, like ash out of the sky, over the tortured clearcut to the north.

The sun sat all day in one angry spot, which showed a cluster of dead crab-apple trees, and sometimes in the wind there was a rush of small, grey birds, taking wing at the exact same time. The potato field was nothing more than stubble and cold earth, and the great bay had turned black and solid.

Karrie had gone away to a community college and Tom was alone. He would take walks down the dry lane, in the afternoon, while the sky was red, and come home, seeing Maxwell sitting near its doghouse with its tin dish.

That fall there was a large ten-point buck roaming the chopdown, and by the second week of November Tom was in the woods every day crossing Arron Brook and waiting for it above the small interlinking deer trails.

The path to Brassaurds' lay through thick woods, where the buck had left scrapes, and once in a while Tom would see the tawny bronzed back of the two year-old doe just out of sight along the upper ridge.

The path to Brassaurds' never seemed to catch the light of the weak sun that filtered in strange dark sadness in Arron Brook's pools. Old deadwood and fallen leaves and parts of broken machinery lay along this trail, where the wind seemed to whisper. And halfway along the path was the old gravestone, half buried and moss-eaten, of Guillaume Brassaurd.

One day during the last week of November Tom put on his boots, took his rifle, and walked far into the woods, almost to Brassaurds' property. He picked up a fresh trail, and in a snow-squall at mid-afternoon saw the buck coming towards him, nose to the ground.

He fired somewhat thoughtlessly, and was suddenly sorry. The buck turned sideways and ran, and Tom followed it, picking up a trail of blood, just before dark.

"Damn me – the poor old boy's gone to lay down," Tom thought. He was angry with himself, because he thought of the doe, and how she was alone. He stood and looked at the trees, and felt sad. Then he heard another shot, from a shotgun, very close to him.

He waited a moment and walked, bent over, through some tangle and brush, and in a few minutes came out on the old deer trail near Brassaurds' property line. He saw the buck down and Madonna Brassaurd kneeling beside it with a scarf about her face, and a twenty-gauge pump in her hands. The buck had its head turned back, its tines dug into the snow behind it.

She looked up at Tom and, taking the scarf down, smiled.

"You sent it right to me," she said.

"No," he said. "It was real sick after I shot it –"

"Oh, but I was the one who killed it," she said. "Karrie's gone?"

"Commun'ty college," Tom said.

"Oh – I bet she's already at you to take upgrading, so you be smart as she is, or she'll fly away from you."

Tom gave a laugh because of Madonna's remarkable eyes fastened upon him. "What are you lads doin in here, poachin moose? I found half a carcass up near Arron – and you'll find a 30.30 bullet in your buck."

"Tom, yer just scared there won't be any left for you," she said.

The Brassaurds always said what they felt others were thinking, and never minded what they said. And the fact that Tom was very protective of animals made this remark scald him. But many untruths had been said about him, just as they had been said about his parents, who were both wild, and he felt the untruths would continue.

"Don't want you up on my property killing moose," he said, though he liked Madonna and always had.

"Do you know who came home last night?" she said, deflecting his statement with customary nonchalance, as she took out her knife.

"No – don't," he said.

"Mike Skid."

Tom didn't answer. The wind blew against his open coat, and his grey eyes watered.

"He's been to India and back," she said.

"Well, he's got time on his hands." Tom smiled. "Don't he?"

She glanced up at him and cursed, her hands over blood, and said: "He's turning into something of a photographer – and is going to put all his photographs out in a book. A publisher has already talked to him. So I want him to take some photos of me – it'd be my chance."

Then she moved around him on the path, and pumped her shells out. "And he is writing an article about the private school he went to and is waiting for the right time to publish it."

Tom had heard all of this before. He felt a little resentful that Michael was now telling these same stories to Madonna Brassaurd.

Tom looked at the air directly in front of him and could see the sky blurred by small flakes of snow.

Madonna bent over to take the buck's testicles in her hands and cut them off, but then frowned: "Tom – you do this – will you? – and I'll give you some steak."

When they were finished, he helped her drag the buck out to the road near her property where she had left her sled.

"Are you going to tag this?" he said.

"Tom, why don't you give me your tag? I used mine up." The wind blew stiff against her old orange cap, and against the deer's dull, sad, staring eyes. Again she looked at him and, with her scarf pulled up over her face, she resembled the bandit she was.

Tom made his way back along the path to his house after dark. Snow came out of the sky in large, wet flakes. There was blood on the path, and the intestines near the river were golden in the cold sharp air.

He for one couldn't travel the world. He liked it where he was. An old piece of machinery covered in new-fallen snow, off on the side of the path, and the old tombstone sunken into the earth with white snow falling on it proved this to him once again. He breathed the air, was happy with his lot. And then suddenly a small flame of angry thought flickered inside him, as he turned towards Arron Brook. Because, having known Michael for three years, things remained unresolved between them.

The first was the remark Michael had made about Karrie, two winters before.

They had gone to the Christmas party at the community centre. Tom walked the floor all night, going by her table. Yet he couldn't find the courage to ask her for a dance. Finally, she got up and began dancing with another girl and Tom, embarrassed, left the building and started home. The snow was piled very high on the side of the road, and snow was still falling out of a black sky.

Michael came outside and, walking behind him, teased him all the way home.

"If you can't ask her to dance, how'll you ever get it in her?"

The remark was forgotten the next day, because Tom knew Michael was so drunk he hadn't remembered anything. And Tom never mentioned Karrie to him again.

The second issue was the way Michael spoke about his past that Christmas night. He told Tom about his former girlfriend.

"Don't laugh," he kept saying, as if he was used to people laughing at true emotion in his life, or as if he laughed at this himself, at the private school he had gone to as a boy. Then he cursed her to the ground, in a show of bravado.

But Tom found nothing at all to laugh about, and felt pity for Michael cursing her. Her name was Nora Battersoil.

"I was wild, I guess. I told her we could go away. I waited for her to come and meet me – we were going to run away together. We were seventeen, eighteen. I had flunked out of school that year, and had fourteen hundred dollars saved. God knows where we would have ended up. But she should have contacted me – the fuckin bitch. I never would have betrayed her!"

"I know about it," Tom said.

"Well, then – do you know why she broke up?"

"No," Tommie said, but he was lying.

Michael did not speak about her any more. He drank from a pint bottle of Captain Morgan's white rum, and, holding a piece of meat pie in his hand, he began to wave it about half-angrily, half-jubilantly. He spoke about being forced to go to private school and having to wear a uniform when he was eleven years old. How his mother and father were small-town snobs to send him away. And how it had ruined his life, because he couldn't make friends there, and was bullied, and then found it hard to make friends here. He stared at Tom a long time, his eyes glittering with drink, his meat pie with a bite out of it, his head cocked sideways. "Yes," he said suddenly, "I'll show you it!"

"What will you show me?"

"You're the only one I'll show it to, you're the only friend I have."

And he took an envelope with the draft of an article he was working on from his inside coat pocket. It was written on regular lined binder pages, in red and blue pen, scratched and scribbled over. Tom initially felt privileged that Michael would show him this article. But as he read it he discovered dark secrets, which ultimately took the form of tattling on others.

"You can't publish this, Michael," Tom said, embarrassed.

"No – I will get them back," Michael said simply. "I don't care, for myself. I just have to wait for the right time. I have taped a dozen of them – I started when I was there. When the time comes – I was eighty-five pounds when I went there and had no one to look out for me."

He spoke about the dorms, the prevalence of deceit, the mean suppers, the sanctioned sexual bullying of other boys, the drama teacher, Mr. Love, who himself was sexually harassing boys, and had forced him to play Juliet and wear a smock and dress.

The night of the play, with the mothers in attendance, during the balcony scene when he was supposed to say, "What's in a name," Michael had bent over, lifted his fine dress up, and wiggling his bum had said: "Lookie here, Romeo – pure Capulet."

He was given a month's detention. Tom looked once again at the article and smiled kindly.

"I wouldn't publish it – if people are going to be hurt by it. It's just not right. If it's going to hurt innocent people as well as –"

Tom broke off. Who was *he*, with his grade-eight education, to say anything? Still, for some strange reason he was very adept at picking out what was wrong with the article. And what he had picked out immediately, which he couldn't articulate, was Michael's ego, his lack of introspection.

Michael took a drink of rum, with great self-esteem, and said: "Well, what do you know – have you been to Ryerson?"

"Well, no – nothing," Tom replied simply, handing the article back. But he did not like the way Michael used his education against him to end the discussion.

The third and most important issue, the one that bothered Tom more than the others combined, involved a suit. This happened at the time of his parents' death. Tom was going to wear the only suit he had, an old light-brown suit of his father's, to the funeral. But Michael took him aside.

"Let me give you mine," he said, and loaned him his new black one. Tom was extremely grateful. Just as he was grateful for everything else Michael did during that period. Unfortunately, he forgot to get the suit cleaned and give it back.

One evening, a few months later, after Tom had worked all day, Michael visited with the idea of going out to the bar in Neguac. He was intoxicated, delighted with frivolity, yet Tom still had had all the inside work to do on the room he was building for Vincent. Michael began to walk behind him playfully, attempting to ruin Tom's concentration.

"You're wasting your whole life," Tom said, after he had warned Michael three or four times to stop. "And you can't recapture it once it's gone, boy."

It was at dusk and because of the yellow sawdust a strange light filtered through the new double-paned window. Tom smiled and playfully grabbed Michael's ear.

"You might not have wasted your life but you still can't afford a suit for a family funeral," Michael snapped.

As soon as Michael said this, Tom knew he wished he hadn't. There was a pause. A board that had been lying across the sawhorse at an angle dropped to the floor.

After Michael's comment, Tom never felt the same towards him. And he could never feel the same again. He walked across the room, to the kitchen, took money from the drawer, 426 dollars, and handed it to him, but Michael refused to take it, saying the suit was not important, and left the house. The next day, Tom had Michael's suit dry-cleaned and sent back to him. They had not spoken since.

Thinking of all of this, of Michael's cavalier attitude towards Karrie, of the pettiness of the article, of the meanness about the suit, Tom frowned, spat, and felt homesick even though he was so near to his house.

Madonna got home dragging the buck on the sled, the rope frozen to her mittens. It was now well after dark, and sparks flew up from her chimney, and a cold wave of snow fell over the field. In this gloom she saw Michael Skid standing near the shed in his long coat and high insulated boots.

She and her younger brother, Silver, hauled the buck inside, sliced holes in its back tendons, and hung it from a rafter. Then she began to scrape the hide from it, starting at the rump and moving down towards the head. As she worked she walked about in her tight boots, and had her scarf pulled down across her mouth, with bits of blood on her face.

Michael came in.

Silver sat in the corner with a small pickle jar of moonshine, sharpening a knife on a whetstone.

"I met Tom," Madonna said.

"I hope he's well," Michael said.

"Seems to be," Madonna answered. The three of them, at one time or another, had relied upon Tom for advice. But they had drifted away from him, each in their own way, and had come independently to the same conclusion – that Tom was too reasonable, too practical, and youth never had time to be reasonable. Still, he was the only man Madonna trusted.

It was sometimes painful for Michael not to go over and see Tom – but he would stand on his blood oath not to, unless Tom made the first sign. He knew he had hurt Tom because he'd spoken rashly about the suit. Yet he pretended to others that in some way Tom had belittled him.

Unknown to both him and Tom, they frowned at these memories at the exact same moment.

"I haven't seen Tom in over a year," Silver said. He was a small man of eighteen, with a strangely old face, like an elf. When he smiled his face crinkled.

He had spent close to a year in hospital because of depression. Madonna had taken care of him, travelled back and forth to the psychiatric hospital in Campbellton, and now regulated his medication. He had been teased a lot as a child and was beaten by his father, and at sixteen had had a breakdown. But now he'd been home for the last few months and things had returned to normal.

Madonna was secretly very happy about getting to know Michael Skid. For Tom, whom she had once loved, had gone off with Karrie.

Her idea was that in some way, no matter how slight, Michael's superior knowledge of the world would rub off on her. He would take her picture and it would be printed in a magazine. She had battled a long time to make some kind of a life for herself. This life was fine, for now, but there was another, more brilliant life that she expected. And her beauty and her body would get it for her.

This was Michael's third trip down in two days. When he came downriver before, he had always stayed at Tom's place. Now that he was coming to see them instead, Madonna didn't want to risk ruining it. And so she had begun to flirt with him, and tease him. As Madonna had once told the parish priest, there wasn't a man she couldn't have as soon as she decided to. This was perhaps very close to being true. She knew it was true with Michael. She knew it would be true if she wanted, with the parish priest.

She worked for a while in silence, and now and again Michael would come over and help her haul the hide away from the fat, and stare at her as the lantern glowed against her face and old woollen shirt fastened with one pin at her breasts.

"What's that?" Michael said after a while, looking at the pickle jar full of liquid.

"Shine," Silver said.

"Moonshine – where did you get it?"

The wind blew, and the light flickered as Madonna took the hacksaw and started to saw the buck's head off.

"Gail Hutch's shack," Silver said.

"Take me down and I'll get some," Michael said.

Madonna looked at him, her eyes giving a slight perceptible start, as if to say: *Why would you want to go there?* But he picked up his gloves, which were lying on the bench near an old can of mosquito repellent, and put them on.

They set out on their way, walking the road in the cold wind, Michael walking behind Silver at about three paces.

"For Christ's sake, help me get this cocksuckin head off," they could hear Madonna roar. "And don't go down and wake up that little boy! – You mind what Gail says! And if Everette is there, you two stay away from him. He just got outta jail and is crazy as arse."

Michael turned and waved, and laughed.

Gail Hutch lived far down the road past Oyster River bend.

She had a child of five, had come back from Quebec, where she and her son had lived for three years, and she now paid rent to Dora Smith. She had also had asthma and kept an inhaler, which she would haul on at intervals. Sometimes in the night she would begin to suffocate, and her child, Brian, would wake, frantically searching the room until he found the inhaler for her. He would sit beside her smiling and wiping perspiration from her forehead as she took her puffs.

Now her brother, Everette, talking and happy, sat at the table. His eyes flitted here and there. He was just finishing a long monologue about religion, which he liked to discuss. These discussions invariably worked their way around to the nature of power, and what made him, Everette, violent. He was fascinated by his own violence, and always held the belief that he would commit a great crime, that he was a man who didn't like to be violent, but could not help it, since people got in his way. Any other reasoning was beyond him. Everette's most telling trait was his conviction that everything else was beyond him. As if, in lacking compassion, he proved himself.

Twice in the past few years, Everette had been in jail for assault and robbery. He had got out of jail this day. He owed a large sum of money to his cousin Daryll, who was both younger and even more volatile than himself, and Everette's mind was racing, trying to decide how best to get something from someone while giving nothing in return. He could stall Daryll because of Daryll's respect for him, but only for so long. The five thousand dollars had been neither his nor Daryll's to begin with. It had been stolen by them in a series of robberies, the last one, two years ago, at Wholsun Breau's store on the inlet. When Daryll went to jail, Everette had spent this money on a motorcycle and accessories before he was sent to jail himself. Now both of them were out. So Everette had to pay back his cousin, who was serious business. He felt the best way to do this was through selling drugs. He could market the drugs for triple the profit, and he was calculating this as well. But in order to bring in the money for Daryll, Everette wanted four-thousand-dollars' worth of uncapped mescaline. He would cap it, then up the price, selling it for fifteen thousand and make some ten-thousand-dollars' profit himself. But he had no means of earning the initial four thousand as yet. In his wallet was twenty dollars, which he always kept. So he needed some way – besides bullying and frightening his sister – to get the rest. This was what Everette Hutch was thinking two minutes before he met Michael Skid on the night of November 19, 1973.

A table and a heater sat in the biggest room of the small two-room shack where Gail Hutch lived. On the table sat a pot of stew, with bone-ridden stewing meat and two potatoes. The smaller room contained a portable toilet, and Gail, twenty-four, was trying to tape some plastic over the one window at the back of that room where the air and snow filtered through.

Gail's welfare had been cut off recently, and was "between two provinces," lost in bureaucratic red tape.

Her husband, who had been an assistant manager of a small Sobey's store where he wore a white shirt and a bowtie, had died at nineteen of a brain aneurysm, when Gail was eight months' pregnant. Since that time she had been on her own, with a grade-four education.

Gail's little five-year-old boy lay sleeping on the one bed, sunken down in the middle like a folded piece of paper.

A statue of the Virgin and a picture of the Madonna and Child rested on the table as well, which gave precedence to the idea of religion being an opiate of the people, a controller of the poor. It certainly controlled much of Gail's life and thought since her husband's death. And when it did not, Everette's presence did.

The place smelled thickly of spruce bark and tar.

Everette was about thirty-six, bald, had a scar on his cheek that was black and red, and wide, dark eyes. He moved slowly – his hands now and then made signs for something and Gail would run to get it. She had prayed most of the month of November for him not to come to her when he was released from jail. But he had made it directly to her shack that afternoon. And now he was half-drunk. So none of her prayers had been answered.

The door opened. Michael and Silver entered. Everette looked at Michael as he sipped from a small pickle jar of moonshine.

"Your father put me in jail," he said. The air was hot where they were. There was in Everette's look a peculiar expression of outraged morality that is the bare bones of every criminal face. Michael sensed he had to do or say something to prove himself very quickly.

There was a moment when Silver started to go to the door. "C'mon, Michael," he said. He put his hand on Michael's arm, but Michael shrugged him off.

"You'll find I'm not my father," Michael said, moving towards Everette as he said it.

Michael then took out a slab of hash wrapped in paper, and cut off a chunk.

"I'll give you this for some shine."

Everette was startled by this. He picked up the hash, smelled it, touched it with his tongue, and said, "The case against me was for that new prosecutor, Laura McNair, to get her wings. A just-out-of-college quiff. I'll get her back the last thing I do."

Everette was talking about the assistant prosecutor who had helped send him to jail. Michael knew Laura McNair. He had taken her to a dance one Christmas when he was home from private school (the date had been arranged by his mother) and had kissed her on the cheek. Now, at this second, he had seen the underworld and how it spoke about *his* world, but he was unperturbed by this, because he felt he had the wit to side with the underworld. Men like Michael always felt that by holding no judgement they could flit back and forth from one world to the other.

"That's how things go," Michael said, shrugging. He then moved his left hand towards the white jar. "Won't blind me, will it?" he added, with it close to his lips, glancing over at Everette.

"Means it's good," Everette said, not looking up from the block of chocolate-coloured hash and waving his hand. In that wave was the one other trait he exhibited as much as rough power – a certain indefinable hatred for those about him.

The hash was worth five times as much as the shine, so Everette was pleased. Everette, pleased with how his comment sounded, said it again.

"Means it's good."

Everyone in the small, meagre shack, in the middle of broken windfalls and trees, began laughing, and their laughter, filtered by yellow light, caressed the snow and reached almost to the dump in back of them, where a rat burrowed down to suckle her nine young, her favourite, one with a small, black, slick face.

Silver stood near Michael, agitated and restless. He hadn't had any moonshine as yet because Madonna had been keeping an eye on him. But now she was at home and he was here. When the jar was passed to him, he tried to remember what they had told him at the hospital about peer pressure, and how miserable he had felt just a year ago when he was sniffing glue. He closed his eyes and bolted it back.

"Eeeeuhhhoo!" he called, banging his foot on the floor, and waking Brian, the little boy.

Although he was only a few minutes from Tom Donnerel's and could go there at any time, Michael spent the rest of that winter at Madonna and Silver's place. And once in a while they would meet Everette as they came and went. They were always pleasant with him and he with them, sharing a toke of hash oil, which was plentiful, and a drink of moonshine, and going on their way.

Michael, all during this time, lived with Silver, began, at the exact moment she wanted him to, to sleep with Madonna, grew his hair even longer, and read many books of popular philosophy, which continually reaffirmed Michael's overall perception of himself as a good and caring and decent human being. He inquired about renting a farm and buying some chickens and living in a way like Tom Donnerel lived back on his farm.

Each time Madonna, who now looked upon Michael as her boyfriend, wanted to encourage a reconciliation between the two she said: "Why don't you ask Tom to help you out? See if he can get his tractor going up next spring and plough those fields for you."

Michael would frown, close the paperback book he was reading – a Kurt Vonnegut novel or some other popular book – light a cigarette, and say Tom's advice about anything was the last thing he was after. So Madonna would only nod, smile, and in a moment curse Tom in agreement.

Michael had one or two run-ins over the winter, and gained the reputation of being a rich boy from town, devil-may-care, because of how he drove his old car down a ditch one day for a quarter of a mile.

"And he a judge's son," Everette Hutch said, feeling obligated to be as startled as everyone else. It was also known that Michael said nothing bad about anyone. And this attitude served him well along the road.

But one night in February, just after the incident with the car, Mr. Jessop stopped Michael on the road, near the gas bar. He was an old man, who had conducted his own life a certain way, and now wanted to give advice to a young man he admired – or hoped would admire him. He remembered Michael's father as a young boy, and he was one of the few to know the true story about Michael's former girlfriend, Nora Battersoil.

What Jessop said made Michael realize that people were watching him, which annoyed him slightly. Mr. Jessop started slowly, clearing his throat and breaking out into a rather loud, nervous laugh every two or three seconds.

"Madonna and Silver – look up to you a awful lot. They are always talking about how good you are to them, and how you are helping them out. Silver was in hospital, and Madonna had to take care of him – so you are –" Here he paused, laughed, and tried to think – "a real blessing to them. They had nothin in their lives – and look up to you. I mean it would be real good for them if you could help them see things the right way."

"Oh, of course – I'll do what I can," Michael said as snow fell out of the sky onto his head and shoulders. It was the casual and presumptuous tone in Michael's voice that made Mr. Jessop frown.

Mr. Jessop told him the following story:

"I knew your daddy – I was building yer cottage when you was in diapers. Once I met Lord Beaverbrook – I had three men workin for me and Lord Beaverbrook he said: 'Be careful if people look up to you – you have an added responsibility –'"

"Well – I'm not that fond of Lord Beaverbrook," Michael said, as a youth who wants to clarify all his opinions immediately. Mr. Jessop gave another abrupt laugh.

"No – maybe not, but even *he* had his points – however, let me tell you, those poor little Brassaurd buggers never had a thing. Never had a bicycle – a toy – nothing. I always thought they needed a guide – a person to show them – and I was hoping *you* would. I was hoping you'd get back with Tom Donnerel – you two were close once. He's a good lad, and he don't like that Everette Hutch. You have a right attitude about things. They will do what you say. So don't lead them astray. Like with that Everette Hutch. There is nothing in him for them –" Here he gave another short burst of laughter.

But Michael felt he had already done whatever he could for them, and treated them kindly. He gave them hash oil whenever they wanted, and helped Silver split four cords of wood, and talked to them about Kurt Vonnegut. And except for teasing Madonna now and again, he was straight with them. He felt loyal to Everette Hutch now because of the opinion Michael felt Everette now held about him. And this made him feel a sense of security. As well, he saw a pedestrian quality in Mr. Jessop, emanating from his nervous bursts of laughter, which he hated.

Michael thought he was very responsible towards Silver and Madonna in his own way. Yet, he liked the notion that Mr. Jessop, pedestrian or not, thought he, Michael, was superior to other people. It made him think once again that he would do his article on his former school and put everything in its proper perspective.

The next night he took Madonna and Silver to a restaurant and ordered a meal, and spoke about India and London, England, told them that Heathrow Airport was as big as any town on the river. He saw how Madonna watched to see which fork he was using. Madonna had to pay for herself and Silver because Michael didn't have enough money at that moment. And she opened her purse, almost in delight, as he sat there.

"We should do this a lot more often – I like to dress up –"

By the next week he had forgotten about his conversation with Mr. Jessop, except for the fact that he now had a certain dislike for him. And he went and asked Silver a favour.

"You think you could get me some blotter acid?" he asked.

Silver looked at him a moment, and then shrugged.

"You're the boss," he said, "but I don't want to get back into all this – I'm not s'posed to – my head gets all mixed up. Already I got some bennies – so –"

Then Silver shook his head and smiled, as if he himself

shouldn't be worried about himself if Michael wasn't worried about him, even though he might be destroyed.

"Well, I don't want you to do anything you don't want to," Michael said. "It's just for some friends of mine. I got into a little argument at the tavern with them and said I could get it. I guaranteed them. They are having a party in town tomorrow night."

"For you, no problem," Silver said.

Michael handed him forty dollars, relieved because he did not want to lose face with his friends from town. Still, Silver had to clear this with Madonna.

"He wants some of the blotter acid Everette has – there are some kids who want it for a party, I guess – and are relying on him, he says. They take it and sit in the graveyard and babble."

"Michael must understand that Everette Hutch is crazy. Does Michael know that? Once he starts dealing with him he won't be able to get rid of him."

"Oh, I think he does – he must understand who he is. I mean, his own father put Everette in jail for cutting a man, so he must have understood it."

Then, with Madonna's permission, Silver went to Everette. He stood in the shack and looked at Everette from under furry eyebrows.

"I don't understand what Michael Skid would want to do this for," Gail said.

"Oh, he's just selling it to some of his friends," Everette said, happily, because he had just thought of something to do with the money he owed, and how he could get that money. "He don't like to be known as the judge's son. He pretends, don't he? But you three come to see me if you want to make some *real* money – I mean twenty thousand dollars."

"Twenty thousand," Silver said, in disbelief. He had never in his life come close to twenty thousand dollars.

"We can make twenty or thirty thousand this summer if Michael has his sailboat. Now I'm not saying we will use the sailboat – but we *might*. But don't tell him anything yet."

Silver looked like a man who not only cannot believe his sudden good fortune, but who thinks it all came about because of divine forces in his favour.

He used to like Tommie – but Tommie's too much a prude, so now he likes me, Silver thought about Michael, as if he, Silver, had done something very special to warrant this consideration.

Then Everette added in a whisper, "You get me a date with Madonna – let me see her sweet little pussy, just once – and you'll be my partner. Here – see?" And he hauled out a folded twenty-dollar bill.

Silver said nothing. He only nodded, his grin fading. And he left soon after.

Throughout the winter, Everette wanted Madonna to sleep with him. This was the real reason he spent so much time at Gail's instead of at his house in Chatham. And this was one part of the ongoing tension that Michael did not see or understand that his recent presence had placed on Madonna Brassaurd. Already his relationship with Everette Hutch had created problems for this young brother and sister, who had made a pact of loyalty with each other when they were left on their own.

Silver came home, and Madonna quietly listened to him speak about some fantastic plan involving the sailboat and all the money. She listened pensively, and now and then snapped her gum slowly. Then she said this:

"We should go and tell Tom. Nip it in the bud. I don't like this – Everette will use Michael. Michael is smart – we both know he's smart – brilliant even – at talk. But he don't *know*. He's not smart the same way *we* are smart. Nor is he smart the same way Tom is smart. Everette'll get Michael to go to jail for the exact same amount of time Judge Skid give him. We should go to Tom and get him to help us."

"Tom is too big-feelinged to help us. He won't even look at Michael now," Silver said. "Besides, Everette isn't smart enough to think of a way to get Michael to spend time in jail."

"Who says he has to think it? It's in his nature," Madonna answered. "A part of his blood. He'll never be able to *stop* doing it." Then they both laughed at this because it seemed so true. The wind blew down the flue, the fields were raw and flat in the twilight.

Suddenly what they had just said sobered them. They both stopped laughing.

They sat in their little house in silence, as they had when they were children, frightened of the bogeyman, and of all those things that went bump in the night.

THREE

During that winter Tom walked down to the mailbox at the end of the lane to look for letters from Karrie. When he got one, about once a week, in a pink envelope with a happy face drawn on it, he would put it in his pocket, go over to Jessops' farm where he would do the afternoon work, feed the pigs, and send the cows out for a walk. Then he would read his letter.

One day Mr. Jessop brought him out a piece of warm cornbread his wife had made, and Tom sat near the barn door with his letter in his hand and his cornbread on his lap. Mr. Jessop wanted to talk.

"The people say they are going to get the police – if they don't stop being rowdy," Jessop said.

"Who?"

"Your friend – and Madonna and Silver – throwing a big hulloo about somethin – roaring and fighting." Here Jessop spat. Tom felt a certain kind of hollowness. He felt childish, as if Michael and Madonna were doing these wild or impractical things just to spite him.

"Well, that's too bad," Tom said. "I hope he don't get himself in trouble. I hope they all grow up." And he nestled himself down to read the letter.

"Maybe you could talk to him?"

"*No*, I don't want to. Maybe some day. But not yet. He said somethin to me you don't say. I didn't expect him to. It was a – betrayal."

"Listen," old Mr. Jessop said, "I ran for four elections. I won one. I seen a lot. Our values are no longer important to him. That's what it is." Here he spat again. "But when you throw out one plate of values, you have to go get another. If it's not Tom Donnerel, it's Everette Hutch. And that's the choice he *wants* you to know he has made. Madonna too. Maybe they don't see it that way yet themselves, but there it is."

"It don't matter none to me," Tom said. "I'm no big fan of Everette Hutch even if they are, so don't you worry – no one'll bother you."

But after the old man left, Tom thought. The road had become a very different place in just four months. He tried to remember how it had all happened.

Silver, who had been in hospital in Campbellton, came back. Everette, who had not been here for a year, after beating a store clerk, got out of jail. And people whispered that he was back too.

Michael had come back from his trip. With his money gone, and nothing much to do, he came down to spend the winter. And the road, with the river that ran beyond it, filled with trout, and the fields of corn, and the gracious elms, had suddenly become less idyllic.

Tom felt that nothing would be askew now if he and Michael had remained friends. But unless they came to *him*, the three of them would not be able to stop until something desperate happened. This thought came with the feeling on his skin of dry winter air, and he opened the letter.

Dear Tommie –

You didn't phone the other night – I spose you don't love me no more – I was in by 9 o'clock waiting to hear from you. I went to the movie – like I told you I would – anyway, the movies nowadays have nothing but sex in them, and swearing and cursing and no *LOVE*.

I just want love. Love is all there is.

So you remember Joyce Taylor's wedding dress – she got it at LeClair's in Moncton. I am thinking of having a similar one made up. I spose you don't remember what the dress looked like, even though you were the usher. But mine will have a train – hers did not – we have to start going for instruction. I don't like the priest – he's so old fashioned make you gag but even so – we have six months instruction so if we could start it maybe – the next course starts in August – then I would travel home next year every weekend? And we could be married (if you still want to) the next spring.

I can't wait to get home anyway – where everything will be normal again. You always are there to cheer me up – you know the sad feelings I sometimes have about cruel things – the old world is a pretty rotten place – I saw a man lying right on the street yesterday peeing himself and no one would help him – he was drunk I spose – but I'll be home soon, so say hello to all of the people – Vincent and pat Maxwell, and no drinking – or smoking! or taking chewing tobacco – ugggg!!!!! A happy face and an X and O – Love Karrie

Tom shoved the letter into his shirt pocket and went into the back room where the smell of cowhide and the smell of ice was ever present. He went to take some plug but didn't.

The next night he borrowed Jessop's truck and drove to the community college in Bathurst to see Karrie. He waited for her to come out of the stone building, saw her coming down the stairs with a boy following her and grabbing at her scarf. She tossed her pretty head this way and that, in a teasing way. The boy fell back a few steps, as the wind blew over the ice-riddled streets. Her small black winter fairy boots slipped along on this ice as she walked. She was almost to the truck before she noticed him, and gave a startled look, her scarf hanging down either shoulder. That startled look bothered him, and he glanced slightly away as she turned and waved goodbye to the boy.

He had thought that she would be delighted to see him. And he supposed she was, but getting into the truck she spoke only about the test she had to do the next morning on office management and said that her feet were freezing.

She had a small room in an apartment she shared with three other girls. Entering it he felt suddenly that her life here was foreign to him, and foreign to the Karrie he had known on the river. He saw her knickknacks, the picture of her deceased mother, the small decorated china plate she liked, her underclothes, panties and bras which she picked up hurriedly when they came in, and a small slice of pepperoni that she offered him, delighted that she had something to offer.

"No, keep that – look what I brought you," he said. "Jam from Mrs. Jessop, and homemade rolls – cheese too."

She sat down on the bed immediately and began to eat and he watched her. Although he didn't like to, he asked her about the boy.

"Oh, he's no one. He's doing a drafting course, so I see him because our room is just next door. Sometimes the boys like to come over and tease us – well, you know boys," she said, putting jam on a roll and looking at him.

She paused, and smiled prettily, her head cocked just slightly, as if questioning him.

"What's wrong?" she said.

"Oh, I don' know – just a long way to come fer an hour," he said.

"I know," she said, and again, as it had been the first night he spoke to her, the word *know* was said sensuously. "But it's just my test," she said. "I have to study for it tonight –" She paused and reflected on something. "Tom – when are you going to get a haircut?"

"Oh, I been puttin it off – I didn't get to town," he said, reaching along his neck.

"Well, it's getting long again, isn't it. You don't want it like Mike Skid's all-greasy long hair."

She smiled, put the roll down, and came over and sat on his knee for a moment. The door of her room was half-closed, and it was almost dark. He realized that in another half-hour he would have to leave and drive home.

"Are you going to take upgrading next year like you promised?" she asked, rubbing his nose with hers.

"Maybe – if you want me to," he said.

She smiled, held his face in her hands, looked at him intently, then gave him a lingering kiss that tasted like jam and butter. Then she suddenly leaned forward so he could kiss her eyes, like a child who has just seen something that has scared her.

"There, that's better," she said. "My eyes are kissed all better again."

And Tom hugged her, knowing he was profoundly in love.

At this time Michael was firmly established with his new friends, but they realized that at any time he could give this life up for a safer, more sedentary life. And in certain poignant ways Madonna tried to stretch the boundaries of her relationship with him.

Sitting on the opposite side of the table from him, in her small house, she would shake her head and say: "Someday I'd like to see your house – I've never been in a house like that – well, I was at a house where I made curtains once – Rita Walsh showed me – but other than that, no, I've not been in a house. Now Karrie Smith has a nice house I guess – I been down there."

Michael would nod.

"Some day Madonna is goin to get her own bicycle," Silver would say, smiling. "She never had a bicycle before, didn'tcha, Madonna."

"Well, I don't care about no fuckin bicycle now, Silver, for Jesus Christ sake – I'm nineteen fuckin years old –"

Madonna would blush, embarrassed that this secret about her childish wish to have a bicycle was now revealed.

"Well, I'll get ya one anyway someday, ya stupid quiff – I tol'ja I would."

"Silver got on pills and tried to knife himself, and went and stabbed hisself in the leg – and now he's back into sniffin the glue."

"Ya ya ya ya ya, so what the fuck," Silver would answer, angry that this had been told about him.

"Stay away from my fingernail polish is all I'm saying."

"Ya ya ya ya ya."

One night, near the time Tom went to visit Karrie, Everette came to Madonna's house. He mentioned that a friend of his was coming to trial for rape, and wanted to know if Michael could put in a word for this man. And for the second time Michael heard the name of the girl he'd once taken to the school dance: Laura McNair. She was prosecuting this friend of Everette's.

"I want you to help him out if you can," Everette said.

In ways in which he himself never understood, Everette's entire life was obsessed with and dealt with institutions and the courts and the law. His eager face showed this as he waited to hear Michael's answer. It was as if this obsession were a chess match, where the morality of right or wrong, or the sense of right and wrong, never mattered, but the idea of *winning* or *losing* was paramount. In this way, all things were simply business to him.

While maintaining his friend's innocence, he casually mentioned that the rape victim was deaf and dumb, aged twenty-two, and had a four-year-old son. They had been hitchhiking, and her son witnessed the entire assault. The man had been sure he would get off, because the woman could not speak to defend herself, or to say no.

But Laura McNair had got enough clinical evidence to support the case against him, and the man was no longer sure, so he had gone to Everette. And Everette, as a matter of course, had come to his new friend, Michael Skid, who was "a good guy."

"Could you please put in a good word for him with your dad? He is the best of lads," Everette said, and his face looked touching and reflective. "I know your father – I hold nothing against someone doing their job. As you know, he put me in jail and it was fair and square. I was reckless and did a reckless thing that I is – is ashamed of. But this man is a friend of mine. He never did nothin to that woman – she was beggin for it. He just took her back to the lane and give it to her as she wanted."

"I'll try," Michael said.

Everette came over to him and squeezed his arm. There was a seductive quality about this. He remembered how Silver had squeezed his arm trying to get him to leave the shack the first night he had met this man.

The case was odious to Michael, but to have Everette's friendship was a certain valuable plus.

Then Everette lit a huge chunk of hash and put it to Michael and Madonna's nose.

"Here you go."

Madonna began to giggle, but moved away when Everette tried to hold her around the waist.

In May, Michael decided to go home to Newcastle. He wanted to do more research for the article on the private school he was committed to write. There was a certain moment when it became clear to him that he should take this no further. His father wanted him to take a job collecting soil samples for a mining operation in Labrador. It was far away, and it paid well, and there were no temptations. Michael knew this. His friend Professor Becker asked him to go back to university in September to begin his master's. But Michael knew Professor Becker liked having students around because he wanted to be seen as youthful and boyish.

Still it was time to go.

When he told his friends, Madonna said nothing. She only tore paper from a cigarette box and then set it afire, so the smoke came up in front of her brilliant eyes.

"So I think I will go back up to town," he said finally.

"Well, I'll come visit you, okay?"

"Sure," Michael said. "Anytime."

However, when he went down to say goodbye to Everette he got a different reaction. Everette looked disturbed, even irritated. And it pleased Michael to see such a reaction.

"You're a friend of mine – what are you doing? Summer is just starting and you're thinking of leaving – wait until the summer is over – you know I'd love a trip on that sailboat of yours – just once." Then he looked at him, and smiled, "Well, if you have to go – I wish you could wait – but I understand important things – always important things keep friends apart. Look, if you don't have the money, we could pool our money and booze and drugs together so everyone would get a share." And here he lifted up a pickle jar, poured a tiny bit of moonshine out, wiped the jar clean, and took twenty dollars from his pocket.

"Now, that's the pickle jar – and that's the money, and it's *your* money – so you don't have to spend the summer up in Labrador, working for that mining company your father wants you to. Anytime we have something we'll just pool it together!"

Michael smiled, and was happy he was so well thought-of. But he didn't know how Everette would have heard about the job in Labrador. As he started towards his car he heard a short shrill whistle, and turned to see Everette coming out behind him.

"Come here – just for a moment," he said.

Michael hesitated, shrugged and went back into the shack. Everette sat at the table smiling, a huge grin on his face.

"You didn't think you were going to get away this easy, did you?"

"What do you mean?" Michael said, feeling nervous.

Everette then said that Michael owed him at least *one* favour.

"One favour – okay," Michael said, smiling, "One favour before I go. What is it?"

It was a warm, white night in May, with some snow still at the edge of the woods. The birds were singing late into the evening, and tamaracks were budding behind them, while a whiff of dark smoke rose from the dump a little ways away.

"What?" Michael asked.

"I want my chopper back," Everette said. "My Harley."

Then he picked up a hammer and tossed it against the wall, so close to the little boy's head that it surprised everyone, except, it seemed, the little boy himself. "And I'm not paying 426 dollars either."

"Why, where is it?"

"Ken's shop," Everette said.

He wanted to get his bike out of the shop where he had taken it to get it painted. The shop was across the river on a back street behind a half-dozen houses. The man had threatened him, Everette said. The man had used him, and tried to "besmirch Gail's name with bad language and called Gail a slut." (Here her little boy looked up.) The man was out chasing Gail even though he had a wife at home. Here Everette shook his head as if he couldn't go on.

Michael formulated a vision of Ken as a conniving, machiavellian, unprincipled man who was trying to steal Everette's bike and ruin the Hutch reputation in the neighbourhood where they grew up.

"Always it is the same," Everette said. And then he ended by saying: "Will you come with me? I need you with me. The man's as much a bastard as that Tommie Donnerel. I tell you about Tommie – we owned a fishing camp together – put money in a pickle jar just like this – but his drunken old man kept interfering, and finally stole the money, so I ended with nothin –"

Michael did not like to hear this. Yet he felt for some reason he did owe Everette at least one favour. He did not know why he felt this. He felt in fact that he owed him a great deal. Cicero once wrote that men are sometimes grateful when men of power do not kill them, and Michael had read Cicero before – read that very line, and felt it could never pertain to him.

Michael sighed. That night Michael's parents were having a special dinner, and had invited someone to meet him, as a surprise.

"Okay, but I have to get it done – and get on home. And then I'm done with *all of this*." Michael smiled.

"If we get caught – we're in a scrape," Everette said simply, looking down and spitting between his legs, tapping his boots on the dusty floor, and then looking up and yawning, to watch Michael's reaction.

But Michael was not at all frightened of this, not at this moment with the sweet-smelling air, the feel of springtime, and the feel of his own strong body.

Michael caught little Gail Hutch's look at that moment. She had been waiting for days for him to talk to Everette, to try to get him to settle down. With her hopes dashed, she went over to the bed and sat down, stroking her son's hair.

The smoke from the dump seemed solid and pleasant as they left and drove to Chatham in Everette's truck.

The shop was small and cramped. There was the smell of earth and oil and wood, and the gleam of four or five bikes in various stages of being painted or repaired. It looked like the shop of a man who bore no relation to the description he had just suffered.

The door was wide open and Everette's Sportster was sitting near the front, behind a small Honda. They moved the Honda and rolled the Sportster towards the truck, lifted it quietly, tied it down with bungee cords, and moved off.

"He didn't even do the job right – the tank is streaked, there's no flames painted – I'm going to have to do it meself. And why would he not guard it? Anyone could have come in and stolen it."

"Won't he know you took it?" Michael said, and Everette looked over at him with gleeful savagery. Michael remembered when, in the winter, Everette had tried to steal Mr. Jessop's little baby pig, and then had taken a pitchfork and thrust it into its side so it squealed in terror. Everette's eyes were exactly the same now.

"Don't worry, Michael Skid, I got something good on him," Everette said emphatically.

What Michael did not understand, what Silver and Madonna and possibly Tom Donnerel did, was that Everette Hutch kept tapes on certain of those whom he considered his well-to-do friends – for future embezzlement and blackmail – such as the tape he was wearing at the moment, inside his left boot, as he smiled.

FOUR

Michael went home to his parents' three-storey brick house and met Laura McNair. She was the special guest and was sitting with his father and mother in the living room when he came in.

Dinner was over, and though he didn't mean to be, he was abrupt with Laura. He answered her questions simply and vaguely and felt bored.

Just once the name of Everette Hutch came up, in connection with some ongoing investigation, and Michael blinked monotonously. And when Laura asked casually if he ever saw Tom and Vincent Donnerel any more, he flushed.

"I don't know why everyone hates Everette Hutch, why he's blamed for everything. He's as good as most of us," he blurted. But though he tried, he could not do what Everette asked, to plead for the man accused of rape. And so he became sullen and looked bored again.

At one point, when his mother mentioned the re-zoning law for the industrial park coming into effect in August, he called the mayor an embezzler. Laura had dated the mayor's brother in grade eleven, which made her laugh in embarrassment when he said this. She then said she had to go.

But when she left he knew his mother was angry.

"She's just lost her brother Lyle – he was killed two weeks ago –" his mother said. "How could you ever be like that? Is that how your new friends who we never see, and who never come to the house, and all look like refugees, just like you, taught you how to be?"

At that moment the whole evening, Laura's sad laughter when he spoke about the mayor, the way she looked about the room at nothing at all, as if she sensed he was attacking her, took on a far different meaning. And he realized how close he once was to her.

So he went to visit her the next day. The McNair house was the last house in a cul-de-sac. The presence of death still clung to it, and the spring air amplified this, with the sweet smell of lilacs and the trickle of a little manmade stream, placed tactically behind their hedges.

The graciousness with which he was brought into the house also signified a kind of rehearsal and mourning as did the coloured stone wall, Mr. McNair's nervous volley of movements and nods.

Laura came down from her room and the two of them sat in the den and spoke. She told him her brother had died trying to rescue someone from the river. He and two friends had been on their way home from first-year university. They had stopped to have a beer near one of the old bridges and lit a smoky fire on the shore. The ice was still moving out, and the water was high.

"You know what kids are like. We have to watch them nowadays – there are so many things they can get into," Laura said, and she squeezed her hands together. "One boy walked out over the old bridge. He turned to wave and slipped, and Lyle ran and jumped in to help. He was always helping others. But the water was too cold. He tried to help his friend onto one of the ice floes, but the boy panicked and grabbed him about the neck, couldn't let go. Both of them were gone."

Her brother had been everyone in the family's pride and joy, and had died in simple unplanned heroism.

"I wish I had been there," Michael said. "I'm a very strong swimmer. I wouldn't have allowed him to drown. I would have gone out with him."

This brought tears to Laura's eyes and she started to cry. "I know – I know – I know – I know what people are like in this community – people risk their lives for each other in a second – I know you would have. I was waiting for him to arrive home when Constable Deborah Matchett came and told me." Then she whispered, looking at him and smiling, as if this was what he had come to find out. "I was friends with Constable Delano for a few months – but it was a very silly mistake. We both know it was a mistake, you see. He still tries to protect me, though, and now that Lyle is gone he is often here worrying about me. So you'll probably see him around, protecting me." Here she sniffed, held the Kleenex to her nose, gave a surprised cry at her own vulnerability, and looked about. "Oh my God – here I am talking about my problems –"

"Don't be silly," Michael said. He looked at the curtains, the fine ordinary collection of Royal Doulton, and the well-creased, vacuumed carpet with just one small piece of lint. Outside the day was warm, the street dry. He suddenly disliked police officers like Constable Delano who would take advantage of her.

In the trees jays squawked. Laura's mother came in and sat down for a moment and asked about his family and if they still owned their cottage. Mrs. McNair was a tiny lady with red lines in her tired, long face, who looked at him and Laura in timidity, as if she expected another jolt or shock at any time. She asked Michael if he remembered once taking Laura to the dance.

"Of course –" he said. And instantly he remembered her young brother Lyle that night, peeking his nose about the door of the den. Their eyes met just briefly – and that was the only connection Michael had had with him.

When he stood to go he shook Laura's hand.

"I'll see you again," he said. "If I knew you'd be around – I'd change my ways," he said, laughing.

"Oh," she said, surprised. "Yes – okay." Because she didn't know his ways. And she took more Kleenex.

Michael stayed home for over a week and a half. He mowed the grass, painted the outside of the garage, and cleaned the deck chairs. He chipped some golf balls and now and again met his father for a round at the golf club. All about him now was talk of the man named Everette Hutch, the man from downriver, who had stolen his bike back from Ken's shop. Once or twice Michael would say, "Oh yes, well, I know him, and he's not so bad."

"Yes, well, that's like knowing Mephistopheles," one golfer said, looking at him and smiling. Then he teed up his Titleist and drove the green.

His father would ask him about Laura, and he would say, "Laura is fine," or "Laura is sweet."

But just as his mother was making plans to have her over again, and just as he was thinking it would be nice to see her, Silver phoned him and said that Michael had to come down for a lobster boil at the Hutches'.

"Madonna wants to see you tonight," Silver said. "She has to."

"I don't know if I can."

"For her sake – just tonight – just for one night!" Silver said.

And Michael, knowing he could have Madonna again that night, instead of waiting on Laura McNair, perhaps for months, went back downriver.

He arrived at nine o'clock at Gail Hutch's shack and learned that Everette was planning a robbery. He was startled, but tried not to show it. He also was in a conflict of interest, and wanted to stay out of any involvement.

Everette explained that a certain businessman had travelled back and forth to Tracadie, stopping at Hutches' one day a week for a bottle of moonshine and to talk about baseball or hockey.

"He thinks I'm a friend of his," Everette said, "but he cheated me – and now I'm gonna cheat him."

In a way, Michael realized, things had changed slightly but emphatically. Madonna and Silver were now more under Hutch's control. Silver was sniffing glue much more.

Michael also knew that Everette wanted him to hear what he was saying about the robbery so he could gauge his loyalty.

Everette was relying on Madonna to help lure the businessman into a trap, and "get him" by using her body. Any money was to be put into the pickle jar. The man wouldn't dare tell on them because he had a wife and kids.

"Just flash him yer tits –" Everette kept saying.

Both Madonna and Silver Brassaurd were terrified of Everette Hutch. Neither would ever have bothered with him if it wasn't for their friendship with Michael Skid. For days Madonna had balked at the notion of playing a part. And for days Everette had asked Silver to talk "some sense" into her. Today she had asked Silver to get Michael to come down, and to help her out of this.

Now she and Silver waited for Michael to speak.

"Don't look at me," Michael said, when Everette logically explained how the robbery was not only necessary but of good conscience, designed to take back money that Everette felt he had been cheated of, that the man had the courts on his side, but Everette had *right* on his.

"This is something you have to decide, Madonna," Michael said, finally, after seeming to weigh it for many moments.

"Michael," Madonna said, brokenheartedly, "what are you saying?"

But Michael only raised his hands as if to wash himself of it and he took a drink of rum.

"Don't look at me," he said, laughing.

Madonna did not know why Michael and Everette were laughing, and tried not to be embarrassed. She looked at Gail, frowned, and shook her head. She had waited all day for Michael to come and help her. But he had not come – at least not the Michael she expected or knew. His laughter suddenly made her blush. It was as if he had told Everette what she looked like naked, or that he could always make her come. She looked from one to the other.

The little boy sat in the chair near the door, listening, and Gail kept her eyes fixed on the far wall with her fingers folded.

"Well, I'm not robbin nobody," Madonna said, as if it was the only answer she could think of, and her eyes darted Michael's way once more.

Everette then took the faded blue picture of the Madonna and Child that had rested on the table and, holding it up, said: "Look, yer so saintly a cunt, what we got here is a picture a you."

"You shut yer fuckin mouth," she answered. Then, taking a lighter from the pocket of her shorts, she grabbed the picture and burned it in her palm. The picture crinkled as she dropped it to the floor.

"Ya'll burn in hell now," Everette said.

"Well, I was always teased – so I hate that joke, and that is why I burned it."

Silver felt ashamed that he had not stopped them from mocking his sister. He did not know why they would treat his sister meanly all of a sudden. Especially Michael. And he was worried and angry because of it.

The little boy looked up at them, without much expression.

"Why won't you help me?" Everette said despondently, rubbing his bald head. "You help me get that man who stole from me. I tried the cops, Michael," he said plaintively, "I really did. So Madonna, you help, and I'll make it worth your while. We can get three or four hundred off him. We'll pool all our resources – in that way, anytime you need money it will be here – and anytime you need a toke it'll be here – and if I need the sailboat for a day, I can have it. That's how people should live. Like the communists."

Michael then Everette both burst out laughing at this.

"Help them," Silver suddenly blurted. "Help them – they would help us."

"Wait till next week and I'll think about it –" Madonna said quietly.

Michael and Everette both looked at her and smiled. She sat down near the boy and patted him on the head.

"But if I do it for you, don't you touch your sister or her little boy ever again." And she crossed her beautiful legs, wearing terry-cloth shorts, without panties.

"I treat everyone okay," Everette said.

Michael looked up, wondering why this was said, and what it was he didn't know.

It was May 18, 1974, the day before Michael launched his father's sailboat, *The Renegade*, into the great bay, the day before Karrie Smith arrived back home.

FIVE

By the summer Tom was working full time at his farm, back
on the low river, and fishing in the bay. He had for the times
rather conservative views, short instead of long hair, and loved
country and western music. But these qualities only reaffirmed
Karrie's belief in him, because she herself was afraid of so much
that was becoming fashionable.

Tom believed in the Orwell aphorism, without ever having
heard of it or Orwell. That is, that so many who were rebels against
the status quo were often rebels against a sense of integrity in their
own natures. He believed this about Michael Skid. But he tried
his best to keep these thoughts to himself and say nothing.

However, Karrie was home and things were better. She had
had two dates while away that year, but as she told Tom they were
only to parties where others were going, and she got home both
times by ten.

He felt he shouldn't be too upset about these dates and so said
nothing about it.

Sometimes he and Karrie would walk the cool path through

the woods to the bay and back, holding hands. Sometimes he would take her to the drive-in theatre in her father's car. On Saturday nights, they would generally be home before midnight, and see each other after Mass on Sunday morning. At the end of August, they were to start premarital instruction on Friday evenings.

Only once or twice had he seen in her something which he did not like, a contrived sentimentality over her family's lot in life and for herself. But this was always swept aside by his love and concern for her.

Karrie began to practise writing the name Donnerel in her diary. She had been into his little farmhouse, into his kitchen and living room, the TV room with its dozens of magazines. She came and went whenever she pleased, took money from the drawer if she needed it. But she had not climbed the stairs to the bedroom. She felt it proper for proper girls to wait.

At her own house things were not good. Her stepmother, Dora, ran the family, and her father, Emmett, would say nothing when Dora put her foot down, so sometimes on a Friday night, just when she was getting ready to go out, there were a dozen things she was asked to do.

On occasion, the thin little Hutch woman would come over to clean the toilets in the gas bar and wash the floor, and Dora would get her to do the same in the house. Since Dora owned the shack Gail lived in, she was not paid for this, but there was a certain amount of rent money deducted.

"Comme ah sa va?" Dora would yell at the child, because Brian had learned French before he had learned English, "Comme AH – SA VA – diddly POOP," she would say, and give a knowing smile.

Gail was trying to save money to buy that shack at the end of a woodlot, that sat amongst the black spruce in the blazing summer heat, where no wind from the bay did reach.

One day in July Karrie went with Tom to the bottom field where he had to get the tractor and bring it up so he could hay the top field. The crop had been early and he was almost a week late.

At this field near the bay the hay was wild and smelled of salt, while paths ran off the edge of the cliffs towards the red muddy shore. The tide was low and smelled sulphurous, and gulls pattered here and there on the beach. Far off in the inlet an old wharf log jutted out and, farther still, a cargo ship lay off the strait, turning towards the Atlantic Ocean.

Hot wind blew at Karrie's dress.

The tractor, red with a broken seat, had a poor clutch and a worse fuel line, and Tom was having a hard time starting it.

"Well, forget it and walk back with me," Karrie said impatiently, trying to keep her hair out of her face.

"Don't rush me – just five more minutes – this fuckin thing," Tom said.

"Don't swear, Tommie Donnerel," she said. But he just looked at her.

"Be quiet – I'm trying to get this done."

Karrie turned impetuously, looked at the flat metal clutch pedal and cursed it, and went along the short, cool path that led from the field. It followed the bank for a way before it turned along a cascade of trees towards the church lane.

Karrie kept looking back hoping Tommie was following her, and once, as she looked, she tripped over a root and fell over the windswept bank. Her head landed near a piece of barbed wire, and her forehead grazed a rock. For a moment she did nothing but stare up at the sky.

She would have to walk back up the hill, and her dress was covered in mud and clay.

She stood and tried to grab at the crab grass above her, but when she put weight on her ankle she felt pain and cried out. The bottom of her foot was bleeding.

"Tom – Tommie!"

There was just wind, and he didn't hear her.

And then farther down the beach, she saw Michael Skid. He had rented one of the old farmhouses near the clam beds, a farm that sat in a desolate area of the shore.

Small trees surrounded his farm, and a river ran beyond it. There were always people at the farmhouse. They came and went as they wanted, and there was always a party. Music haunted the road after dark, loud talk, and fights would break out. Sometimes she could hear Madonna's voice.

Michael came up to her. He had long, dark hair, and wore a wristband of brown beads. His skin was tanned. The most insistent discrediting of him had come from her stepmother, Dora, who had told her Michael and his friends believed in free love, and were mixed up with the Brassaurds, and that he wasn't very nice to his mother.

Karrie now pretended she did not notice how Michael looked at her. He put pressure above the ankle, and taking a bottle of moonshine from his pocket, poured some over the scrape on her foot while holding her leg by the calf.

"Can ya walk?" he asked, sounding even gruffer than Tom. And then he began telling her of the story of a wounded osprey he had saved that morning. "I wouldn't let anyone hurt a thing," he said.

She looked down at his hand as it rested on her calf, and she smiled. Then she tossed her head, in the same impetuous manner as she had ten minutes before with Tom. But only she realized this.

He was trying to act as if he wasn't from a town of just five thousand people, or from a house in the centre of this town. And she knew this, because she'd heard he'd been to India and had even climbed a mountain.

But she too always pretended, pretended she wasn't from the little house just above them. This sentiment was part of the one aspect of her personality that Tom disliked.

51

Her stepmother had often told her that Michael did nothing. He was wild and had piercing eyes, and was just like a judge's son, and while she was in community college he and Silver had stolen one of Mr. Jessop's pigs.

But once when they had seen him, Dora demurely nodded and smiled, and later said in front of Karrie's father she could understand why women liked him. And this to Karrie seemed insulting to her family.

Now Michael leaned above her, and she rested back on her elbows and looked up. She studied his face. There was not only a masculine quality to it, there was a feminine quality to it as well, about the nose and mouth. And suddenly she felt that he probably thought highly of himself and very little of others.

"I was carrying this to drink – but it's more useful here," he said. And then he took a drink and laughed. He looked at her, and stared straight into her green eyes. She blushed because in his look she felt he had already determined her as a country girl who would be easy to impress, while she knew immediately that he would only think that way if he had no concern for her and was not once Tom's friend. If he was wild, so could she be. Neither did he really seem disconcerted by her pain, although both he and she pretended he was.

A gust of hot wind blew across them, smelling of charred wood from a forgotten fire, and caught at her dress just slightly.

His right hand lingered a moment on her calf. She understood even more that there would be a desire by both of them from this moment on to play a part for one another. She was suddenly afraid, half hoping he was going to kiss her.

Michael helped her back to his farm, while she rested on his shoulder and hopped on one foot. She carried her scuffed shoes in her hand.

When she looked up at his face there was a slight grimace to it that was mocking. What was more unusual was the fact that this mocking look was expected by her – and couldn't be otherwise. So she didn't look at his face, but instead at the insole of her shoes.

He sat her on the picnic table in the front yard, and then after he had wrapped her foot with great care, telling her he had learned to wrap feet in India, he convinced her to go up to the long verandah where they would be in the shade.

"Tommie," she said, partly as a question to herself, looking back down the shore, where a lighthouse stood in solitude against the glimmering water.

"Tommie Donnerel," he said, as an answer to himself, without batting an eye.

"I know you know my Tom," she said in an old-fashioned way.

"No," he said quietly, "I know my Tom." His voice sounded hurt.

They sat on the verandah now, staring over the red clam bed – in the distance the sun was a disturbing red over the grey water – and as smoke from a dwarfed fire rose across the inlet, Michael told her that he was reading great works of literature and philosophy, which took up more time than anything else. With that he tipped the bottle again. She looked at him a little in awe, though she didn't want to, and he noticed this.

Behind them, in one of the farmhouse windows, coloured glass chimes clinked in the breeze.

"I'm reading the Kama Sutra," he said. "It's all about the best way to have sex. I don't know if Tommie has it at home."

She smoothed her dress, looked at him questioningly, and he gave her a small sip of moonshine.

"I know nothing whether he does or doesn't," she said, and noticing he was wearing a small pearl earring, looked away.

As he spoke, his right leg, the one with the bandanna, moved out and touched her dress.

Far away they could hear the sound of the tractor as it made its way towards Tommie Donnerel's farm. Karrie stared at the smoke, squinting slightly.

And then Michael reached out and took her fingers in his hand.

"No diamond yet," he said as he let her fingers drop.

"Well, maybe someday, maybe not," she said pertly.

"That's right – keep him guessing."

Then a man appeared at the door, talking about the barn. Karrie knew who this man was. He was Silver Brassaurd, who lived by Oyster River with his sister, Madonna. But he pretended not to recognize her. He was very drunk and kept lurching against the door frame, which he held on to with the fingers of his right hand. He was very upset about something just now. How peculiar his hand was, Karrie thought suddenly, for no particular reason. His hair was almost the same length as Michael's. He was angry with Michael and wanted him to go to the barn and see to something immediately.

There was incense burning on the table inside the old foyer, and Silver's older sister, Madonna Brassaurd, came around the corner wearing nothing but a T-shirt.

Karrie looked down and away and blushed. She blushed as much at Madonna's beauty as anything, and at how casual this beauty seemed. How vulnerable and yet powerful she in her near-nakedness was.

"Oh, don't mind, I'm taking her picture – that's all," Michael said. "For a magazine – aren't I, Madonna?"

But Madonna's brilliant eyes seemed to bore into Karrie's soul and she could not look up.

Later Karrie was able to walk on her own. The ankle was swollen, but not broken. As she left the yard, Michael waved and turned away as if she had never been there. She didn't wave back. She limped up the long road to the main gate, where there was a smell of wildflowers in the ditch.

"He ain't so hard to figure," she said to herself.

That she felt she understood Michael was true, that she disregarded certain things she understood, because of her vanity, was a secret also true.

That evening Karrie told Tom what had happened, and how much she disliked Michael, and how conceited he was. She did not tell him about the moonshine poured over her foot. She did not tell about the conversation, or the questions, or how Michael wore a pearl earring.

Tom said nothing. He lifted the wheel off the hay cart and set it aside as she spoke. She could see the huge sweat marks under the arms of his shirt that seemed to amplify the dust on his back and on his sunburned neck.

He knew Michael, he said. They had once been friends. He wished him well. He looked at her squarely but said nothing else.

For a few weeks things went on as usual. Karrie would walk to the barn and meet Tom and sit in the shade near a great oak tree at one side of the field. She began to insist that he do what he had put off the year before, follow her suggestion and go back to night school so he could graduate.

Each day she would bring him lunch, and watch him work. He would wait for her to come, watching for her to appear by the side of the fence. But she would become bored and trail away in the afternoon, and he would go down to her house after supper. Now and again she would say something that Tom realized had come from someone else.

"I knows all about that suit," she said one day carelessly. "Tom, it was nothing to get in a big mix-up for. Mike is ready to forget it."

For Tom it was as if quite unexpectedly someone had scalded him.

"How do you know?" he said.

"Oh, Tom, I just heard," she said.

"Well, I'm a fool, that's all, but let's not talk about it," he answered. But he was stung deeply. A moment went by. A great wind blew off the bay and against the bare picture window in the Smiths' small, modestly adorned living room where they sat.

But he couldn't look at Karrie. He felt betrayed.

The next evening she wanted to go to church. So they went to seven o'clock Mass.

She prayed with her gloved fingers against her lips and her head bowed. Now and again she would look at him from the corner of her eyes as she prayed. He watched her, the laced-up blouse open at her neck, the small silver cross, the light freckles on her skin. He breathed her in, in the dusk of the old church, while the priest, feeble with age, tottered before them, and the altar boy, almost asleep, would look out at them with drowsy eyes and then scratch his behind.

After church, as they went out the front door Tom saw a man standing beyond the graveyard next to the steps leading to the shore.

"Do you want to go over and talk to him? He's been waiting over there for you," she said.

"Who?"

"Michael."

She smiled as if this little plan of hers and Michael's had been ingenious.

"I'm going home," he said. "You're getting mixed up in things – things you don't know about. It might a been just a suit to you – but well – 'cause it were my parent's funeral, for fuck's sake!"

"Oh, Tom – don't get all up and angry," she said, and tears welled in her eyes.

He turned and went up the lane. She stamped her foot. "Oh Jehosephat," she said, and followed him home at a certain distance.

They sat in his living room that evening, watching TV. Karrie had her arms folded and her chin lowered. They never mentioned anything about what had happened. But when he asked if she wanted some tea, she said she was tired and had to go.

She told him that the next afternoon she would bring him some clams and they would barbecue them for supper.

"Why can't we just cook them?"

"No – I want it done on a barbecue," she answered.

The next day Tom watched the blue sky, the horizon, and waited for her to come.

He set the barbecue up, and wanted to go and see where she was, but had to help the farrier – who only came once every three weeks and whose time was valuable – with the new mare.

"Come on," the farrier said. "Stop sniffing after her and she'll come along." And he laughed, spitting tobacco on his brown leather apron.

Tom didn't get out of the barn until dark. He had tried to rush and hurt one of the mare's legs. And then he had to poultice it. He could see small lights far away on the other side of the bay. Everything after dark without Karrie was lonely, and he could smell tar, and smell blood from a dead animal, still warm on the highway.

Karrie was not at home. Her stepmother, Dora, answered the door of the house, with its tiny peaked roof. She looked at him with just a slight hint of mischief, as if being a stepmother gave her a peculiar licence mothers did not enjoy.

"Oh, *ain't* she with you? Magine-magine-magine. I always thought she'd be with you," she said.

There was the trace of malice about her mouth. And he remembered that, although she'd been nice to him this past while – when he had taken them out to dinner at the Portage Restaurant in the spring after he had a big lobster catch, she'd shown a sugary graciousness towards him – most of his life she had disliked him intensely because he was one of the Donnerels from back on the swamp road, whose father was a drunk who killed both himself and his wife driving off Arron Brook bridge in a three-quarter-ton truck.

Tom walked over to the store for a pack of plug. The first he would have since Karrie got home.

Karrie's aunt, a French woman with tiny shoulders and heavy-rimmed glasses, who was changing the fly catcher over the ice cream freezer, seemed worried for his sake.

"Oh, she's gone with dem – the lot of dem."

"Them who?" Tom asked.

Her look became sad.

"Oh dem ones – she's wit' all of em. I don't know what they have or what it is they do. On that sailboat they have," the woman said, waving her hand, as if at the dead flies on the fly catcher, and, looking at Tom suddenly, as if he were at fault.

"I said it was a shame not to tell you – Dora said it's not our business." And again, unknown to herself she looked at him as if he were to blame.

Tom tried to look nonchalant but couldn't bring it off, and he turned and walked out into the dark.

Far down on the shore near the clam beds he could hear faint sounds of singing and talking. From beyond the point he could see Michael's twenty-eight-foot sailboat in the last of the light on the water. It was an old sailboat, called *The Renegade*, that had been swamped twice during the last two years.

Michael had swum out to it in rough seas after it went adrift one time, and Tommie remembered this now because he had been certain his friend would drown, and mixed with this memory were faint flickers of admiration.

He remembered that two hours later *The Renegade* in rough seas came towards the wharf, its bilge pump working, and Michael straddled up at the wheel.

"Tommie Donnerel," he had said, out of the cold late-August wind, "I just did what you couldn't do."

He'll be all right with Everette, Tom thought suddenly. *He'll understand how things are and no one will take advantage of him.* Yet everything for Michael already existed, so he threw it all away, while everything for Tom had been a struggle since he was fifteen. And Tom understood this as well.

Tom didn't take the road, but crossed Arron Brook at its highest point – just where he'd shot at the buck the fall before – and went through the woods. At places, the water came up to his waist and, though it was midsummer, the brook was still roaring, and since the rocks were slippery he had trouble crossing.

He got home, went up the stairs and lay on his bed, in torment, soaking wet.

A song came on the radio.

"*I gave you everything and you flew.*" The line resounded in the dark, and it plagued him for a long time.

Tom stayed in the barn and worked and waited for Karrie the next day.

A few hours passed. And then a few days. The stalls were swept out, the shovels placed in the corner, the long barn floor was spotless and smelled of sun and shadow, horse and oats.

The house was quiet, as quiet as it was when one waited out the warm afterscent of a thundershower.

One day, in the third week of July, he hitchhiked up to Douglastown to enrol in night school, and on his way he thought of Karrie, and how she had told him she would drive him in her father's car.

He thought of this, standing on the side of the road, with the marks of a comb through his short blond hair.

He walked half the distance before being picked up by the milk truck. He saw Silver Brassaurd roar past him in his Pontiac without acknowledging him. And then at the door of the school he decided not to enrol.

He had lost his nerve without Karrie there. He could not understand school. He could not understand history. He had always been hindered by shyness, something that was so often never taken into account in these matters. And the smell of the school, the dogged smell, yanked him back to when the snow piles sat for months along the endless road.

The attitude of the milkman who had picked him up was synonymous with the attitude of others. People now seemed apologetic when they saw him, and he hated it. Some looked away when he passed them. Some, like the milkman, couldn't help drifting into a slightly pleasure-filled smile.

He could tell in an instant that people were diplomatically avoiding the only subject that was on their mind.

Even Vincent was different in Tom's presence, as if he felt something bad was happening.

Vincent went down to the road every day and waited for Karrie to come along, or he sat in the grass near the barbed-wire fence.

Tom did not go back to Karrie's house. Nor did he go down to the gas bar. He went farther down the road to buy his plug at Wholsun Breau's little store near the bay.

Two more weeks passed like this, and no one would speak to him about her. When he went to the horse-hauling at the community centre, he stayed until well after ten at night and she didn't show up. Even for the light horses the next afternoon she was absent.

Then on the night of her birthday, August 4, he put the diamond in his pocket, took the tractor, and drove recklessly down to Michael's farm, only to find that no one was there. The doors had been boarded shut, and an old clam bucket sat on the beach waiting for the tide. The sailboat was out. The barn was solid and quiet, the new picnic table deserted.

Tom went back to the tractor and, with tears of anger and hopelessness flooding his eyes, he drove back up the lane.

At three o'clock the next afternoon Vincent ran across the field to tell him that he had seen her.

Tom was piling hay into the barn, and looked at him. "Where?"

"Over there I do," Vincent said.

The day was hot, the sky dark blue. Beads of sweat stuck to Vincent's shirt and his pants. His pants were torn at the knees, and he had a large straw hat that he wore with a string about his neck.

Vincent pointed far away, as if the distance he was pointing was, to him, the most important aspect of the information he was giving. There, on the flat blacktop lane that ran from the farm all the way into the centre of the province, far down that road was a small solitary figure with her quart jug.

"Blueberry," Vincent said. He smiled again, closing his eyes automatically, his teeth perfectly straight and white, and there was a smell of manure in the wind. It was as if her love of blueberries had caught her for them.

Tom threw down the hay bale, turned and walked, faster and faster, and finally broke into a run across the dried field stubble. All the while he did not know if he should be going towards her.

He reached the property marker at the back of the field, and he could now smell his own sweat, and something else – fear. He did not know why, but he was very afraid. He watched her a moment. He could not bring himself to imagine why he had not seen her for almost two weeks. And yet, besides this, he was afflicted by a kind of agony of delight.

He did not walk up the road but climbed the old bare barbedwire fence and went into the woods. Here it was cool and he could smell the shade. He tried to think. He couldn't. He felt himself begin to shake, as if he were cold.

"I'll give her one more chance," he kept saying to himself over and over again, without realizing he was saying it.

On his left, the roadway where she had walked was dusty and white. Patches of the road were shaded, and in amongst the trees were the remnants of the old forest-fire growth, where blueberries now flourished.

Tom, thinking he was going to tell her off, knelt instead and picked as many berries as he could, using his shirt as a catch-bag. He picked enough to fill a quart jug, and stepped onto the lane. He squinted in the sun and at first he didn't see her.

Then he realized he had come into the road ten yards above her. She was standing behind him, and had been watching him for some time. The first impression he had was that she was very sad. There was a mixture of kindness and sadness in her eyes. He thought of how he'd kissed her eyes that night in Bathurst when she had sat on his knee.

He then thought of her father and her stepmother, how one day the week before they had driven behind his tractor, and impatiently honked as they passed him. He was filled with anger at this now-obvious slight, at the idea of the stinginess of the stepmother, and how that would influence Karrie about a wealthy man like Michael Skid. This was what he reflected upon as he stared at Karrie, and he now saw in her those same qualities he had always disliked in her family.

"I'm sorry," he said. He did not know why he said that. At this moment she looked inscrutably upon him, while at the same time bending over slightly to scratch her leg below her billowy white shorts. He had once teased her about those shorts, saying he could make two sails with them. She was wearing makeup and he could smell her perfume on the air. It was a delicate fragrance just lingering upon the sweltering heat.

"So you were spying on me," she said. She smiled, but her lip trembled just a bit.

"He's not our people," he said. "I can't tell you what I know – but I do." He was saying something that was diminishing himself in his own eyes. That is, he wanted to tell her about Michael and Nora Battersoil – her own cousin – but even now he couldn't bring himself to. He stopped short, almost apologetically.

"I mean, his farm means nothin because though it's twice as big as mine he don't work it – the hay will rot – the stalls are broken – why do he need it? He got that big sailboat from his dad.

"I could play the geetar – he could play the geetar but it would be different. He got money comin in, but he likes bein poor. I tell ya somethin else – ya's a play toy for him, if ya thinks yer not."

But when he said this, he was admitting to himself and to her that he believed perhaps something had gone on. She gave a slight start with her eyes, just discernible to someone looking into such eyes as he was at the moment.

He pictured himself at this moment outside of his body and saw a man of five-eleven with a thick neck and strong shoulders, scratched by branches and abrasions from days of work, standing before her like a child. He could even feel the presence of cars miles away on the highway, and see both him and her as tiny figures in the middle of nowhere. So, too, he felt a kind of light throbbing from the heavens as he spoke, just as he noticed the startled look in her eyes.

It was excruciating the way she stared at him. She did not defend Michael. Her green eyes were wonderful again – her hair reddish. Suddenly he recalled he had heard that there was some girl Michael teased and called "cinnamon girl" – and now, only now, did he realize, like a vague fact coming out of the blue sky and turning into one more stabbing dart, that it was her.

If only she had not gone with him that day to get the tractor, if only – the clutch – if only it had worked. He suddenly thought of the clutch and the piece of straw under it, and how unimportant it all seemed then. And he remembered Madonna telling him that Michael had come back home.

"He's nothing like me – and if I see him I'll break his back," he said.

He wanted to frighten Karrie the way he was now frightened. But everything about her was inscrutable. And in this agony there was a terrible and conscious realization that his love for her depended now upon this agony, and somehow always would. And then suddenly, and most terribly of all, he remembered her praying at church, with her gloved fingers fumbling in front of her mouth the night she had tried to trick him into meeting Michael. He now felt small and pathetic in her eyes.

"Here," he said, flinging the blueberries high in the air. In a moment they fell, shadowing the road.

She turned with her quart jug and walked down the lane as if his wasting the blueberries was what she had been waiting for, the act that confirmed everything she now felt about him.

Tom stood on the road where the heat was scorching, and the old burnt trees in the distance stood like spikes against the shadow of other trees. Everything was silent, except for the faint ticking of insects. He watched Karrie move away. For a while she walked slowly and then suddenly she started to run.

He could not comprehend that this was actually happening. He turned and went into the woods. He sat on some cool moss and then began to grab at it, as if it were hair, staring down at the roadway as if he were drunk.

After a while, he went home. The tractor sat exactly where it had been, the field was dazed, and just the slightest hint of a breeze came from the faraway bay.

Vincent was standing exactly where he had left him, holding little Maxwell. He had a smile on his face, thinking that some enormous reunion had been accomplished.

"Go away, Vincent –" Tom said, at first feebly, and suddenly raging because he felt he was being spied on in a moment of weakness, he went over and hit him.

Vincent stumbled and put his huge arms up, the little dog cried and scampered about them, jumping up and barking, and the picture Vincent carried of himself and Tom and Karrie at the church picnic, when they had all helped at the rings, fell out onto the dirt.

"Good," Tom said, when Vincent started to cry.

And now he thought there was only one more thing to do. He would go and get drunk, although he had got drunk only once since his parents' death. He went to his room and snatched the diamond, put it into his pocket, and, getting on the tractor, he drove along the back road. He intended to throw the diamond from the bridge over Arron Brook, but he couldn't bring himself to do it. The air was heavy with the scent of full summer, the puddles were dried and cracked, and now and then a toad moved under a leaf, a rabbit darted ahead of him and disappeared into a shadow.

When he got to the Brassaurds' he almost sideswiped their old Pontiac, which was on blocks near the back steps.

Sitting on a bait bucket, staring at him, was Madonna Brassaurd. He stopped the tractor near her, and stared at her loose white top, tied at the middle of her stomach in a knot. She had her bathing-suit bottom on. She was smoking a cigarette. There was the foul smell of low water and eels that lingered on this road all the way to the Hutch shanty near the back dump.

"How's she goin right there now?" he said, but he could tell his voice sounded distraught. She looked at him, and he could tell she knew everything – even things he did not know, and even knew that his coming here was a signal that he had fallen in his own estimation.

65

He stepped from the tractor, its huge back tires white with dust and mud, his green shirt dust-caked and covered in sweat, and he went inside.

He did not feel welcome. He himself hardly drank, and he had at times, just as he did last fall, lectured them for poaching deer and drinking.

Tom realized now what he had known all along – that the Brassaurds had been part of Michael's arrival back home as well. They cleaned his farm for him, helped launch his sailboat, ran to do things for him. He realized that three weeks ago he could not have cared. And now it seemed that every word he had heard about Michael – from the moment Madonna met him in the woods the fall before, to Mr. Jessop speaking to him in the barn – was a warning to him that he had intentionally put out of his mind.

Silver Brassaurd smiled when Tom asked for wine. He was called Silver because of his silver tooth, which was blackened at the gum. It was then that something he had first begun to see when he looked at Madonna and now saw in Silver's smile came to him. That the Brassaurds, since they knew all about this affair, would be the ones to help everyone through it, would lend an ear to everyone.

Silver nodded in the wise way unthinking people have when they sense the moment is theirs, and ran into the other room to get Tommie the wine.

"Make it a lot or it won't last," Tommie yelled. He wanted Madonna to hear him, outside.

Six

When Karrie began to run away from Tom she could see herself – the quart jug in her hand. She could envision how people might see her running. They would be at the store perhaps. She would walk towards them with tears in her eyes, and the boys who she had once flirted with would look at her, standing about Bobby Taylor's new Chevy, with the large back tires.

"Oh damn," she thought now, "I'm crying," but also thinking what a nice effect this would have on everyone who saw her. That they would know – not right away, but upon reflection – that she and Tommie were *through*.

Then she remembered a rude boy at community college (the boy who had hauled her scarf) who had taken her to a party and had tried to get fresh. When she told him about her boyfriend, Tom Donnerel, he had said, "Oh, you won't marry him. Someone else will have you long before him – you're the type."

That statement had bothered her very much at the time, and now it bothered her more.

The lane was hot; the trees still and moribund. After a time she stopped, looking back quickly, hoping that Tom would still be there. But he wasn't. And suddenly the emptiness created a pulse in the sky, where a haze rose off in the distance and she, too, was slightly afraid. She took two steps back towards where Tom had been, thought of poor Vincent and the little dog, and how she had a picture of them in her jewellery box, and then turned and walked quickly, arms folded like county girls do.

An idea had formed of late that Tom had done something wicked – against *her*. And she had played upon this idea for the last two weeks with Michael, and with her father and stepmother.

The previous two weeks had been the most eventful in Karrie's life. She was always discussing great issues now, and saying wonderful things about life. And everything was fitting into place, as if she had come into her own.

With Michael she had feigned being in a predicament over Tom's cold behaviour, and feigned needing to come to Michael for advice. Yet though she and Michael pretended it wasn't, it was very much a predicament that both of them knew would not exist unless they themselves *willed* it.

At first Karrie wanted to believe that Michael's and her relationship revolved around the principal idea of getting Tom to reconcile with his friend. Later, when she saw how hurt Michael was, Karrie felt sorry for him, and angered by Tom's stubborn meanness. Yet behind all this, there was a subtle but marked game being played between her and Michael, that both of them knew.

She thought, as she walked, that Michael would not let her go back to Tom ever again, even if Tom did get violent. There would be some kind of confrontation, but she did not know how that would turn out – only that Michael by the power of his voice and his brave eyes would finally win.

Why did she suddenly think of court? Perhaps something

would happen – she would have to go to court – then Michael's father, the judge, would come – everything would be solved. The judge would put his hands on her shoulder, calling her his daughter (or something – that part was still vague.) Then, in her mind, years passed. They would be in a large brownstone house. Trees, children.

Her own father seemed to think of some injury against her, and so did her stepmother. Karrie was silent in the house. And for the first time she felt very powerful, and sensed that they were both in awe and perhaps a little afraid of her.

"Well, it's a shame," her stepmother had said, a week ago, a slight smile playing at the corner of her lips, where tiny black hair could be seen. "I don't like to see anyone *hurt*."

She remembered how outside of their house the bay was black and steely, and far away a buoy-light could be seen. Down the road was Oyster River corner.

Her father had sat licking the filter of his cigarette and frowning at some memory, with grey suit-pants high up on his waist, and counting the money he kept in a tin can beside him. This was the money her father and her stepmother were saving for their retirement. They kept it locked behind the bookshelf in the den. It was money that came from rigged gas pumps – especially the diesel pump, which the local trucking companies used. It was not that they had rigged these pumps themselves. The calibration had been set wrong by the previous owner five years ago, and only Dora was astute enough to notice this. When Emmett went to telephone the company to report the mistake, she rushed in and stopped him.

"Don't be a godalmighty fool – we are not the thieves – they did it. We're going to make an extra seventy cents on a tank of gas." And her face turned beet-red and she looked over quickly and suspiciously at her stepdaughter. "You keep your little Smith mouth shut up tight, Karrie," she advised.

As long as they were careful about this they felt they would not be caught. It would only be a problem to explain if it were found out they had kept extra profit for themselves. And though Emmett felt guilty and though Karrie was at times burdened, they maintained complete silence. And Emmett and his wife would smile at each other at times across the table late at night.

As Karrie walked away from Tom she thought about this. And then thought about the night before, her twentieth birthday.

She had not meant to meet Michael, but it was destiny. This is what she told herself. It was what her stepmother had told her the week before.

"It's just destiny, dear. Don't fight it."

"But I feel some bad about it," Karrie said, at that particular moment not feeling bad at all. "We were s'posed to start our instruction at the church." And she blessed herself.

But Dora snapped her fingers quickly in front of Karrie's eyes, startling her. "Think for once of what *you* want. People like you and me never think of ourselves, dear – think of yer own self –" And she suddenly smiled, snapped her gum, hugged her stepdaughter coldly, and her lips quivered slightly, so Karrie had to look away.

Now, Karrie remembered Michael as a young boy who swam out from the wharf without a thought to get a wounded seagull – and it seemed as if she'd *always* been attracted to him. Yes, she was the one who always took his side, and never allowed people to talk about him.

Her stepmother had bought her a new silk blouse that she had worn on her birthday.

Karrie had also been singing the song lately: "*Many a tear will fall – but it's all in the game of love.*"

She did not tell herself that his family was well known and wealthy – with political connections in Fredericton, an uncle who was a senator in Ottawa, and sailboats and trips to the Bahamas – her stepmother did.

As she ran away from Tom, smelling the thick, bland heat, remembering Tom's poor troubled face, and what he had done with the blueberries, she felt that she had finally met someone who understood and respected her.

SEVEN

E veryone called her the cinnamon girl. Michael gave her that name during her first trip on the sailboat.

"Oh," he had said gravely, "you won't be Karrie here – you will be – oh hell, I don't know – the cinnamon girl."

There was such gaiety at everyone else's expense – there was such disorder, fighting and cursing and nudity. There was such high revelry at nothing at all. There was such a pretence of concern for their friends, the world of affairs, the marijuana laws, that seemed upon reflection to be tired and sad.

Sometimes as they sat on the sailboat, it drifted to the port side, and they could smell the Jessops' farmyard.

"God, those horses," Michael complained about the odour.

"Them aren't horses, boy – them are cows. Them is the smell of money."

Michael studied her in a particular way when she corrected him. There was just a slight look of aversion on his face. Then he just bent over, and with his hand on the inside of her thigh he kissed her. She opened her mouth slightly and felt his tongue.

He was only the second boy she had ever really kissed. Then he drew away and playfully squeezed her thigh.

"Now, stop it," she said. "What am I going to do with you?"

And she began to laugh again, with a marked fear at doing something inappropriate, and then moved a lock of hair back from his face, and shook her head, as if she was exasperated.

She decided then to go back to Tom, where she felt she would be safe. But on her way to Tom's the next afternoon, she came out on the road, and spied Vincent waiting for her, looking down the highway holding Maxwell. Far up in the field she heard Tom's tractor, and her heart was no longer in it. She turned quickly and ran, all the trees passing her at the same instant, and didn't stop until she got to the bay.

"I'll go with you – to Prince Edward Island," she said. "If you want."

"Well – as long as we enjoy it," Michael said in an almost ice-cold fashion. And she suddenly gave a short embarrassed laugh, and looked at Madonna.

On her birthday, Michael took her to Prince Edward Island. He had to talk to some people there, or Silver (who seemed to be upset about something) did. But while the rest went to shore, she remained on the sailboat, looking down the teakwood stairs into the cutty.

She kept walking back and forth on deck hoping they would come back soon, and her attention was drawn to three young teens on the wharf who kept asking her if she owned the sailboat.

"My boyfriend does," she said suddenly, filling a glass with white wine.

She then looked across the strait to the far-off shore she had come from, and took a drink. She promised herself she would be back home by six. When Michael came aboard again, she found herself talking about Tommie.

"Shhhh," Michael said.

He took her hand, and led her into the cutty.

She looked at his face and it was filled with a quiet strength. She could understand why he was likable. And all the *rude* things she had thought about him. But she now felt Tom had told her those things. But she was free of Tom, if she wanted to be.

There were many things in the cutty and she tried to remember them. Bottles and small hash pipes, clothes tossed here and there, a map on the wall with pins in it, showing where he'd been in the world, a chart of the bay, and the overriding scent of suntan lotion and of a faintly soiled mattress.

Silver Brassaurd was on deck, cursing to himself about something important, and now and again he would peek down the stairs, his bottom teeth protruding from his mouth.

The sailboat rolled in the waves and Michael sat beside her, squeezing his strong slender fingers on her back. He told her a story of riding out a hurricane off the coast of Africa, while she sat and drank.

She drank almost an entire bottle of wine, and now and then as he continued rambling on, she ran to the cupboard in the cutty to pee. She kept falling back and forth laughing while the door banged open and closed. He went over, helped her to her feet, and pulled her panties up.

"I've never done anything like this," she said, staggering and laughing.

Michael then got upset about something that had happened on the Island two or three weeks before, and began to hit his fist against the wall behind him. When she turned in fear to stop that fist she fell against him. There were tears in his eyes, and he was drunk as well, and she was frightened.

"Why are you fooling him?" he said, "He was the only friend I had – or is it me you are making a fool of?" He smiled.

She jumped up in a start to run away, but when he hauled

her back to him she started kissing him apologetically. She kept kissing him, on the mouth and teeth, on his bare chest.

"I'm sorry, I'm sorry – this *wasn't* supposed to happen between us at all." And then she said quite suddenly: "I'll go out and get you some blueberries tomorrow – I'll bake you a pie."

And he began to laugh, that laugh he had, which always frightened her.

Later, there was phosphorus on the green bay. The swells were high and they went on deck. Actually he got up first, and went above first, leaving her alone to dress.

Far away they could see the lights from the road, and she could make out the one light over her father's gas bar. She called Michael to show this to him, and when he came over she leaned her head against his arm. Then he smiled and gave her a squeeze, and told her he would be back in a minute.

Riding in the wooden dinghy that was being towed behind them, dead drunk, was Silver Brassaurd. It was dangerous to be out there now, with the strong wind. If the dinghy ever came loose, there would be no saving him and he didn't even seem to care.

While she was looking at him he would roar and yell at the waves, then sing. Then as Karrie was watching he took a plastic bag from his pocket and shoved it up behind the dinghy's rear seat. For some reason, as Karrie watched she thought of herself as a little girl hiding marbles from her cousins one Sunday afternoon. Yes, she had wanted all those marbles for herself, and perhaps, who knew, that's what Silver was hiding as well. Some marbles for himself. Something he didn't want to show anyone else.

When she turned around to look towards the bow, she felt that she belonged to all of them. This was a very warm feeling.

But then she caught a glance from Madonna Brassaurd, who was sitting on top of the cutty, smoking a cigarette and tipping a bottle of wine. And Karrie remembered, dizzily, that with all the wine she'd had, she'd been naked when people – both Madonna and Silver – walked in and out of the cutty.

Madonna simply stared at her now and the look unnerved her. She realized it was because she had always, as had her step-mother, felt superior to the Brassaurds, and Madonna's look said she knew this.

Michael had to climb up at the bow to get the spinnaker out. But it had been broken on an earlier trip, and bowed under his weight. He wore old cutoffs that were very loose so that the top of his butt showed. And he was cursing about something as he seemed to swing far out over the desperate water.

She remembered when they'd been on the hard, long seat how thin his ribcage was. She had tried to stop him, at first. She remembered too how much it hurt her at first, and how she'd been unable to stop moaning, so he'd held her mouth.

Now in the dark she could only hear his voice – and for the rest of the night he didn't speak to her. He seemed to be respon-sible for everything and everyone. The idea that he was Michael Skid seemed to be implicitly woven into this responsibility to care for those about him.

No one spoke to her again, and she felt very lonely. She kept trying to talk with them, but it became quickly apparent she had done something that they all thought was dishonest, or at least she felt they did. Just once, when she was moving back towards the cutty thinking she was going to be sick, Michael's eyes caught hers, and she looked away.

Eight

From the day Tom threw the blueberries, everything about Karrie's situation changed and was to become worse and worse from the moment she ran away from him.

When she ran from Tom that day, she did not go back to the sailboat, but the next day, she went down. As she got off the dinghy she felt that they had been having a conversation about her.

"What are youse saying about me?" she said, laughing, but her laugh was a nervous one.

Michael looked up at her and she thought his smile was cold or annoyed. She remembered his smile on the beach when she had first met him. It was the same smile.

There were other young women on the sailboat that day as well, and they were all going to Portage Island. She was angered that they would go there and not invite her.

Michael got up and moved around her, as if he were very busy. He told her they were casting off, if she wanted to come. But she stubbornly said no and asked someone to take her back in.

She went back to shore and looked out at the boat. No one waved back when she waved – so she picked up a stone and pretended to throw it at the boat and laughed. Then she yelled out to Madonna: "Madonna – I have something to tell you – wait till I see you again. But I'm not going to tell Michael – la-te-dah."

She watched Michael disappear into the cutty, and then soon – ten to fifteen minutes later – Silver Brassaurd pulled anchor and the sailboat began to drift, as she heard the squeak of the sail being lifted.

Going home, she borrowed her father's car and drove quickly along the bay road, watching as the boat became a dot in the sun. Then she turned and drove into town. Town was hot and empty and silent.

She went to the bookstore and bought Michael a book. It was a book of poems by Robert Frost. She wrote in it, "All my love dear one. Karrie." She did not know much about literature, but she did once have a part in a school play.

She was aware of herself walking back to the car, and felt a little hopeless.

And so it started. She could not help but be with, and wanted to belong with him. Or more *to* him. But everything about *them* intimidated her. She hid the book of poems in her room, waiting for the proper moment to give it to him.

She kept trying to do and say the right things, to be *irreverent* in just the right way. But she only managed to repeat what others, like Madonna Brassaurd, said and she was clumsy in repeating it. Whenever she said something it only sounded vulgar and foul.

No one in the group seemed to approve of her, and she became nervous and her face started to break out. Once, when she was with Madonna, Karrie said: "I'd like to know what to do to be more like you." And she smiled timidly.

"You have to know not only how to fuck – you got to know who to fuck," Madonna said. "But he fucked you good, didn't

78

he?" Though she laughed, as if joking, and though Karrie laughed also, Karrie felt deeply humiliated.

She began to feel that belonging to someone who didn't care at all for her was her destiny. Soon she began to feel, in a secret part of her, that she had cheated Tom, and had cheated the plans for her future with him, for nothing. It took her some weeks to begin to admit this.

The evenings began to pass, and there was never an easy moment for her. The idea that she had been dishonest came principally from Madonna Brassaurd. And no longer did Michael act in an easy way with her. There was nothing easy between them now.

Soon she hated the boat, and all of them, and yet she was forced to go there. That is, she was forced to go there in the hope that she had got all those impressions of Michael and the rest of them wrong. That they were not mean people, that Everette Hutch, when he once came by, didn't hate her, or hold her family up to ridicule because of the shack Gail rented. That Michael didn't take his side and glare at her as if she were a "slum landlord," as they teased her about.

She wanted to prove to herself that it was exactly as it had been before, like the night they went to P.E.I., that Michael was an angel and she was an angel and they would fly above the world together, over the sorrowful trees.

She kept going back to the sailboat so her father and stepmother wouldn't be disappointed. And she kept going there because as long as she was there, she had a chance to change their minds about her, to prove something to Madonna and Michael.

For days and days Michael didn't want her. He seemed very upset with her. He told her that there were things that she didn't understand. She could not seem to break through.

"If you only knew," he said to her one night at his farm, "of the trouble I'm now in – you would run away."

"What trouble?"

He moved his hand through his hair and looked at her.

"I'm in trouble – but you can't tell."

"Is it Tommie – is he bothering you?" she said.

"Don't you realize you've betrayed him?" he said.

She jumped up and ran to the door. She had just brought him down a set of sailboat chimes for the house, and had placed them near the window in the living room.

The old Mexican sombrero sat on a chair, and she picked it up and fumbled with its leather headband, her lips pouting.

The next night he was drunk and climbed up on her verandah roof and woke her. He looked worried about something, and she allowed him to rest his head on her shoulder when she opened the window, then cup her breast.

"Please don't do that here," she said.

He wanted to come in, and began to make a commotion.

Instead she snuck out the back door and down through the cool, dark garden in her bare feet. They went down to the field where she had left Tom that day with the tractor, and right on that spot Michael pushed her down drunkenly and lifted her nightgown. She was very silent and passive, because he was so drunk.

After that night, "cinnamon girl" took on a peculiar, odious meaning. Madonna used it, and she could not stand to hear the way it was said. Also, after that night, and more importantly, she was frightened of her father and stepmother's terrible hope – of her as an investment for them.

She kept pretending that they were her friends and that everyone loved her. That this was the age of friendship. So her father and stepmother kept making small talk, wanting to know what Michael was really like – asking her about what a sailboat ride was like.

"Why don't he come around?" her stepmother asked the afternoon after he had come to her bedroom window, with a smile that told her that Dora knew he had been there the night before. Karrie was walking down the hallway, and froze in midstride when Dora spoke.

But when Karrie gave the excuse that he was busy refitting the sailboat, that's all that seemed to matter to Dora.

"Oh, the sailboat – when can I get on it?" Dora said.

The hallway smelled of stale summer air and Karrie glanced into the dining room where her stepmother sat, her cheeks shimmering slightly.

She went upstairs and, staring at the small freckles on her arms, began to sob in spasms. What was she supposed to do now?

NINE

After he left her on the road that day, Tom went to Brassaurds'. The wine was brought out. He hit the bottom of the bottle, took off the cap and took a drink. It was warm sherry wine, called Hermit – or Uncle Herms, as those who drank it with frequency called it. It gave most blackouts and made many violent.

There was the sweet summer smell of clover along with the smell of river water and eels. For many moments Silver, still hungover from the night before, looked upon his imposing guest with sorrowful, even bashful eyes. They talked about haying, they talked about the tractor – the clutch plate – Mr. Jessop's prize pig. They talked about the lobster season. Until Tom had drunk half the bottle.

"What's going on down there, Silver?" Tom said. He was staring at the corner where the fridge was. "Tell me everything – the whole of everything. What's Mike been up to with her? Anything?"

Silver didn't answer for a while.

"I don't know," Silver said, and he shook his head piteously.

But then he kept right on talking, in a whisper, as if confidence were required with Tom, when the story had already been spread across the entire road, so that even Dora had heard all about it. "She was naked with him last night –" he whispered. "Now, maybe he didn't do it yet – but I think he did it to her last night," Silver said, shaking his head.

Though Tom took in everything he kept staring at the fridge. His whole body began to shake as if it wasn't his, as if he had no control over it. He picked up the bottle again, couldn't get it to his lips, and the wine spilled down his chin.

"Don't be wastin good wine," Silver said, and he took it from him and drank. "I got a good glance 'tween her legs – and her hair isn't so cinnamon downstairs. Go ask Madonna."

Tom looked over at him, but Silver, in communicating his story with such profound and vulgar naiveté, had no idea why Tom was looking like he was, and so he only whispered a little more urgently.

"Oh ya," Silver continued recklessly. "It was the bet he made me that he could fuck her by her birthday –"

There were two awful sounds from Tom's throat, and he looked so terrifying that all of a sudden Silver stopped speaking, tipped his chair back, and snuck away, trying to be as careful as he could – for he had just seen a monster.

Silver went outside and the night was hot. The trees waved slightly and the road smelled of tar. He went and leaned against the Pontiac. He began to shake. He was suddenly frightened for himself.

"He's going to kill someone," he said.

Madonna looked at him, unmoved by the statement. She loved her brother – because he was her brother. But she had no use for anyone now. Very little talk about love or violence ever moved her. Not as it had when she was a child and had loved everyone in hope. She blinked and took a drag of her cigarette.

83

"Go in and sleep with him," he said. "Take his mind off of *her.*" And he said *her* in an urgent voice.

"I'm not sleeping with him," she said.

"Why not – what's wrong with him?"

"I'm on the rag," she said.

"He won't care."

"I do."

And so the argument continued in hushed and urgent tones about whether or not Madonna would go in and sleep with him, while the tractor sat like a giant sleeping animal nearby.

What was poignant about this argument was its defiling nature; for once, a long time ago, she had waited for Tom to ask her to a school party and had bought a dress by working on the weekends sewing curtains for Rita Walsh.

She thought of this now, and the smell of those curtains in town, as one sometimes thinks of their lost innocence.

She had gone to the dance with someone else. They went in a car to a camp and there was a group of boys. Thinking of this, as if stung, she said once again: "I'm on the fuckin rag – so I'm fuckin no one tonight so leave me the fuck alone."

"Yer a different girl than you used to be – not doin me no favour," Silver said. And he walked away a few feet and sat on the grass, looking over now and again at his sister. Then he opened a bag of mescaline and looked at it.

"This is the stuff Everette told us to sell now. What are we going to do? We have to tell Michael what we're being forced to do."

Madonna stood, ripped the distributor cap off the tractor, looked at her brother and said: "Useless fuckin men. The last thing I want to do is tell Michael we're selling bad drugs."

Madonna wanted desperately to start a new life. But she could not start a new life on the residue of her old, past life. This was the sad truth she now knew. She had struggled since she was six years old, always thinking that around one of the pale-blue turns, on a sky-blue day, her new life would happen.

And so the argument ended, and the night was still soft with all its stars.

Silver walked up the old Arron Brook road, past the Jessops' cow-corn field. He didn't know what to do. He felt he had all the decisions to make.

Madonna went into the house while Tom was drinking his second bottle of Hermit. He asked for hash, so Madonna rolled some in a cigarette and gave it to him. He took the whole joint.

Then he asked for pills – he didn't know what kind of pills, but Madonna realized he was probably talking about the mescaline going around. So she told him to lie down.

"The mescaline is filled with shit," she whispered. "We're selling it – because we have to – not because we *want to* – Everette got us into it."

She went into the back room with him. He stumbled and fell against the cot, with its old army blanket. He took out the diamond and, leaning on one knee, tried to put it on her hand. She smiled and lay him down, putting the diamond back in his pocket.

He asked Madonna to take off her bathing suit. She lay down beside him and put her head on his chest, and for an hour or more every time he tried to get up she pushed him back.

He reached down and realized that she had actually taken her bathing suit off, but she was wearing a strap and Kotex pad against her warm and somehow angelic body.

After she fell asleep he went outside and lay in the grass for over an hour, and later he could hear Madonna talking to him, but didn't answer her. Then he got up and stumbled to the driveway and tried to start the tractor.

And then he began banging his head against the tractor housing and slipped, cutting himself.

Somewhere – they were either near the tractor or near the Pontiac – Madonna was holding him, and he was shouting at something. He didn't know what it was.

Afterwards someone said it was near dawn, and Silver appeared in the dooryard bare-chested, smoking a cigarette.

Madonna's eyes were deep and mysterious, the most spiritual thing in the whole little yard.

By noon hour Madonna and Silver were asleep in the old house, and Tom had gone. He had washed his face and hair, and had gotten the distributor cap back on the tractor. He started out for home.

The day was quiet and warm and he drove the back road, his shirt tail flapping in the wind, his chest bare. Now and then he would look down beneath the engine at the asphalt. His head was woozy and he felt sick.

When he came to the great field of cow corn owned by Mr. Jessop, he pulled the tractor off the road and took a junk of cord from under the seat.

The field spread out for a quarter-mile in each direction. The corn was now waist-high and shimmered in the early-August breeze. Sky birds flew above and the sun beat down. This cow corn had the density of *life* that Tom had sought and thought he had attained, and he began to walk through it as if committed to do some crime. This crime was to go to the end of the field where he used to hunt partridge and hang himself with the cord.

He had no emotion except that he wanted and needed to do this as quickly as possible. For a good four hundred yards he was in a daze that glowed inside a yellow ball of light. Now and then he would come out of this daze of yellow to stop and look about. And finally the daze, the ball of yellow August light, subsided. He was hampered by the growing corn, and he stopped to inspect its shoots, noticing some small yellow breaks in the stalks, and wondering if he should not go and tell Mr. Jessop about a better quality of insecticide that he, Tom, would have used if the field were his. And, taking two or three samples and inspecting them, he looked at the cord still dangling over his arm and was surprised by it. Then suddenly ashamed, he flung it high in the air, like a black snake, and it fell beneath the ball of sun into the corn, making a stinging sound.

Then he left, determined to be by himself.

TEN

For the next week his brother was away and Vincent was alone and as scared as a boy of five. He tried to feed the mare and the stud. He tried to do the work. He sat every night in the barn talking to the horses, coddling Maxwell the dog. The horses were getting thinner and crankier. He didn't know what to do. He kept telling them about Tom and him, and how they had gone to the church picnic.

By week's end he needed tobacco for his pipe, but he was frightened to go and get it by himself. And he was waiting for Tom to give him the note he pinned to his shirt.

Every now and then the mare would move and Vincent would tell it to stop. He was sitting inside the door shaking. But the mare kept moving and flicking its tail.

Once he stood up, pretending he wanted to hit her, and saw that when the mare's muscles flinched along her flank it was because of blowflies. So he took a carrot and fed it, tears in his eyes as he looked at its yellow teeth. He wept and sat on a bucket. He wailed so that the Egyptians heard him.

He took heart that in the morning the farrier would come and help him with the animals.

Then he looked through the black pouch for more tobacco, but could only find a few strands.

He went towards the house. His door was on the far side, facing Arron Brook. He opened this door with a great deal of dignity. A picture of his parents sat on the night table. A large picture matching the one he carried in his pocket of him and Tom and Karrie sat on the mantel. In the far corner was a pet gerbil that Tom had bought him, named Snowflake. His little dog Maxwell looked up at him mournfully.

He sat in his chair and thought. Then he opened up the dresser drawer beside him and looked into it furtively for any tobacco that might be left. Then he thought he would go and see his Aunt Libby.

For a while he smoked the last of his pipe tobacco and thought of the gerbil and how he had gone to the pet store with Tom. And how Tom, having to hold Vincent's hand, talked to the young salesgirl whose name was Sally.

Vincent stood and went out, closing the door, locked it with a good deal of ceremony, and walked down the dry, rutted lane towards the road. Already the stars were out, in the last of the white sky, and all the trees were silent. And he made sure he had his key in his pocket, because Tom told him not to lose it.

He would go to the store and ask for tobacco, and say: "Put on Tom's account." That's what he would do, and this is what he was trying to remember.

PART TWO

ONE

On a sunny Sunday back in June Michael went over to Gail Hutch's shack. The day was hot, with the smell of pine cones and dust, in the little yard that sloped so that when it rained, water gathered in pools just outside the door and remained there in perpetuity.

He went inside to find the large pickle jar to take out forty-five dollars to pay his phone bill. He had been working on his article again and was phoning former classmates, taping what they said. Many were nervous to come forward, to tell him their views – some might even have felt culpable in what Michael was trying to expose. And this gave him a secret sense of amateurish journalistic power. He would not interview his drama teacher, Mr. Love – but he would go to those closest to him. They were older now and so felt freer to talk.

He felt that he was ready to make a breakthrough, if he could keep his concentration, do his job without a lot of interference. Then he would publish this article in the fall in the Halifax *Chronicle-Herald* or the *Globe and Mail*, and punish those, including his parents, who had forced him to go to boarding school when he was a boy. This was the whole point of his article. To punish others, to close the school for good. It was his ambition from the time he was sixteen. And though it was right and just for this school to be exposed, he still had twinges of doubt. It was exactly what Tom had told him he should not do, if to injure others was part of his motive.

Thinking of these things Michael stepped into the small, dark shack. But the jar that had always been visible – which had, when he'd last counted, over seven hundred dollars in it, most of it money that he and Silver had earned helping load lobster traps – wasn't there. He began to search the main room, whistling.

Everette was lying in the dark far room on a mat. He put his hands over his eyes, and looked out at the sunshine.

"Who's there?" he said, as if to make it clear he was not expecting or wanting visitors.

"It's me," Michael said. "I've come to get some money."

"What money?" Everette said, sitting up. He walked out of the gloom and into the main room in his underwear. It was the first time Michael had seen his muscular body, covered with ink tattoos. "There's no money here," Everette said. He was angry that Michael had woken him up. "How can you expect us to make a deal if you keep grabbing at our funds?"

"What deal?" Michael smiled.

Everette looked into a drawer and began shaking some seeds back and forth, looking for enough grass to roll a joint. The sun came partially into the shack and the flies soundlessly moved at chest level in and out of the sun.

"The deal I told you we were making –" Everette said.

Later, when Michael went back to the farm, Madonna and Silver listened to him, staring out at the dull, sunbaked shoreline.

"He says we have a deal of some kind – which is part of our investment. Do you two know about it?"

94

They both looked at him and shook their heads.

"He mentioned a deal – once or twice –" Silver said. "I mean – about earning twenty thousand. I don't know."

"Well, Jesus Christ, I just lost three hundred dollars," Michael added.

And again the three of them looked at each other.

"Tom always said –" Madonna began.

Michael raised his hand. "Come on," he said. "We'll leave Tom out of it."

They had pooled their resources and their capital at the end of May. That was the main reason Michael did not take the job his father had secured for him for the summer. Everette had spoken of this collective as a way to ensure everyone had a good time, and to ensure that Michael was able to stay downriver, instead of going back to town.

They had, until this moment, believed that it was working wonderfully well. But the real problem was that neither Silver, who waited for Michael's instructions, nor Michael himself wanted to blame Everette for doubledealing them.

"This is what we have to do," Michael said to Madonna and Silver. "We just have to talk to him – calculate what he has taken – if it's not in our best interest we'll break it off."

"Breaking it off – now – would be good," Silver said, his forehead reddened by the band of his old leather hat, and by the sun beating down upon him.

The bells of the church pealed for Sunday Mass, and they could hear cars driving down the church lane and parking. The sound of children, the slamming of car doors, all sounded depressing.

At this moment on this particular Sunday the idea of his article seemed depressing too. One man from Sackville kept saying, "Michael – if this comes out – if this comes out – talk to Terry about that incident – that was his fault – you talk to him."

This was a boy, who was now a lawyer, whom Michael had secretly detested. It was strange, but Michael felt sorry for him now.

Now, turning to Madonna, he asked: "What do you think Everette has up his sleeve?"

"A way to earn money."

"By doing what?"

"By selling drugs – but sooner or later he'll want us to sell them for him."

Michael looked at her. He squinted slightly. He immediately envisioned two scenarios. Everything would be fine and they would get away from Everette as soon as possible, or they would get caught and end up fined or jailed. But there was of course a third possibility that enticed him – and this was that they would actually make a lot of money – and that Everette *was* doing all of this for them.

They decided to talk to Everette that night. They drove over in Silver's old Pontiac.

Everette was very used to inquisitions. And he claimed that all the money was safe and hidden and, in fact, he could have charged them for the lobster that they had eaten one night the month before.

Then he offered advice. He crouched on his haunches, drawing some numbers in the sand with a stick he had picked up at the side of the woods.

As he drew these numbers, in tens and twenties, he spoke.

"We have about three thousand now – but I need another thousand. Then we can get fifteen thousand in uncapped mescaline for four thousand dollars."

He said that they should all keep tabs on how much each one earned or spent. But they should start earning some money, because he could not do it all by himself. It was as if he had taken over a part of their lives they had not willingly cast his way.

And this was done as naturally as all other things that he did, so that *not* to go along with his scheme, of getting mescaline from certain people he knew, and selling it on the Island in a month, would display deep ingratitude.

"It'll be the biggest deal I ever worked on," he said, smiling at them.

To Michael it didn't seem possible that he had not heard of this deal before, but, so as not to embarrass himself or Everette, he kept pretending he had. And he felt at that moment that this was exactly what Everette was relying on, that is, Michael and Silver's omission to ask the pertinent questions, or demanding *out* of a deal that had not been fully explained to them.

In the evening air was one other notion – and this notion, as the three of them stood side by side, was this; they themselves realized they were weak, and had no qualities that would allow them to escape, or stand up for themselves.

As Everette spoke, Michael could only look at the knots on the old birch stick in Everette's hand.

Michael sat in the shack later that Sunday night, looking at the vicious stingers outside the window and wondering how all of this had happened.

"This'll get me outta my scrape with Daryll," Everette said. "That's the first thing we got to worry about."

Yet no one knew why they themselves should be worried about this.

They then went back to the farm and sat in silence.

Madonna wanted to ask Tom's help in getting their money back, but Michael could not bring himself to.

"It is an awful good deal – if he can get fifteen-thousand-dollars' worth of uncapped mescaline for four thousand – it's a big profit for us all," Silver suddenly said. "I don't think we should worry – he's a good guy."

Being called a good guy in Everette's world always came when someone had just done something dishonest.

By the end of June, Michael was worried whenever he went to his parents' home lest Everette come visit him there.

He remembered how casually mistrustful Everette's smile was every time he looked at anyone.

He also felt obligated to Madonna and Silver, who had already put their savings into Everette Hutch's hands. They had put in about twelve to fourteen hundred dollars. And now they waited with innocent faces for Michael to tell them what to do.

One day after a party, Michael went over to pay Everette for a certain amount of marijuana.

"What about the other fifty?" said Everette.

"What fifty?"

"The other fifty – the interest for the pool – it's for all of us. I told you the other night – Daryll is patient but his patience will wear out – and how will I explain to him that you are welshing on us –"

"Do I owe another fifty?"

"Gail – what does he owe?"

Gail looked abashed and tried to speak, but Everette cut her off.

Everette smiled and rubbed Michael's head playfully, as if he were trying to keep Michael in line, implying that he had caught Michael just then trying to take advantage of them.

"Oh oh oh oh oh – I'd better not tell Silver this, or he'd be some disappointed in you," Everette said. "You know he doesn't have that much. And he worked for a week hauling traps for the little money he got," he added in a pious whisper.

The idea that Michael would ever be thought of as duplicitous in anything was infuriating to him, especially at the tail end of that false and pious whisper. But his fury was only spent in Everette mockingly pointing a finger at him.

98

"Come on," he said, smiling a sugary smile. "Admit it – I caught you!"

And Michael could not help but smile at this falseness, a smile which made the accusation seem true.

"Ahh-ha – you see that?" Everette said, pointing the smile out to Gail.

Michael then went back to Brassaurds' and told Silver that if Everette ever said that he, Michael, had cheated them, they should not believe him.

But this made Silver suspicious. He sat on the grass, looked here and there, and spat.

"Where is the pickle jar?" Silver kept saying, pulling grass up with his hand. "Where is that pickle jar? I'd love to have a look at it. I put my money in it, and it's been a month and there is not a cent. We have to buy groceries – what in Christ are we doing mixed up in this? What are you and Everette doing?"

Both he and Madonna felt betrayed. Michael did also, but now they both suddenly suspected him.

Still, Everette said the one deal that would allow them to recoup all of this money, and more, would come through. That he and his cousin Daryll Hutch could be trusted with this.

By the early summer, this deal was constant in Everette's conversation. And he spoke about it as if *they* were the principle investors, so that almost every cent Michael got from home, he gave over to his friend, because now he had committed himself.

One night he was at his parents' house. His mother left fifty dollars – two twenties and a ten – on the ironing board, and Michael, going out the door, picked it up. And, instead of keeping it for himself, he went down to Everette, thinking: *I'll give him this, and prove it.*

He had no idea what he was trying to prove at that moment. There were two other men with Everette that night. One was Daryll Hutch, the other a biker from somewhere in Quebec.

Michael tried to be nonchalant and brave. Now it seemed imperative that he show them who he really was.

"Look, I've got some money," he said, laying it on the table. But Everette, in agitated conversation, only looked at him and looked away.

"Hello," Michael said to Daryll. But the man said nothing. It was a terrible moment, for the moment said this: *Pick the money back up, put it in your pocket, and leave – prove to them who you are.* But he could not do it. This was the conversation in which Everette convinced Daryll to wait a while longer for his money by telling him how they could rely upon Michael Skid, on his sailboat – and that they could do three or four runs that year. He also convinced Daryll to put in five hundred dollars himself. With this windfall he had collected almost all the money needed for the initial buy, and had himself given exactly the one twenty-dollar bill he always kept in his wallet.

A week went by. Michael went to visit his parents again. Just before he left, his mother mentioned the money.

"Did you see any money on the ironing board?" she asked. "I was sure I put it there."

"Money – why would I take your money?!" Michael yelled. His mother flinched and smiled timidly. "If you think that I steal – well, I'll never come back."

"I didn't say you stole, dear. I would never say that."

And the same feeling he had from the time he was a child, that he could have his mother do his bidding, overcame him. He looked furiously put-out, and, turning at the door, said he would go downriver and stay there, if this was how he was going to be looked upon at home.

"No, dear – come back – please," his mother said, holding the patio door open. But he didn't go back.

Downriver he could see only his mother's timid smile, and tears came to his eyes.

Everette asked them over that night. And things were again the way they had been in May. That is, Everette seemed once again happy to see Michael. Michael, who had always felt warm in this man's presence, was glad of this turn. What he didn't know was that this turn had come because Daryll said he would give Everette another month.

"Michael," he said, "come in – please. Gail, get Michael a drink – how are you boys? Close the door get out of the rain – cold tonight." And he smiled at Madonna and shook his head.

They sat and drank for quite some time, while Gail's child sat in the corner near the door, yawning continually, and having the perplexed, bored look he often had when Everette spoke.

"My father had to walk twelve miles to work," Everette said. This came after he'd been speaking for a long time about hardship, callously mentioned names of adversaries long dead, speaking about being turned away from school, about trying to take care of his sisters and brothers, with his father working and his mother ill, about eleven kids living in an upstairs apartment overlooking the wharf.

"When the eleven of us got running back and forth on the floor the old lady who lived below us said it was like a herd of rats over her head," he laughed. "She was a kind old lady to me but she died when I was still a kid. I always thought – didn't I, Gail? – if she hadn't died I might have got on the right track about things."

"I'm sorry to hear that," Michael blurted tenderly, and looked about, his eyes shining.

There was a pause. Everette looked like a man who had just demonstrated his internal fortitude, and he nodded and drank. Yet, in every way possible, in every way that counted, the men he spoke about – the biker from Quebec who would bring the drugs across the border to him, Daryll, who had just gotten out of jail, and others – were violent, untrustworthy, and dangerous.

Everette then told them that the sailboat was the key. He wanted it for one night, to take the drugs across the strait to P.E.I., where certain people were to wait for him on a patch of dune, miles from any police or any spying eyes. They could make a fourfold profit on the east side of P.E.I., where a lot of back-to-the-landers were. And of course in Charlottetown also. He couldn't see selling the drugs in New Brunswick, because he was being watched, and trusted no one. Here his eyes glittered. Nor could he travel to P.E.I. by car and ferry, because of the RCMP. He was afraid they had a tap on his line in Chatham and were tailing him whenever he went anywhere.

There was a pause. The trees outside blew, and far away they could hear the cawing of a crow.

Michael said it wasn't his sailboat – it belonged to his father, and his father was a judge. "I'm sorry – I can't risk it," he said, and smiled naively.

"I can't take *The Renegade*?" Everette asked.

"I'm sorry," Michael said, still smiling.

"You've been talking about this deal all winter – you've come and gone as you pleased, this is your side of the bargain," Everette said, astonished, and he looked about quickly at the others to see which way they were leaning.

Michael had not remembered talking about anything. Everette was silent a long time. The crow kept cawing.

"Who's been talking about this deal more than anybody else," Everette said, looking up suddenly, "if it wasn't Michael?"

Both Madonna and Silver looked sheepishly about and shrugged. It was the moment for them to unite in force against him. But they could not. Not after Everette had talked about hardship, not after he spoke about living in an apartment over-looking the wharf.

"All of this money is ours – *ours*," Everette said. Suddenly his hands seemed to shake just slightly.

"How much is in the deal?" Silver asked, in a voice that sounded as if this were the main question, the answer to which would allow them to decide whether or not the sailboat could be used. Yet even this question was answered enigmatically.

Everette looked at Silver with a pleading expression. "It's something I can't disclose," he said, and he looked quickly at Michael again.

Michael was furious with Silver for asking this, as if Silver could make any decision about *his* father's sailboat. He suddenly saw his position and felt sickened. The last thing he would have thought was that he would do something for money.

Finally he said: "I'll do it – once – and that's it – but I'll only sail it – you have to do all the other stuff."

"Only sail it – well, that's better than nothin," Everette said, laughing. They all began laughing.

But when Michael, whose mind kept racing, wanted to know certain details about the plan and why Daryll had looked at him so coldly, Everette became impatient and said: "We can't have a moment to party without him talking business." And everyone laughed again.

It was June 21.

All of a sudden Michael had became an active participant in a scheme he had once thought was simply Silver's talk, a scheme he thought he was superior to, just as he had always believed he was superior to people like Madonna and Silver, and to people like Tom and Vincent.

He had always believed he was superior to every one of them. That he would have some fun in the summer, and though he had never thought about his future, he always believed he would soon go up to town and once again see Laura McNair. He had already, in the back of his mind, chosen her as his wife. And this was partly because of the fatal heroics of her brother Lyle, whom Michael admired the more he thought of him, and partly because he knew she was in awe of him, and was pleased by his own impulsiveness.

There was a fine smoke from the dump, where the young rat with the slick black face spent the evening.

"Why didn't you say something to protect me in the shack?" Michael said, when they were back at the farm later. "NO – you *couldn't,*" he said. "You leave everything up to me!"

"We should just go see Tommie," Madonna said, "if we want out of this. Tom would bust his head if he thought we were in trouble, and he wouldn't be afraid of no Daryll Hutch neither."

"Don't you think I can handle it?" Michael said. And to himself at that moment he suddenly sounded like a child. And he felt like a child.

"I used to think so," Madonna answered. "Up until a month ago – Silver and I believed everything – *now,*" she added with certainty, "just go to Tommie – just for us."

Michael didn't want to humiliate himself by doing this.

"No – I'll do it for Everette once and get your money back for you and then we're out of it. If you two get some money out of this I'll have done my job – that's what I figure."

Madonna just puffed out her cheeks and crossed her beautiful legs.

"I don't mind for me," Madonna said. "But Silver's nerves – are bad again and he's sniffing my goddamn Cutex."

"Tell Silver not to worry, I'll take care of it – I will take care of you both, I promise," he said goodheartedly.

"No money will come of this," Madonna said. "Everette won't give us a cent."

In early July, Everette brought them into the shack and told them: "It's comin. But you guys have to cap it – at your barn – that's the safest place to do it. I tried to think of somewhere else – I can't move or the cops will be on me – so – take it to the barn. No one bothers you down there –"

Then, in a rash moment, drinking wine, he admitted something. He stood and walked about the shack, shaking his head as if he were remorseful and needed an act of contrition. He admitted he had stolen from them all – not only five hundred dollars, but six hundred more, and the two cheques his sister had managed to get from welfare. That is, all of Silver's money, all of Madonna's, and most of Michael's went towards paying for the mescaline.

"There was nothing I could do – I just had to act. Now everything will work out. If I left it up to you –" here he reached over and rubbed Michael's head – "the money would've been all pissed away. Now we'll make about four thousand each – and that's just the first of it."

Michael and Silver laughed, as if Everette had their interests at stake and could read them like a book. And for that second, all of the anxiety they'd felt over the last month was forgotten.

But at the moment when everything was going well once more, when the plan was going to take place, Everette went out celebrating and got drunk, lost control of his bike, the Harley Sportster he was so proud of.

TWO

Everette lay in the hospital in a coma, half the skin on his side torn away and his head cut open. They were worried about his brain swelling. The last rites were given.

His face was covered with bloody wrapping and gauze which left one eye and part of his forehead exposed. There was yellow fluid coming from his ear.

Whatever else the accident said to Michael it said that Everette had done nothing to prepare himself for *this*. That the drug deal they were talking about did not prepare him or anyone of them for this. That the way Everette held things over other people, bullied his sister, lived in self-torment, did not prepare him for this. Other things in life, all other things, were more important.

The morning of Everette's accident was the last time Michael took any drugs.

But still Michael no longer thought of the fear he had of Hutch, but of how much he was obligated to him. And he thought, too, that if he did just one more thing to prove himself, with Everette now dying, he would show himself to be the friend Everette needed him to be.

Michael had, without knowing it, replaced Tom with Everette. This unseen fact had much to do with what happened over the next few days.

The group that gathered to keep the death vigil was monitored by Constable John Delano, who had been tracking drugs all spring long. Delano was looked upon in Michael's group of new friends as a narc and a rat because, besides being an RCMP officer, he was their age. Michael felt this most of all because of John's friendship with Laura McNair. He felt it because he was supposed to, and because he hadn't taken time to think in any other way.

Delano watched Michael as if he were an unknown equation here. Michael noticed his glances and fumed.

"Who does he think I am?" Michael mumbled three or four times, within earshot of the constable.

Michael went to Delano and told him off. He assumed a particularly moral attitude when he spoke, and felt quite empowered. "The only thing you have is a uniform, nothing else, and you're letting that suit puff you up."

"I'm sorry you feel that way, Mr. Skid."

"Well, I do feel that way – because – well, because that's the way I feel," Michael said. He put a coffee to his lips and tried to drink it, but his hand was shaking. The air smelled of antiseptic, linen, and urine. The hospital corridor was awash in darkness even though it was eleven in the morning.

Delano looked at Skid. He knew how much Laura McNair admired him.

"Michael," he said. "Come on – how can you be fooled by *this*?" He waved his hand in a quick arc and smiled slightly, as if he were calling on Michael's integrity. He was also calling on him to do something – and that was to give up his posture. This was just hinted at in his smile. And it was this smile that Michael reacted against.

"Who are *you* to take notice of who visits Everette?" Michael snapped. "Just because my family has a special position and I've been to private school doesn't mean I don't understand people like Everette Hutch –" He wanted to continue, to keep going, but Delano looked away, embarrassed by this extravagance, and then looked at him again. He stopped smiling.

"If this is a time for histrionics," Delano said, calmly, "sit in the waiting room, where some of his friends might listen to you."

And Michael flushed with anger and embarrassment. He went to the waiting room, feeling he had lost a valuable piece in an important chess match. The worst of it was, until that moment in the hospital, he did not know a chess match was being played, that it was being played all summer long.

Recklessly he said to no one in particular: "I guess we all have to watch ourselves, for we're all suspects now – if we say hello to someone they are a suspect – well, Laura McNair speaks to me and I to her –" He felt pleased that he was able to include Laura McNair within this web of surveillance.

Michael's posture flew in the face of Constable Delano – that very constable who had found Everette Hutch bleeding and unconscious, brought him to the hospital, and therefore had saved his life.

Delano, standing by the nurse's station, didn't acknowledge his remarks. But later, when Michael was alone in the corridor getting another coffee, Delano came over to him and, placing his short red hand on Michael's left arm, said: "I will tell you this much – Miss McNair is a friend of mine, and has had a difficult time. She has lost her brother, her mother has a heart condition and is in and out of care. She has also received death threats – probably from the man in that room. Her father worries about her day and night, and they have not let her mother know. That's why I'm here. You might also think that I'm a terrible man and that it's just a few grams of hash. Well, I don't care at all for a few grams of hash –"

He said this perfectly calmly, and Michael felt another personal sting of anger.

"I would never threaten Ms. McNair or anyone else – you'll soon be proven that!" Michael said, smiling. "And neither would my friends. If you're jealous of me being with Laura McNair, that's not my fault – every one knows how you're bothering her."

He went to go by him, but Delano responded, with pressure still on Michael's arm and a look in his eye that was for Laura McNair's benefit. "One must not be speaking on their friend's behalf without examining their friend's motives."

"Everette's motives are all sincere," Michael snapped. But strangely at that moment he was not thinking of Everette Hutch; he was thinking of Tom Donnerel.

Michael went back to the waiting room. He sat there for another hour and could not bring himself to drink the coffee he had bought. He kept talking about Everette with Everette's friends – how kind he was to everyone who had dealings with him, the way he would give things to you without a thought.

Gail was praying, beads folded in her hands, while her old aunt recited the first decade of the rosary on her knees. After Michael had stopped talking, Gail turned and gave him an urgent smile: "Yes – you are right, Everette can be kind, and good – at times. I do love my brother very much. But if God takes Everette *now* – instead of next year or the year after – but takes him *now*, *all* of us will be *free*. It will be best for Everette as well, that he goes and faces up to what he has done – before his creator – now. So pray with us for that –" And she blessed herself and continued with a Hail Mary, kissing the crucifix on her rosary.

A woman even older than Gail's aunt sat in the corner, looking from one to the other and trying to hear what was being said about her son. Until the second day, Michael did not know this tired little woman, with a kind, intelligent face, was Everette's mother.

By the third day, the doctor advised the family that if Everette did not come out of the coma soon, he would probably not live.

"I'm sure Delano will love to hear this," Michael said bitterly, but for one moment he himself felt a twinge of relief. He also thought, strangely, though he did not want to, of all the money that would *not* come their way now.

Word had moved quickly through the small, violent neighbourhood where Hutch grew up, and people began to collect in the waiting room. Men who by nineteen had the look of cold, impregnable silence in their eyes were staring, in the cramped waiting room, at Michael, as if everyone knew of him.

Two of Everette's uncles came by to collect fifteen dollars their nephew owed them.

The uncles were twins, both wore hearing aids. Both smelled of wine.

"Here," Michael said, taking fifteen dollars from his pocket, and tossing it towards them. "Take it!" And he looked over at Daryll Hutch glaring at him.

"But – it's fifteen dollars apiece," one of the uncles said gleefully.

"Fifteen apiece," the other said.

Michael didn't have any more money on him. But just then John Delano came in and placed fifteen dollars in the second man's hand.

"Here," he said. "You can't be bothering a dying man for money – now go home."

"No, no – I wouldn't," the first uncle said with ingratiating piety. And both men, in ratty pants and worn shoes, nodded to everyone and slinked off.

"What are you staring at, Daryll?" Delano said, noticing Daryll

Hutch's continuous self-aggrandizing stare. Then John smiled. "Well, don't be bothering Michael Skid here – he's a good friend of your cousin's."

Daryll got up and left the room. He did not come back, and it gave Michael a great feeling of relief.

But he was agitated by this also, agitated by Delano's thoughtful generosity after having just argued with the man. And he remembered what Gail Hutch had said: "Pray with us for his death now." And remembered Everette's mother's silent accepting nod.

He went back and sat beside Everette's bed.

In the early-morning hours, when everyone had given up hope, Michael felt Everette's hand grab and clutch his. His face was bandaged. Only one eye was free of wrapping, to glare about the room.

Michael jumped up and went to the waiting room.

"He's awake –" he said softly. Gail, half-asleep, only nodded in acceptance and, with her mother, stood and went in. The old aunt broke out laughing.

When Everette was well enough to speak, he brought Michael close and whispered that his bike had been sabotaged by "certain people," and that because of this Michael would have to take over the deal. He said that Michael had to do things for him.

"You have to become my legs – while I'm in here," he whispered hoarsely with a tube still in his throat, and fluid draining from his ear running onto a white napkin pinned to his johnnie shirt. "Take over – you have to make the big deal – it's coming through – but here I am – you have to go in my place! Please!" he said. "I wouldn't ask you if I didn't trust you – if I said anything to you – to bother you – I'm sorry – but I had to do it – no one would believe me – and I couldn't trust Silver – only you. You have to go up to New Carlisle – it isn't as far as you think – Daryll will tell you where to go – a place we can be safe – then cap it in your barn – you and Silver – take it to P.E.I. – on *The Renegade* – bring every penny back –"

For moments Michael did not respond. How could this have happened? How could he have gone from being on friendly terms with someone to replacing that person in something he did not agree with.

"I don't know," Michael said.

"Shhh," Everette said, trying to look about him, to see who else was there. "You have to, Michael – who else can I trust? I've never had nothing in my life – my whole life –"

And Michael remembered how Everette had stolen the money to buy the drugs for this deal, and for some reason it made Everette seem vulnerable.

"Okay," Michael whispered, "I'll do it – this once but never again."

"Everywhere is death," Everette said. "People have to get closer to each other – they have to start trusting each other or we is all lost!"

Michael nodded.

Everette then sniffed and seemed to reflect on what he'd said. "If you can you bring me in a gun," Everette whispered hoarsely and took his hand again, "I want to get John Delano if he tries to arrest me."

Michael suddenly felt his face go numb. It was said with such casual rage. He looked at Everette's red and blistered arm.

Michael said he would see. But he had no intention of bringing Everette a gun to shoot a constable or anyone else.

He went home and stayed with his parents for a day or two. He did not know what he should do.

He went downriver. The danger at least gave him a certain feeling of accomplishment.

That night he spent waiting in the woods, down a dirt road on the border with Quebec, far up by the Padapedia River for Everette's drugs. He managed to bring the bags of uncapped mescaline and hash, the three-thousand-dollars' worth of blotter acid, back to his farm by three in the morning. He fell asleep in a slumber on the verandah, looking at the stars, thinking of Spain, and thinking too of how terrifying all of this was.

It was by accident the very next afternoon that Michael met Karrie on the beach. By this time everything was ready to go. He would deliver the drugs and get fifteen thousand dollars and bring it back to Everette.

"Every penny," Everette whispered to him, sitting up in bed and eating his supper, with a tube still in his arm.

Everette ordered Michael and Silver not to wait for him. When Michael got back to the farm that night Silver was gloomy.

"It's his deal –" Silver said, sourly. "I've been thinking of this all day. If anything goes wrong, we're screwed. Just leave the drugs for him – if we're out money, who cares? The hell with it. I'll do what you say – here I am – I'll do what you say." He was saying much about what he thought about himself, by his posture, which was huddled and bowed.

All along Everette had told them they didn't have to know anything about what was happening – and now *they* were the ones forced to carry it out.

There was a pause. Their eyes met, and Michael knew exactly what Silver was thinking: that he, Michael, was a weak middle-class boy from town.

"Take the drugs to the boat," Michael said.

Silver, standing in bare feet and cutoff shorts, looked at him.

"Take the drugs to the boat."

"Fuck!" Silver said turning about. "You know Everette doesn't care for you. His cousin Daryll – you can't tell me that lad hasn't killed before. Not a cent will come our way. We bring that money back to Everette, who will see it? So what do you want me to do?"

Yet Michael felt obligated. He remembered his promise.

"No – we have to do it," he whispered. "And then it will be over."

Silver looked at Michael sheepishly. His only comment, as he walked away mumbling, was, "Why do you think he is *still* in the hospital? It's over three weeks. He should be out by now – but it puts everything on our shoulders. He has worked all summer long – to *make* us do this for him. He never intended to do anything himself. Why didn't you listen to Madonna and go to Tom three weeks ago? He wants you in jail – Madonna told me that last fall – he wants the judge's son in jail!"

"Don't be ridiculous –" Michael commented angrily.

So little Silver went by moonlight and put the drugs in the boat.

They left for the Island three days after he first met Karrie. Mist still clung to the trees and over the water. A great marsh hen flew in the silence over those trees, and the boat slunk, listing slightly to port, out of the flat inlet before it was daybreak. There was a moment when both of them were singing and laughing and sharing a bottle of wine.

But before the sun had reached full in the sky they had gotten becalmed. Not a breath of air. So Silver started the motor, but it died as well.

Hours went by. At times they dragged anchor, at times they floated free.

Silver tried to get the motor going and had it in his hands most of the day. The carburetor float was sunk and the lines were filled with dirt. And Michael fretted about the time, and about the danger.

Then they began to argue and bicker, each blaming the other

for everything, including the weather. At 3:30 in the afternoon Silver pulled so frantically on the spinnaker mast he snapped the rope and pulley.

"What are you trying to do?" Michael yelled, noticing the spinnaker cracked along the boom.

"I'm trying to save your arse," Silver said.

After this they worked in silence at opposite ends of the boat, the drugs sitting midship on the starboard side in a small cardboard box.

At nightfall Michael was approaching this box when, without any warning at all, the coast guard hauled along their port, four miles off their rendezvous point.

Michael, seeing only floodlights and hearing the blowhorn telling them they were about to be boarded, panicked and threw the drugs overboard in front of Silver's startled eyes. Silver still had the carburetor in his hand from the old inboard Chevy engine.

Michael was ashamed of this. It was his one lapse.

The coast guard had come alongside to throw them a towline, and hauled them to within five hundred yards of their rendezvous. But they had no drugs to sell and could not make the meeting. Waiting for them was Daryll Hutch and two other men.

"It's gone," Silver said. "It's gone – I can't believe it – I saw it with my own eyes – all the caps just disappeared. It took me four days to cap it. I was in the barn day and night."

He sat down on the deck and began to laugh. His whole body shook up and down, and no sound came from his mouth, and Michael at times did not know if he was laughing or crying.

Then Silver began muttering and cursing. He was outraged. But still he stayed by Michael's side. He would not, ever, desert him.

"You know what?" Silver said, throwing a cigarette into the water. "Let me tell you, okay? We're dead. If Everette finds out we don't have the fifteen thousand, we're dead. He already thought we cheated him in our little pool."

"Oh, don't be crazy, Everette is our friend. He'll understand. I know how to handle him. No one kills for fifteen thousand," Michael said.

"What? No one kills for –? Let me tell you something and you listen, you listen very carefully: Everette is on the fringes of real bad people he's been in and out of jail with. He liked you only because he could use you, you and your boat. And he would kill you for fifteen dollars."

Michael said nothing, but he felt humiliated, and immediately took the towrope in his hand and tossed it off as the coast guard blinked their lights goodbye and moved to the north. The wind had come up, and the small waves danced and jabbed the keel.

Everything they did was done to erase this one mistake.

They could get no more hash or mescaline. They had taken a trip to Fredericton to try to find some on the quiet, from Michael's friend Professor Becker at the university there. Becker had a pleasant, uncaring smile and liked to talk about his female students and Timothy Leary. He had a dark tan. He sat in his office with his sandalled feet propped on the desk, clicking some worry beads in his hand and smiling, looking now and then at Silver, and then giving a glance at Michael, his desk overflowing with papers and books.

But Becker had nothing to give them, though he liked to garnish his talk, and therefore his life, with all of the proper sayings of the time. Once when he left the office, Silver looked over at Michael with the look a disappointed child might have.

"He's talkin nonsense," Silver whispered.

Becker came back with an expensive hash pipe and three small chunks of hash, and locking the door and opening the window passed the pipe around.

Professor Becker then waited until Silver walked back to his Pontiac and, taking Michael aside in the afternoon corridor of the long empty university building, whispered: "These look like dangerous people you are dealing with," he said. He himself looked thrilled at the fact that Michael would know dangerous people, and he asked if he could go and visit the farm.

"No," Michael said, smiling at him, "it's not a good time for you to visit."

Becker looked grave, accepted this with a nod, and walked back to his office, turning at the door to shake his head and wave.

When they got home from Fredericton they found out that Everette was back from the hospital, staying at Gail's and convalescing in the sunshine. Michael could only think of how Everette spoke about others who had cheated him. How when they once witnessed an accident of an elderly couple from Toronto along the coast road, Everette had stood and talked with concern to the police. When he came back to his van, he smiled and winked and said: "That's how I like to see the rich die." Yet Michael had *not* reacted against *that*.

This night, on their return from Fredericton, Michael asked Karrie to take Tom to church, so he could meet him after. He wanted to ask Tom's advice – to come clean, to try to start over. He walked to the graveyard and waited. He could hear the out-of-tune organ during Communion and he stepped a little closer to the church.

Unfortunately, Tom turned away from his entreaty and Michael was left waving into thin air. He was angry and bitter that Tom had deserted him. For a moment that night he thought that Karrie had also deserted him, and did not think he would see her again. And part of him wanted to pay her back for this.

In the end there was nothing else to do. He and Silver had to go and meet Everette.

Everette walked with a cane, and wore a white bandage on his side, and white corduroy shorts, which showed his legs to be thick and muscular. All this made him look even more powerful and oppressive.

He called them in and said: "Where's my money?" Resting his hands on his cane he studied them. He was actually old enough to be Silver's father. To him, drugs, hallucinagens, had absolutely nothing to do with freedom of expression, or values, as Michael believed they had. Drugs had only to do with business, commerce, money, and the using of people like Michael who desired to be gullible about themselves.

By this time Everette had found out everything. He knew that the deal had not happened, that they did not have his money. He also knew how he would react once they told him. He knew how Michael now viewed him with fear, how this new reality was, in fact, the only reality.

He knew for instance that they had gone to Fredericton and whom they had seen. He knew that they had not come to visit him because they were scared. He knew too that this was the first time he had ever asked them to do something for him. He didn't remember all of the other times.

So there was no sense in pretending any longer. And Everette took a certain delight in his posture of having to get tough. And he wanted to give them examples how he could do so.

Silver stood near the shack, looking off in the direction of the trees.

"We'll get it," Michael said, after admitting what had happened.

"Why did you go to Fredericton?"

"We went to Professor Becker. He's a good guy – but he's got nothing much right now."

He expected Everette to laugh and say, "Well, we'll figure a way out." Or even tease him. And he smiled, waiting for Everette to smile.

But Everette didn't tease him at all. When he stood up, in the late-afternoon sunshine, Gail came running up with his tea. He looked at her, Everette did, rushing out the door towards him, and he simply backhanded her with his left hand. She fell against the door, and lay on the ground.

"Don't you fuckin get up," he said. And she lay exactly where she was.

Michael wanted to react – help her – but for the first time in his life he was truly scared.

THREE

The next few weeks were lived in worry and desperation. And their trip to the Island the night of Karrie's birthday was a trip in the hope of getting something going again. Silver insisted they take this trip, because he had people to see there. What Michael didn't know was that Silver was being forced to sell bad mescaline for Daryll Hutch and that he had seven-hundred-dollars' worth of it in his possession, or that this is what he had hidden under the seat of the dinghy.

All during this time Michael was seeing Karrie too. Long before the trip to the Island he was warned to stay away from her, not only by Silver, but by his own inner voice.

"Why do you have her about?" Silver asked him one day.

"Because she doesn't love Tom, and it's better if he finds this out now." He frowned, and took a puff of his cigarette.

Underneath this concern for her was unmasked carelessness and cynicism for no one more than for the girlfriend of his former friend. He did not look upon her as a human being so much as a plaything.

Silver knew this and looked at him silently, and shrugged as if he were disappointed.

"I care very much for her," Michael said spontaneously, noticing Silver's shrug. He batted a mosquito away.

"No," Silver said, "it's just because she's Tom's. It's Tom you care for. Not her. Tom though cares for her – he would crawl on his knees all the way to Manitoba for her. So why don't you leave her alone, let Tom have her? Why aren't you nice to Madonna no more?"

"I am nice to Madonna," Michael said.

"Just get this summer over without no problem. Take a look in a mirror! Everything is going wrong now – it's not the time to have a fling with Karrie Smith. I don't like her parents – I think Dora is a weasel snitch, who will try to find out what is going on here."

It was only after the night of her birthday, the night they went to the Island, when it became clear to Michael that he cared nothing at all for Karrie, and that what was done was all done for the reason Silver had said. But by then Silver treated it all as sport, and so spoke of it as such. "You fucked her good," he said. "I heard her moaning."

Michael told him he didn't want to talk about it – and never to mention Karrie's name again. Silver could see he was upset about what he had done.

"Don't worry, you did him a favour – you just broke her tight cunt in," Silver said. "Why don't you go back to Madonna – she'll suck your cock until you turn inside out."

Silver said this without any other inclination than love for his sister and devotion to his friend.

That same night, Michael left and went out along the bay. He started out in one direction, but was pulled in the other, and walked almost to the wharf, then turned and started back. After a half-mile, he could see the faint glittering lights of his farmhouse, he prayed that Karrie wouldn't be there.

The black trees were solid and nothing entered or left the woods above him except warm draughts of daytime air that had been caught in the spruces, and some flickering lights from fireflies under some secluded branches. The bay was heavy, and warm seaweed rolled onto his feet.

It was almost dark and one swallow flew next to him in the thinning late-summer air.

"I can't see her again," he decided, "I can't. Let her go back to Tom." And he stopped and sat down, wondering how he ever got into so much trouble.

He smoked a cigarette and was ready to go home when far out in the waves, which were rising steadily, he heard some shouts for help. In fact the shouts sounded as if they had come from Karrie herself.

He stripped off his pants and waded into the water, and began to swim towards the noise. He took much water against him and felt the swells move him in the current. He had to bear down and swim hard to reach the shouts. Far across the bay he could see the twinkling of lights, from cottages and houses, that always seemed so sad and so distant.

He swam out far enough to see a boat turned over, and two children in the swell. One was Amy Battersoil – Nora Battersoil's fourteen-year-old sister – the other, a small child of four or five years old.

"Jesus Christ, Amy! What are you doing with a little boy out here?" he roared, his head bobbing in the waves.

The little boy was trying to be brave, but was constantly swallowing water. Amy was trying to hold him up, but he kept slipping out of her grip.

"You'll have to get up *on top* of the boat," Michael said, lifting her with his strong right arm out of the water. But she fell back down and, when she did, took the boy with her.

"We're going to drown!" she cried, which made the child cry. "No!" Michael yelled. "No! You're not going to drown on me." He grabbed her once more, twisting her arm to get it off his neck and throwing her onto the top of the half-submerged dory. "He's gone," she yelled. "Owen!"

Michael looked frantically towards the stern of the boat and saw a child vainly trying to swim towards it. He swam the length of the boat, coming behind the boy and, taking him in his arms, he passed the child to the girl.

"I'm going to push you in," he said. "Hold on to him – I'm going around to the back again and push you in."

For over fifteen minutes he pushed, and twice he felt he could not endure because seaweed had wrapped around his legs. But little by little the outline of the beach loomed closer.

When he got close enough to shore to see it, dismal and grey, he stood up and hauled them in, a pelt of seaweed across his thin strong arms.

Then he found his pants and covered himself, wiping water from his hair. And then he turned on them.

"Jesus Christ – Why were you out there, Amy?"

Suddenly she started to cry. She explained that they had gone to the wharf to look for starfish for the little boy. They'd begun playing in a boat, which was tied to a rung of the ladder, but the rope came loose and she couldn't paddle back. No one else was there.

She kept hoping that the waves would wash them into shore, or that someone on the road would see them, but neither happened. They had been drifting for two hours. When it got dark the wind came up. The boat began to toss and fill with water. The little boy had stood up to call out and the boat tipped.

Michael was still angry but said nothing more about it.

"How's Nora?" he asked.

"Fine," Amy said. She looked cautiously at the boy, and then at Michael, and said nothing.

"What's your name?" Michael asked the child.

"Owen," the little boy said. Then he looked down at the ground, the waves still washing over green rocks near his shoes, and began to cry.

"Oh – don't cry –" Michael said. "Don't ever cry. If you are ever on this shore again, I will show you where I go to read – I read up against the red cliff – up there." He pointed, and noticed his hand was cut. "And if you ever come here and walk up the shore it will sound like all the rocks themselves are talking to you because I read aloud, and there is an echo. I read good books too – but perhaps not as good books as I should." He smiled.

Then he patted the child's head. He led them through the woods, along the old path to their home, and shook the little boy's hand, without going onto their property.

He then walked through the dark woods, feeling elated. Far off there was the smell of wood smoke. Far off there were the sounds of boys and girls having a beach party. Far off – far off was his new life. Which he knew someday he would have.

When he got back to the farm it was very late, and he was startled by Silver Brassaurd.

"He thinks we sabotaged his bike – he thinks it was us who wanted to kill him – he thinks we set everything up to steal from him, and that we went over and sold the drugs in Fredericton – he's going to get Daryll to take care of us unless we get all his money back by September 10. Told you," Silver said. "Told you." He said it as simply as a man does who is proven right, even at the moment of being hanged.

FOUR

Michael went to see Everette the next day. He was asked by Gail to wait in the dooryard while Everette ate. So he walked up and down the drive like a servant.

A cool autumn-like wind cut the blueberry field across the road, and there was the lingering scent of a dead animal. Everette's sky-blue bike rested on its kickstand in the yard. Although scraped and battered it was still rideable. Michael had taken Karrie out on it once.

When Everette came out he hobbled over to the old picnic table, picking up a birch stick before he sat down. Michael stood behind him.

"Everette –" he began.

"It's your trouble – once that is over you can come about again. But as it stands now, it's your trouble – with daily interest –"

Everette sniffed and spat. The wind blew again. He made no movement in either direction.

"Well, no matter what you think of me I want to ask you a favour. It's the only favour I will ask. I heard Laura McNair was getting death threats. Don't threaten her – I mean, she's just doing her job."

At this, Everette turned and thrust the birch stick into Michael's chest, smiling. "You're the one who sabotaged my bike." Then, standing, he walked towards the house in insolent anger at Michael's presumption.

"I was waiting for two years for that deal, all the time I was in jail on 'count of that proper quiff Laura McNair and your old man," he said at the door. "And you ruined it – if you don't have the money back to me I'll confiscate your boat."

A single white trail of smoke came from the dump, and Michael was left to ponder all of this with a sorrowful grin on his face.

Though he had decided not to see Karrie again, and tried to pretend it had never happened, and though he hoped she and Tom would be married, and felt he had done a miserable thing, he went to her house, when he was drunk that night, and had her come outside.

She was having her period and made a feeble attempt to stop him, but he slapped her hands aside and she lay passively in the field as he lifted her nightgown.

He remembered there had been quite a bit of blood on her after he removed her Kotex. She had tried to stop him and then had just given in, so he hauled her Kotex strap down and threw it aside. This had pleased him, and had aroused her.

Yet now he disliked that aspect of things because he thought of Tom.

The next afternoon she came to the sailboat, with a book of poems by Robert Frost.

Her hair was done up, and two strands fell about her ears. She wore small earrings, and a dress, and looked forlorn in the drifting smoke. As soon as she got on the sailboat she began picking up the dishes – some of them had not been done for days. "You've got to take care of this here boat – my parents want to see it." And she turned to him with a self-conscious little grin. "What's this?" he said, quickly, flipping through the pages of the poetry book.

"Oh, I got that for ya," she said.

She kept her head down as he began to lecture her quite calmly about poetry and Allen Ginsberg and Professor Becker, who had once met Henry Miller at a party. And Henry Miller always did outrageous things, he said. His voice was emotionless, and she became scared. He was thinking that Karrie was in danger hanging about with him. And Tom would be outraged if he knew she was in danger. Only he could not tell her this. He wanted her to go away for her own good. Forever.

"But what's the use?" he said, cruelly. "You haven't read a book."

"I did." She looked up proudly, and then lowered her head. "I read *The Moon Is Down* by John Steinbeck," she said, giving a forlorn little smile. The breeze came up, and the loose sail fluttered. Her blouse was clasped with a silver brooch in the shape of a sailboat, with her name engraved upon it, that she had bought to please him. She had bought chimes made of sailboats which she'd placed in the farm's living room. All of this he disliked.

"I do not want to be controlled by *you*," he said.

"I control nothing – in my whole life," she said, still hanging her head. "I've never controlled nothing but my bird feeder."

He looked at her, started to say something else, and couldn't. The sailboat drifted off port in the wind, and there was the smell of acrid smoke.

He could feel the first traces of rain, and he smelled her perfume on that air.

"I have to go – Silver and I – you can't come today."

"I'm sorry," she whispered, still with a cup in her hand.

"Go away," he said. "You'll end up getting in trouble here."

She looked up at him.

Suddenly, he asked her about Tom. His voice began to shake a little.

"I haven't seen Tommie in a long time," she said.

"Well, he's a better man than me," he said. "You don't know, but I do; there are very few men like him. You should go back to him."

"But I can't – because I betrayed him," she said.

"Oh, well, he'll get over that – sooner or later – you can't betray someone forever."

He lit a cigarette and went down into the cutty. He stayed there until he finished his cigarette, and then coming topside he saw her wading across the sandbar towards the cows at the Jessops' farm, the light cotton dress soaking her back, so her white panties were visible, her hair now falling down her shoulder. He threw the cigarette butt into the water, and watched the black flow erase it completely.

FIVE

Karrie went back home, and realized how the house, the chairs, the faint odour of her blood, now all conspired to show her as a fool.

The room she slept in, the unmade bed with its impression of her body, seemed to mock her, as did her collection of tiny doll chairs and suitcases she had kept on her dresser since she was six.

For three days she brooded. She didn't eat with the family – she didn't see them.

"You're getting thin – what's the matter?" Dora said suspiciously.

"I might be getting married," Karrie said, so matter-of-factly it startled her.

The curtains blew in the August evening. Across the paved drive at the gas bar, she heard some boys talking in the dark night. She became lightheaded. A great transport truck filled with dried fish pulled in. And this transport truck with its dried fish, stinking of salt, startled her.

Instantly she wanted to say that what she had just said wasn't true, that she was not really getting married, and instantly her voice failed her. She simply stared wide-eyed, and then touched her finger to her nose because of the unpleasant smell of fish.

"It's not settled *yet*, of course – I don't know if I want to. He's so damn wild, Mike, with his long black hair. But do you believe in love at first sight?" She smiled at this thought, and placed her hands on her lap. "I believe in love at first sight on certain occasions – if the man and woman is really mature," she added. "But they have to be really mature – and not sit around all day listening to George Jones." And she laughed. "They should listen to some Bob Dylan too."

"Yer so growed up now," Dora said, staring at her stepdaughter, "Way more sophisticated, I must say." And she smiled. She always stared at Karrie with a false love that hid meanness and self-interest. Karrie could see this. She understood how powerless she was now, powerless unless her delusion came true. She also felt the first twinges of rage. She thought of the money that her stepmother controlled, and kept in the tin box, and rage at this meanness overcame her. She'd never had a party given for her in her life. And really, except for poor old Vincent, she'd never had a friend in the house. She looked away from Dora, and cleared her throat.

Then Dora talked about Tom. How she secretly disliked him, and how she loathed that retarded boy, Vincent, with his silly dog. And, smiling slightly, Dora whispered about how big his penis was in his loose pants.

"You can see the whole thing stuffed in there – makes me faint, I must say," Dora smiled.

Karrie tried not to listen, but she knew Vincent was a bother now every day, waiting for her – hoping to see her, knocking on the door, walking about the house or hanging around the gas bar so that Dora had threatened to get the police.

Karrie could not stand to listen to this, so she went back to her room, feeling rage descend down her spine. As she walked from the den, she could see the tin box. She had taken money from that box to give to Michael for gas for *The Renegade*, and none of them even thanked her. And the way Madonna treated her was horrible. And yet it seemed so important to have Madonna love her.

She sat for many moments in her room thinking, quite clearly, as lucidly as she had ever thought; and something came to her in a revelation.

What if his father knew –?

She was prepared to go to Michael's father and tell him what she knew. That Silver and Michael had broken the spinnaker on his boat. She looked over at the round gilt-edged mirror, and saw the start in her eyes. Her eyes were pale blue, large, and her face was white, shaded, just slightly, by freckles.

She thought of having been called "cinnamon girl," and was now horrified at her naiveté. She would tell his father about that! And once Michael was driving a Harley-Davidson on the shore road, and got it stuck, and he asked her to help him push it. So they had to push it back to the house, and she had burned her calf on the exhaust. The pain was excruciating and it left a mark. And all of this she could tell his father. That is, she could tell about how everyone was fooled by Michael, because he tormented her. And he wasn't in love with life – or had big plans. Didn't he know that she knew what his plans were? Only to – to have girls!

But the knowledge that one has been self-deceived comes with a terrible suddenness. Now it was so vivid. The blueberry pie she made for him and brought down the path. She had been so happy to make it – and at the moment she gave it to them, she could feel them staring at her as if they all wanted her to go home.

She thought again of Dora's meanheartedness. The stinginess of the house, the smallness of the talk. Worse, the terrible shanty she kept, where those poor people stayed, with the little five-year-old boy named Brian. She thought of how Dora always made fun of them after she took their money.

She shivered. She was too angry even to begin to imagine what she might do. She could tell the police about the money or how Dora had the pumps rigged so they made three extra cents on every dollar. Or she might take the money from the tin box and go away to Europe. They would never be able to tell anyone because it was stolen money. She would learn to ski. She would have all kinds of friends, but never see anyone from home again! They would see her picture in the paper, and she would have a fur coat and she would sue them and have to go to court and they would be scared to hear her name mentioned!

She did not want to love Michael any more but he would be sorry. Perhaps she would die. They would all come to the funeral. But they wouldn't let him. She could see it all. His dark black eyes, his long hair, his walk which always slightly troubled her. There would be the light of candles, some dead leaves – they would be singing something very new, and everyone would try to touch the coffin.

She tucked her knees up under her and rocked herself to sleep.

SIX

The day he sent Karrie away, Michael left the sailboat and went back to the farmhouse. He lay in bed thinking of Nora Battersoil, and remembered the line from an old country and western song: "*I give her everything but she flew.*"

Later that afternoon Silver came to the house agitated and angry. He sat in the living room. Michael told him he would have to hide the boat – if he could just take it up to Millerton, and hide it at an island he knew.

"The boat is my dad's," he said. He looked as a person does when they suddenly find themselves in a crisis and are ready to ask for help. And this is how Silver looked upon him now, in compassion for his frailty. Silver wore a clean red shirt that Madonna had pressed, and jeans with the cuffs turned up. He looked like a poor and tiny peasant on his way to the county fair. In fact, he was on his way to the church picnic.

"Now," Silver sighed, "Everette thinks we're all working together against him – and that you set him up – and –"

"But I was at his side day and night," Michael said.

"It doesn't matter, it's one way he can use to –"

"To what?"

"To fuck Madonna – do you understand?"

Michael said he wasn't sure.

So Silver just shrugged. "Madonna won't unless he promises to bail us out of this jackpot. That's what's been going on with her. She's been protecting us by keeping her arse covered. Now what you've got to do is *not* see Karrie Smith any more – go back up to town – stay there for your own sake. You must go back home – he won't bother you up there – he's too scared to do that. If you think he'll walk in on you at supper you're crazy – he's a coward. And Madonna and I worry about you because – well – because you've been good to us! So I'll take care of the money. But I don't know about Professor Becker – we should never have gone to see him."

"Who – why?" Michael said. His face was white. It looked as if he had been just hit with a board.

"Because Becker bragged all over the place that these drug people came to see him."

"Why – who – told you –?"

"So Everette sent Daryll to talk to him – the idea is we gave him the drugs to sell. We didn't, but that don't matter. Now Becker is all scared – if something happens he'll be the first one to go to the cops –"

And the concept that it was Silver for these nine months who had been wise, and trying to hang on to the reins of reality suddenly was present in the terrible silence. And Michael looked at him with shame.

"I'll phone Becker tonight," Michael said.

There was the smell of cigarette smoke and aftershave where Silver sat. A poverty, a poverty of spirit, that comes in all guises and has no favourite, emanated from him like it never did from his sister. And Michael felt for him, and remembered even more painfully that the only thing Silver had wanted to do that summer

134

was enrol in a course to become an electrician, and he had wanted Michael to help him apply. Michael until now had forgotten all about this.

Michael could say nothing. For now he had entered *their* world, and this was not what Mr. Jessop had wanted at all.

He phoned Becker, but Becker was neither at his house, a bungalow on a one-way street overlooking the river in the city of Fredericton, nor at his office at the university.

Michael then had four or five drinks and tried to sleep.

Later that afternoon, as he was lying on the bed in the master bedroom, wondering how to escape, to get away, Michael had a phone call. For a few moments he didn't know who it was. Her voice seemed to come from far away, from a planet other than his own, from a place that still entertained ideas of goodness.

"Hello, Michael – I'm having a party – September 9 – could you come up? Don't blame your mother – actually it was my mother – I haven't seen you all summer – so it is me – if you could – come."

He suddenly realized it was Laura McNair. He felt sad for her, prompted by the loss of her brother and by the anonymous death threats.

"Sure – I'll try to make it – I really will – I promise I will," he said.

Later he sat in the old chair in the living room staring at the sailboat chimes Karrie had bought him. Their tinkling in a soft breeze from an open window became excruciating after a while.

He left the house.

The road was muddy. It had rained that afternoon, but now the stars were poking out, and a moon, sliver-thin, hugged the sky behind the trees. He walked through the mud as if he were on high heels and made his way to the gate.

He turned to his left and walked towards the highway, later turning to his right and crossing a huge cow field in the dark. He walked in the direction of Tommie Donnerel's house for the first time in over a year.

He could smell the horses in the night air, the farm was quiet, the barn rested against the trees as always, while the house sat in an open space with its downstairs light on.

There was a new swing on the new verandah, and Michael remembered how he had told Tom he should buy one when they were building. Everything was quiet, even serene. Suddenly he smelled sawdust and felt nostalgic for that time and place that would never return.

If only he could go back to it. He thought of Vincent, who'd always asked Michael to take him sailing, and then he turned to go. As he did he noticed a hand move the curtain and saw Tom staring out the window at him.

He saw Tom's eyes, green and blazing dark in a kind of futile anger and sadness. They seemed to stare away at the infinite vagaries of coming darkness, the crux of the wide oak tree gone soft in the night air, and over all into the possibility of one's own death.

That is what the eyes of Tom Donnerel were saying to him. Yet when they faced him they were bruised and hurt, and reflected a kind of irony.

His immediate impulse was to turn about and leave.

Yet he did not manage to move.

"Come in," Tom said, as he opened the door and turned away.

Michael walked into the small kitchen, with the smell of the night in his hair, and of night air still evaporating on his skin. He wanted to tell Tommie how much trouble he was in. But pride stopped him short, and he only managed a strange, sheepish smile.

Tom sat back down with his dinner. Michael put his palms under his thighs.

Tom had been thinking of a word for the whole day and he

had come up with it. "The real trouble is someday you will have to live the *posture*," Tom said. "I don't know when it will come, but when it does – it will be a hard life from then on."

He kept his head down cutting his steak, while the little dog sat at his feet staring up at him wagging its tail. That was the word, *posture*. That was all Tom wanted to say. And he gave a slight, self-incriminating smile for using such a heady word.

Tom stared up at him, sniffed, and again looked down at his steak, as if he were concentrating on cutting into the plate itself. But there were tears in his eyes. Then after a long moment he shrugged. Even the shrug seemed to relay his pain and acute suffering over Karrie.

"I just came up to tell you that I – love Karrie – as a person – but nothing more – so I hope you can forgive us – because you can have her back – it was all a mistake. It'll take time but she can be yours again – no one meant to hurt you. It is you she loves – not me. Not deep down. She thinks I am someone I am not. But she will see that it is you who are all she ever wanted – and I'll head away and leave you two be."

Tom said nothing. Again his eyes were dark and fathomless. And then he looked up in a kind of self-incriminating mirth, and put his head down.

Again he cut deep into his plate. Again his shoulders moved, and again Michael noticed tears in his eyes.

"I'm sorry – for everything," Michael said. "But everything will work out."

He went over and held out his hand. Tom looked up from his plate, tried his darndest, but couldn't bring himself to take it.

Michael walked back down the lane, away from the house, and its added room, the shingles still golden. He walked slowly, his boots making soft slur marks in the pitted dirt, and turned down towards the lane. He walked almost to the shore, thinking that Tom and Karrie could have a happy life together.

He went to a stump and sat down, wondering what he could possibly do to extricate himself from Everette Hutch, who now said he had let him down? And further, how could he help those who had once trusted him?

"This is terrible," he thought. "I'll kill him if he comes for Madonna – I'll not let them suffer any more."

Yet he felt sick, hopeless, and terrified.

SEVEN

Two days after Michael visited Tom, Karrie went to see him. He was reading, sitting against the red cliff, his shoulders thrust into it as if he were hiding. He wasn't reading the Kama Sutra, however – he was reading Cicero once again, only the subtle significance of this was lost on Karrie.

Karrie missed the sailboat and everything she thought was associated with it – its sanctuary and freedom, her desire to belong, to express the opinions of others, and to constantly think of herself as being harmed. Those things that are always sought by youth.

She walked up to Michael sternly, but then lowered her eyes. Then, like a child, she told him she would tell his father everything, for she was no one's fool. Even if he did call her "cinnamon girl." And then she stamped her foot.

When she stamped her foot, it made a strange thud on the desolate beach. Like a heartbeat. The waves were grey and cold and filled with dark seaweed. Michael's eyes seemed to start, as if his pulse had quickened.

She smiled and then turned away from him, biting her bottom lip.

"*What* do you know?" Michael asked.

"Oh, I just know, that's all."

She walked over to where she had tumbled over the bank two months before, but the tide was high and she couldn't go any farther.

So she stood with her back to him, like a small orphan.

"Come here," he said.

And she turned slowly, then ran towards him.

Later he had the others apologize to her as if it were their fault a falling-out had happened, and not hers. He looked at Silver sternly when he spoke. And Karrie felt very good, for it was the first time she felt that things were not being blamed on her.

Silver stood before her, his eyes cast towards the ground.

"You must stop hanging about with bad people, Silver, or everyone will know about it. You don't think I don't have any information regarding what happened here – the trouble you two are in?" she said, shaking her finger, a bit of authority in her voice, and feeling very happy. "And with Michael's father – a judge – why you're just lucky you're not all in jail!"

Silver glanced up, and looked at Michael as she spoke. And Karrie gave a brief, embarrassed laugh.

Then they went out on the sailboat. But she asked Michael to turn it about. It was past her supper hour and she had to go home.

She smiled and winked at Madonna when he let her take the wheel. She could feel the waves against the starboard side, and kept her legs wide apart and bent a little at the knees to keep her balance; in doing this she looked as she had looked as a child of six when she had placed those tiny suitcases on her dresser, all those years ago.

She began to sing loudly and there were tears in her eyes from the wind. She went home feeling vindicated for the first time since she had gone picking blueberries on what now seemed a long-ago day.

The next day Michael went to town. He sat in the waiting room of the bank. He was dressed inappropriately, in cutoffs and a T-shirt, but he wore no bandanna on his leg.

He went into the bank to ask for a loan of fifteen thousand dollars, feeling dissociated from where he was. The bank's loans officer, one of the young men he had grown up with and liked, looked at him in embarrassment when they started to go over his assets. And Michael stood and left, without completing the application. The loans officer followed him to the door, asking him to come back, but Michael couldn't bear to turn around.

That night he went to see Karrie, distracted and nervous. His eyes glanced here and there as he smoked, which made her nervous as well.

He asked Karrie to take a walk. She was suddenly frightened when she looked at him, seeing how unsure of himself he was. They went into the woods and along the path. Then he turned and coughed.

"I have to go away –" he said.

"What do you mean?"

"I mean it's not good here any more. I've been to the bank but I can't get the money –"

"Why do you need money?" she asked.

"If I can get some money – I can go over to Spain – or out to B.C. I don't like asking you this. I thought you might have some money – you mentioned that you knew where some was – it'll all be paid back once I find a job."

Why he looked afraid she didn't know. Yet as he spoke a small, controlled smile appeared at the corners of her mouth.

"Is Tom bothering you – about me?" she said.

"Partly." He stared at her, and then, blinking, looked away.

"I'll talk to Tom," she said. "So don't you be afraid of him."

"No – talk to no one – no one." Then, knowing he was frightening her, he smiled awkwardly.

"Tom's been violent to me too," she said. It was perhaps the first lie she had ever told about him, but she couldn't help it. It suddenly felt very natural that Tom would have tried to bully them both.

Michael looked at her as she nodded her head and then glanced sideways.

"A little bit."

The last of the evening's light came through the trees in a golden splash and touched her cheek.

"I *will* go to Tom," he said.

"No, no – never mind," she said, and she clutched his hand. There was a pause. A swallow darted, zigzagging up the path as if a scout for God. It felt awkward for him to hold her hand and she sensed this.

"But maybe you can't help me," he said.

"Don't you worry," she said, "don't worry," And she winked. She felt very grown up suddenly, and motherly. "I'll protect you – here, let me kiss your eyes." And she lifted herself up and kissed both his eyes. He stared at her sadly.

"Oh, yes, money," she said, raising her finger in mock indulgence. "I think I can get us some of that dirty ole money."

For once Karrie felt important. And she would surprise Michael with so much money he would never have to worry. And though he hadn't asked her to come, she knew he would want her to go too. So she made up a story about going to Fredericton, and when Dora pressed her she used the only name she knew. That she knew a Professor Becker, whom Michael had gone to see about enrolling her. He was a professor dealing with social problems, who had written an article for a book, and now knew all about her.

Michael spent a few days at his parents', sitting in his large bedroom staring at the wall of books, the microscope from his youth, trying to work on his article and hide from what he realized about himself: that until he resolved matters with who he now called "those people," that is, Everette and Daryll, he had no moral authority to sit in judgement of the antics at his boarding school, most of which were juvenile. He realized this is what Tom must have seen that Christmas night when he had shown part of the article to him.

Yet he could straighten things out. He would ask Karrie to forgive him. He would confess to Laura about the drugs. He must do this, not because he was high-minded, but because he felt he had no other option now. It would be a great relief.

He would tell Laura about the drugs the night of her party. Then the next morning – September 10 – he would go to his father and confess everything, plead guilty if it went to court.

He would forfeit the article and not let recrimination be his. He would do all of this at the right moment. It would mean devastation for himself. It would mean appearing in court and becoming a prosecution witness against Everette, and maybe even against Silver and Madonna. Yet, no matter how tormented this made him, it was the only thing he could think of to do.

His mother was happy he was home, and in order to apologize to him, told him where the money on the ironing board had turned up.

"Do you know where the money turned up?" she said.

"No," he answered, startled.

"It turned up in the pocket of my housecoat – the very next afternoon – I wanted to phone you but I felt so silly." And she looked at her husband, smiling, as if seeking comfort. But a little later, after she laughed and talked about nothing in particular, he realized that she could not look him in the face, and that her eyes were cast downward.

When he got up to go to bed and said goodnight, she raised her eyes.

"Yes, goodnight," she said, looking at him, startled, which unnerved him.

"Well, I'm glad you found it," he said, but he went to the door of the den without turning around.

"I'm glad you are going to see Laura," she called, when he was halfway down the hall.

Karrie spent a good deal of time that last week doing her nails while sitting with her legs tucked up under her in the porch. As the days came and went she thought many times what she must do. And when the day came, she did everything as if she were sleepwalking. She packed a suitcase and left it in her room. She waited until Dora went back over to the gas bar after supper to flirt with the young men, as Dora did every night.

Karrie crossed the den and closed the door. She removed from her brassiere a key that she had taken from Dora's jewellery box. She opened the small hinged drawer at the back of the modest-sized bookshelf, which had three copies of the Bible and four Jacqueline Susanne novels, and took out the tin box with both hands. She opened it slowly and timidly, and her mouth opened in surprise at the amount of money there was inside.

"Oh God," she whispered, and brushed a tear away.

Then she counted some, with her hands shaking. She hoped this would not be discovered right away – she assumed the loose money was "new money" collected over the summer, and she hoped she would be able to send it back to them soon. The majority of the money was wrapped in two large red plastic bands.

She began to giggle at the awful thing she was doing, and for several moments she didn't know whether to put the money back or not, and tears of shame rolled down her face. But they were not so much tears of shame for her part, as for that of her father and stepmother, who'd had the gas pumps rigged, and had robbed even her friends, like Bobby Taylor.

Suddenly she stood and went into the kitchen and wrote a note and placed it on the fridge. Just then she heard her stepmother coming back and ran to put the key back in her stepmother's jewellery box just as Dora came in, and having nowhere to put the money, she shoved it down her panties against her crotch.

When Dora met her in the hallway, Karrie suddenly remembered she had forgotten to put the tin box away, and in panic she left the house, deciding that she wouldn't come back until everyone was asleep to pick up her passport photos and her suitcase.

At this moment, as it had been the first night she had sex, she felt she was unable to stop, even though she wanted to.

EIGHT

Tom was in the barn that evening of September 9.
He'd let the mare run out kicking after her oats, and now
rested against the side door looking out at a pale sky filled with
the first scent of autumn. Everything in the distance was dark-
ened, but the sky, the foreboding sky, was white, and the lights in
the house shone yellow.

When he saw the figure standing within spitting distance he
jumped. She was standing in a white pantsuit in the middle of
his yard.

"Go away," he pleaded.

A bat flew haphazardly against the sky right in front of his
face, and he turned away, feeling the last draughts of heat from
the horses.

The barn was dark and the air was quiet. Two more bats flew
out of the air vent far above them.

"Poor Vincent, I thought I might come visit him," Karrie said.

"He's gone down to get tobacco," Tom said, "so he'll be wandering the road again tonight. He keeps staying out later and

later looking for you. If he tries to get you to come up here – you just tell him no."

He wanted to say something terrible to her, but he couldn't. And thinking this, and remembering the diamond in his pocket, he took it out and thrust it at her.

He had expected to get on his knee when he handed it to her. But that was a ridiculous thought from a long while ago. Now she was a stranger, and he thrust it at her to prove that she was nothing to him.

She took it without a word and stared at it.

"Keep it for old-time's sake," he said in a daze of nonchalance and control, as if resigned now to their new condition and accepting it.

She looked up at him quickly, trying to measure something, and handed the ring back, but he didn't take it. So, after a moment, holding it tenuously in her fingers, she tucked it into her pocket.

"It was you who was following me then – to give me this?"

He didn't answer. She smiled. Suddenly she wanted to feel as if everything would turn out for her.

"Don't worry about me, Tom – I've grown up. You were over-protective," she sighed. "That's what Michael tells me. I guess that's why I rebelled. Michael trusts me. I've met a whole group of new people – wonderful women and men who know what's going on."

She saw the pain in his face, and it reminded her of her own pain a week ago. Her legs trembled just slightly. The mare had gone across the old paddock and rested near Arron Brook. The sky was dark.

He said nothing. He stood with his eyes lowered as she spoke.

"I'll tell Vincent not to bother you again – but he doesn't have his wits."

"Don't worry about me, Tom, please – you're too good a man for me. I'm not a good person – but I'm very independent now

– that's the striking difference between me now and before. Independence for women is what people like us are now after." Strangely, she spoke in a little girl's voice. "And once we get things straightened out here, we are on our way to Spain." She smiled a little vainly, and couldn't help it, because she'd almost never travelled before. Her hair was done up, held with pins, and her eyes were splendid.

Now, as Tom looked at her, she felt a great sentiment wash over her. A new life was coming, the old life drifting away. She thought of how silly she had been, to think of Tom as special just that short while ago. Now he feared her, and she questioned this. She did not understand that he feared her because she was naive, and the naive are always dangerous to themselves and to others.

"We have to go away – Michael and I is trapped here now – always being watched by the locals. I don't feel anything for people here now, Tom. I've grown away from people here – that's why Michael and I is going away – I tried – it's been very hard for me this summer, so please consider that! There is no – no love of poems like I learned about – and sweet wonderful sentiment, and things like that there – that Michael has taken the time to teach me. Tom, I have to tell you this," she said. "I have to tell you that I was scared a ya. I was frightened. Remember when you picked up that wheel, and just threw it against the side of the barn, how it scared me? I thought you were going to kill me."

Tom did not understand at this instant that she was telling him this because she had already told this to Michael and then to her father and stepmother, and so she had to make the story true.

"I – I don't – but I mean – you come here," he said, and he made a clumsy attempt to hold her one more time. When he held her, he felt as if he were suddenly holding some great part of his life that he had lost.

She tore away from him, looked up at his face and turned.

She walked down the dark road. Night had come as silent as a stone. She was feeling happy. She took a deep breath and looked up at the sky.

"Well, that's settled," she thought.

Then she remembered the tin box. What would they do to her when they saw their money missing? How could she face them? She would stay out until late, until she was sure they'd be asleep.

And as she walked she thought instead of how she would tell Michael about her mother's death. And how her mother had been a victim. Perhaps Madonna and Silver would come to say goodbye to them. Karrie would tell all of them how she grew up without a mother: how she went to midnight Mass that first Christmas after her mother died and the old priest, Father Lacey, called her up to the altar and told her she had a pretty dress and when she turned to go back to her seat a sad feeling came over her that was the best feeling in the world, and people were looking at her and crying.

Madonna would then know who she was, and hug her, and there would be tears in Madonna's eyes. And there would be that great reconciliation she longed for with the entire world.

"Please write," Madonna would say.

She would buy Madonna something too – something very special to give her – before they left. She could not think of what it would be, but then suddenly she decided it would be a brooch, just like the one she owned.

Madonna would say: "Oh, I don't deserve none a this."

And Karrie would simply smile radiantly and hug her. Then, of course, Silver. Well, she would hug him too, and tell him to be good, and the train whistle would blow at the exact same time she spoke, just like in the movies, and he would see that she was right, and change his life, and that would be the end of it.

In her mind years passed, and she and Michael would have an argument over something. And then he would come up to her and say: "Yes – you are right – what would I do without you?" They would be in Spain, perhaps. And own a villa there.

Gail and her son. Her *people*. That was one of her *good* acts she told no one about.

Karrie had tried to be kind to Gail and her boy all summer long. But to Karrie, Gail's brother Everette and his friends were those "sad people" she did not understand.

Did she want to go and say goodbye? She thought she might have to go to them to say goodbye tonight!

She had brought Gail pies, and macaroni and cheese, and candy for the little boy. Hardly anyone knew this either. It was her secret. She never minded how dark and sordid the place was, with vicious stingers growing outside the back window. The little boy always seemed to be glad to see her, and one time she brought him a toy.

She had prayed to the Virgin Mary that, if she were a sinner, to count this as one of her *good* acts, and to protect her people, the little boy especially. She prayed that when she went away someone else would come down and help them. For them to be saved from those sad, cruel people you didn't talk about.

The place reeked of gasoline and was dark, and she was always ashamed because Dora charged them so much – sixty dollars every two weeks.

She wanted to do *nice* things for them.

She had met girls from town who were majors at university also. They were all majors at university. And their being accepted by the new world didn't hinge on being able to cook or clean or sew, but on having the right attitude about things, like women's rights. And suddenly she felt she must have this attitude also.

Suddenly she thought of an off-colour joke Madonna told, and flushed. She was such a case, that Madonna!

"Oh, my bird feeder," she thought. "What will I do about my bird feeder?"

She left the highway and proceeded down the lane, limed to keep down the dust from the traffic, making her way through the woods towards the field below her house.

She thought of Madonna's joke, felt agitated, excited and wet.

The wind began to blow, and the tops of the trees waved. The path was rooted, and leaves had fallen over it. There had not been a sinister moment for her this summer. But now, everything affirmed itself suddenly as sinister.

She saw someone in front of her who had a scarf pulled up over his face and he was standing next to a tree.

"I'm not going to jail for you or either is *he*," he said. "So what evidence do you have?"

It startled her. She didn't know what he meant.

"You'll start blabbing – you stupid little cunt."

She smiled, and then her face froze into that smile when he mentioned that awful word. She knew it was Silver, with the silly scarf – the same one Madonna wore hunting.

Karrie had no idea what he was saying.

"Take that stupid scarf off, Silver," she managed to say. She looked around and there was no one near them.

"You're not going anywhere until you promise to give me the evidence you say you have!" He startled her by coming out of the trees beside her, with the scarf pulled down. "What, you take something, to give to the police? What? If Everette goes to jail over this he'll kill us all."

"You wait and see – we are going away! To Spain or something like that there –" She looked at him and became terrified. "I mean – I promise Michael and I are going away – and we won't bother anyone again!"

"Michael! He's the last person who would take you anywhere." Silver laughed. He laughed such an awful laugh.

The trees moved in the wind, and a bird screeched.

Then came a moment when she realized he would not be able to let her go. That this conversation had precipitated an action he had not reckoned on. She realized this at the exact instant he did, and both of them looked at one another, startled.

"Tom," she said. "Tommie!"

She turned to run back to Tom, still trying to smile. There was a blow to her head and she went to hold it, and then fell. She started to vomit. She tried to stand, and she saw his hands. She suddenly remembered those hands as he had leaned against the door the very first day she had gone to the farmhouse.

"Hey, you," she said, to call upon his humanity. "Hey, you just listen." She managed, but she was losing consciousness.

What she was going to tell Michael's father about was the fact that they had gotten becalmed and had broken the spinnaker on the sailboat, and Silver said he wouldn't help pay for it. That was the *secret* she was going to tell, to send them to jail.

And then suddenly, a rage descended upon her. She felt as enraged at the wasted time in her life, the tragic sorrow of her life, which seemed all the more sorrowful because she had bought that poetry book of Robert Frost, and no one would ever get to read it. At the loss of her life, and the child she might have held, as any human being who ever existed. She felt sorrow at the sound of voices calling her name, of those she would no longer be able to help. Then quite suddenly she began to know and to understand. And in knowing, she wanted only these things – to see and hug Madonna, to ask Tom's and her father's forgiveness – to long for a reconciliation between her and the entire world – to hope in love and justice for all humanity – to –

"Silver, don't you understand? You will pay," she managed to say, with a good amount of bravery, and then she closed her eyes, as she saw the terrible rock descend.

He didn't mean to kill her. He would maintain that forever and ever. He only wanted to scare her away, because he'd been worried for two weeks and hadn't been able to sleep, and was sniffing glue and taking bennies.

He hit her nine times, but she was dead after the third blow. He felt her dying, life leaving her. He hit her until a bit of brain came out the side of her head above her ear. Suddenly to Silver it was as if he could see her watching from above as he kept hitting her, as if she was telling him she was dead, and not to be frightened of her any more.

But he kept hitting her, talking to her the whole time. And then the voice above him stopped talking to him, and she just went away.

Then there wasn't a sound. She was curled up sideways, and he rolled her over. There was blood all over the path and on his hands and clothes. He had to do something about that. And he ran. He had not meant to do it this way, but now that he had he tried to force it out of his mind.

NINE

Michael was at the party at Laura McNair's. All evening he believed he was working himself up to an announcement – a full disclosure of what he had done that summer. At first he thought he would tell her while everyone was present. But this didn't seem possible. As he sat looking at her parents, at her, at her friends, time marched along and his nerve failed him.

What prompted this change of heart was seeing Laura's face, the poignancy of her decision to hold a party – Michael had not known it was in his honour until he got there. She was playing her own matchmaker. And she had invited friends of hers, whom she thought could be friends of his – a small man with horn-rimmed glasses who was studying Celtic mythology and pretended to be a wine-taster. A woman who had been to Ryerson, but not when he had been there. A female member of the NDP, who used her womanhood to evoke privilege.

In all ways, her parents were kind, decent people who had not had a lot of good fortune. And he knew, looking at them rushing about, that they thought *he* was. He was to be their good fortune. The worst of it was, he now wished he could be.

Laura asked him to give a speech. The woman from the NDP sat forward and smiled. The little man with the hornrimmed glasses stood in the centre of the floor with his head down, as if terribly embarrassed.

Michael stood proudly. "If only there is time," he said, "I too will have a life."

And he took Laura's hand. Everyone laughed when he said this. It was a strange thing for a man of twenty-four to say.

He left Laura's house just after one o'clock and did not go downriver. At his parents' house he started to phone Karrie, but decided against it. He sat on the edge of his bed, looking vacantly about the room.

"Poor Karrie," he said aloud and felt what he had never felt before – a rush of kindly, innocent feeling towards her.

TEN

Silver had washed himself in the bay, and had thrown the rock into the waves. He went back to his house through the woods, hid his clothes and scarf behind the wall of the shed, where he kept his tool board, and got a clean pair of jeans from the dryer.

He grabbed a screwdriver and tucked it into his pants in case he had to defend himself.

Then he went back to Michael Skid's farmhouse. A few boys were there drinking but Michael was away at a party in town, they told him. This seemed to relieve him quite a bit.

No one paid any attention to him, or to his nervousness. He examined himself carefully. There was no blood at all on his shoes. The blood on his hands had been washed away. He moved those hands nervously.

Then he sat down for a while, laughing and talking, and asked three or four times where Karrie was.

But suddenly he left the house.

When he came to the black spot on the path he hoped that he wouldn't see her. That she wouldn't be there, but would have gotten up and gone home. Yet she was still there. Her blue eyes were half-opened, staring at the sky. One arm was out behind her. He undid her pantsuit and took it off, and then took her panties off. He was thinking of undoing her bra but didn't. He pushed it up over her breasts, and touched them both just slightly. Then he didn't know what else to do. He couldn't enter her, though he thought that was why he must have done all those things. Her body was turning blue and cold and – what was terrible – it was absolutely indifferent to him. He tried to masturbate but he couldn't.

And then he just stared at her, and realized that there was money piled inside her panties, and under her blouse. There were hundreds of dollars.

He picked the money up, and shoved it in his pants, looking back over his shoulder as he began to tremble.

Then he sat a little away from her, staring at her crotch, and its downy, whitish blonde hair, moving almost imperceptibly in the wind. It was impossible for him not to.

He didn't know why this made him feel so sorry for her life, and how precious and vulnerable life was.

He went back along the path towards the gas bar with her panties and a hundred-dollar bill in his hand, and the three or four things he had taken from her pants pocket.

Suddenly coming towards him, smoking his pipe, was Vincent. Silver dropped the panties.

He went off to the side and watched him pass. But Vincent bent over, picked up the panties, and the hundred-dollar bill which had fallen on them too, and looked around.

"Hello," he said. "Hello, you."

Vincent waited for what Silver thought was an eternity. And then he moved off down the path in the direction of the farm. Silver could smell his own sweat, and his body odour, and worse, he could smell Karrie's body all over him. It was her body he could smell – her blood, her urine, her faeces, her brain, all of which had come from her as he hit her.

Worse, he remembered Tom's horrible look that night at the house, when he'd given him wine. If Tom ever knew this he would kill him in a second.

"I have to act smart," he whispered to a tree directly in front of him. *If Vincent finds the body,* he thought, *it could be blamed on him.* "It weren't my fault anyway."

He then continued on the path, and suddenly – for all things seemed to be very sudden now – he decided there must be more money at Emmett and Dora Smith's. He didn't quite know why, but felt there must be.

He went around to the patio door, the one Karrie had stepped out that night when seduced by Michael, and slid it open.

The house was silent, and its unfamiliar shadows bothered him. He went into the kitchen, with its new linoleum, and its brass pot above the stove, and its oven mitts hanging above the roasting oven from a wooden oven-mitt holder that was shaped like a small cat.

He heard the fridge's motor running and turned and saw a note on it that Karrie had written: "Home in an hour – K."

The house was in darkness, the blinds drawn and the gas-bar light shut off. The only light in the den came from the streetlight across the highway that her father was so proud of.

"They don't put a streetlight just everywhere," he had said to Silver one afternoon. "They only do it with more 'portant people on the road."

It was that streetlight that frightened Silver. It was casting his shadow on the couch where Emmett was sleeping, his arm over his head much like Karrie's was now. The man didn't wake, even though Silver had his screwdriver ready just in case.

Silver's hands were shaking and he heard Dora turning over in bed inside. So he became afraid and started to leave.

When he turned he saw the tin box on the small table below the lightswitch, where Karrie had left it.

He took it and brazenly walked back into the dark. As soon as he closed the patio door he heard Dora's voice: "Karrie – get in the house now!"

But there was no other sound, and he turned and went home. He put the screwdriver back on the tool board. Everything had been done, almost.

He opened the tin box. It was filled with money – fourteen or fifteen thousand dollars. For a long time Silver had suspected that they were rigging their pumps, and this money must have been collected over a two- or three-year period.

He counted the money that had been inside Karrie's panties. There was some eighteen hundred dollars.

Then keeping the money in his left hand and looking at it as he tossed the tin box on the wood pile, he went into the house.

Madonna had just come home. He looked at her for a moment.

"Where were you?" she said. "Everette needs to meet with you."

"Just out," he managed. Suddenly he broke out sniggering. Then he told her that he was laughing at a joke. He told a joke that had no meaning to it, and passed her, his body moving sideways. He turned and, unable to help himself, said, almost shouting, "I hope Michael treats Karrie Smith better than Tom did. I feel sorry for her. I think she thinks she's going to go to Spain with him – probably saved the money to go."

"How do you know that?"

"I don't – I just –"

But Madonna had gone to her room.

A minute later he came downstairs and went outside.

Wearing his work gloves he took the tin box, and went up along the path to Arron Brook towards Donnerel's farm. The trees waved in the wind in a constant howl now, and the sound of the brook roared in his ears, as he managed to cross it.

By the back fence of Donnerel's property he was frightened by the mare, who twisted about in the dark and started to bolt, whining a short loud burst, kicking up her hind feet so a clot of soil flew in the night wind.

"I'll kill you too – you scare me," he thought as he unhooked the back gate. Then crossing to the oak tree he lay the tin box down and made his way home.

The feeling he had was one all murderers have. He felt he would be able to forget that this had happened to him, and try to get on with his life. That he would be able to forget it. After the funeral he would tell Michael that everything was taken care of, and to make sure he cleaned the sailboat of any dust or seed.

"A hard night," he said as he passed the tombstone of his great-great-grandfather, who had run away from the English in 1821, and he burst out singing.

He calculated that he could pay back Everette Hutch, get in the clear, and still have four hundred dollars for himself. Though some of this money had blood on it, he knew that would never matter to Everette.

Walking all the way to Gail's he found that Everette had gone to Chatham and so, after one in the morning, Silver went to Chatham.

The earth was soft and warm, and in a large, faded white house behind the park, and behind two other houses, Everette sat. He was a man who looked completely comfortable being who he was, with his large bald head, and his huge moustache.

As Silver entered the room, with its floor uneven and the smell of marijuana, he thought again of Karrie, and how cold her body must be, and he shuddered because moonlight becalmed the room and the table where Everette sat, his jeans covered in motorcycle grease.

"Is this it?" he said.

"This is it all," Silver said, "so you don't have to bother us any more. You leave Michael and Madonna alone."

"How did you get the money?" Everette said now.

"I've got connections too," Silver said, and he tried to sound put-out.

"You're as white as a ghost," Everette said, turning on the light, discounting the blood with a slight smile.

After he counted for a while he took seventy dollars and handed it over, because this had once been done to him when he was a boy, by a man in Newcastle, and he had always been awestruck by it.

"What else have you got?" Everette said suspiciously.

"I've got a diamond too if you want it," Silver said nervously, taking it out of his pocket. "Just to show no hard feelings."

"Put it down," Everette said shrugging.

Silver did. He put the diamond in front of him on the table. Then he sniffed as men do when it's just been proven that they've had far more resources at their disposal then they were ever given credit for.

PART THREE

The next morning, September 10, the farrier came by. The mare had got out on the road and was wandering about, cars had backed up, honking their horns. He woke Tom, who, lying face down across the couch in the TV room, looked as if he had been drinking most of the night. In fact he had been at a bar downriver where he had spent over two hundred dollars, celebrating, he had said, "the end of a relationship."

"You'll wind up just like yer dad if you don't put the booze away," the farrier said. "The Donnerels can't handle it – why, I've cleaned up more after the Donnerels than anyone – if yer going to drink I won't come about – I took a beatin once from yer father for no reason – I won't start it with you, Tom," he said. "A man can take a beatin and still be brave – and I'm braver than the lot of youse," he said, his eyes darting here and there about the room.

Tom leaned up on one arm and looked at him.

"Yer back gate was left unhooked – pretty soon you'll let the place burn to the goddamn ground."

Tom brushed him aside and ran to the barn to get a halter and lead while the farrier followed. Then from inside the door he said: "Don't come in –"

But the farrier went in. He saw Karrie's body, with her arms folded, and a pair of old shorts on, and Vincent, covered in blood, standing beside her with a cup of tea.

The farrier went back outside and sat on the wheel of the tractor. He took a deep breath and looked at the gulls in the grey sky, far away, and cars on the highway trying to manoeuvre around the mare. Everything was very quiet and he could hear faraway laughter from children.

"You'd better call the police," he said.

Constable John Delano was the first to arrive. Tom was sitting on the hay-baler talking to himself. Vincent was standing in the middle of the field under the oak tree, looking at everyone as if something was expected of him, or of the teacup still in his hand. The dog was whining on its chain, and Vincent went over and picked it up.

The farrier was talking to a group of young men who had come up from the road. The traffic had backed up all the way to Oyster River, and people were cutting across Tom's field, which was the colour of mud, while someone Tom did not know was proudly walking the mare along the lane on a lead, as if this was what the excitement was still about.

After speaking to Vincent, who was finally able to tell him he found the body, Constable Delano went down and walked the area where the murder had taken place. He found a tiny shred from a torn bill off the far back path near a tree, where he thought someone might have stood in wait. However, there was nothing to prove that.

But he looked at Constable Deborah Matchett. It was as if the uniformity of the case now had a crease in it. He took the piece of money and wrapped it in plastic. When he stood he brushed off his pants, and walked towards the shore. He walked down the path all the way to the water. There were some motorcycle tracks, and a broken bait box sitting upside down in the sand. To his left he could smell Jessop's cows. On his right the smell of mud and a rotting clam bed. He turned back and came to the spot where the body must have lain. There was a pool of blood four feet from the path that turned towards Michael Skid's.

Sergeant Brendan Fine was at the scene drinking coffee out of a styrofoam cup. He had retraced the steps Vincent had taken when he carried the body back, found where he had rested against the pole near Donnerel's front field, where the girl's hair left traces of blood.

"Did you find the money?" Constable Delano asked.

"No – the Donnerels must have it," Sergeant Fine said. "But we will find it, I suppose." He said "I suppose" in a way which meant he believed that the case was well on the way to being solved, and he arched up on his toes, and had another drink from the cup.

John Delano's eyes gave a slight discernible start in the mild end-of-summer air. And his eyes suggested this: *They are upon a course of least resistance – everything could be proven, the case closed. If I mention any doubt about the Donnerels' involvement, it will start another course that might lead nowhere.*

But Constable Delano had written in his notes: "Imprint of money on victim's skin."

At the Smith residence, yellow ribbons crossed the path behind the store and up to the patio door. Dora had been outside once, to shut off the gas pumps. Then she had gone back and spoken in a grave tone to her husband, who didn't seem to understand what was happening. He sat in the far room, at the back of the house, within view of Karrie's bird feeder.

When the police had first notified him of his daughter's death, saying there was indication that the motive was robbery, he nodded his head. "The thieves found us out," he said. "They were watching us."

Constable Matchett asked what he meant.

"We had a little tin box with some money," Dora said.

"Yes, we found the box – how much was in it?"

"It's what we donate every year to the Salvation Army," Dora said quickly.

"And how much is that?"

Dora's face turned crimson. She did not know how much money the police might have found. She looked sternly at her husband, who had turned in his seat to look at her.

"It wasn't much," she said, quickly picking up a shawl that Karrie used to put over her shoulders and folding it exactly as it had been folded, then impulsively throwing it.

"Over two hundred dollars?"

"It was a large amount," Emmett said, shaking his head.

"But what do you mean – large amount?"

"He means a few hundred dollars – we donate it – but not always to the Salvation Army – sometimes to the Children's Stocking Fund – here and there, you know, anonymously," Dora said. "I like helping people."

"Did anyone know you had this money?"

"No one – besides Karrie," Dora said.

Emmett remembered laughing at a story Karrie had told at supper the night before. But already the body was at the morgue, and was soon to be transferred to Saint John for the autopsy. And realizing this, and seeing birds fly down to the bird feeder, he burst into tears.

"Vincent killed her," Dora said suddenly. "Vincent and Tommie – the bastards – they said they were going to – all summer long they bothered us, didn't they, Emmett – didn't they!"

"Yes, they did," Emmett shouted, convinced absolutely that he had heard them both.

Outside, cars slowed down and people looked in as they passed the house. It gave Dora a grand feeling, especially since she always felt superior to the Donnerels. Especially since it was realized, and mentioned by everyone, that she had donated money.

Constable Delano had what he felt was the unpleasant task of interviewing Michael Skid.

Michael came to the office, early on September 11. The day was bright and windy, and sunlight flooded the room. The treetops and the hedges waved, Michael's eyes were watering, from the walk, and his face was red. He seemed sure of himself. He was smoking a cigarette and offered John Delano one. Delano felt a profound disrespect coming from Michael's gaze. Delano looked through his notes and turned sideways in the swivel chair.

"Well, this has been a hell of a thing," Delano said.

"Hell of a thing," Michael said.

"There was no indication of this, was there? I mean, did she mention to you that Vincent was harassing her? When was the last time you saw Karrie? She was – a friend?"

Michael cleared his throat, "A friend – yes – a good friend – a few days before the murder –"

"Did she say there was any trouble?"

"Trouble? No – well, she said that Tom hit her."

"She did say that –"

"Yes."

"And where did you see her – that last time?"

"On the path."

"On the path – where the murder took place. By accident, or you meet her there?"

"I met her there –"

"So you were good friends –"

"Friends, yes – well, she confided in me –"

"In you – really? About what?"

Michael rubbed his right hand across his face and tried to think.

"I was at Laura McNair's the night of the murder, I don't actually know what happened –" He looked up. Delano went back to his notes.

"Of course – but you were *her* friend – she confided in *you*. So Tom might have been jealous of you. You were going away with her?"

Michael paused and lit a cigarette once again, in the small bright office.

"Who told you that?"

Delano looked through his notes, flipped back four pages and looked up.

"Dora Smith – 'Michael and she were going away – so Tom had Vincent . . .'" He looked up.

"Oh – well we talked about that, you know, just to stop Tom from beating her. Who told you, Dora Smith?"

"Who is Professor Becker – a friend of yours at UNB?"

"Well, I studied under him –"

"And you went to see him?"

"Oh – no – when?"

Again Delano paused, perplexed, looked through his notes. He glanced at Michael. Michael seemed angry, flustered.

"Well, you went to Fredericton and saw a Professor Becker – that's according to Emmett Smith: 'My Karrie wanted to go to university and Michael had spoken about her to Professor Becker last week, and now that's all ruined –'"

"Oh – Karrie *is* confused – I didn't *really* go over to speak to him – it's just – I ran into him –"

"In Fredericton –"

"Yes."

"Yet Karrie *was* confused."

"Pardon?"

"In Fredericton?"

"Pardon? Oh yes – in Fredericton."

"In his office –"

Michael's cigarette was hot as he dragged on it, and he looked at the half-closed Venetian blinds where sunlight splashed through.

"Well, we went to his office –"

"We?"

"Silver was with me."

"Silver Brassaurd?"

"Yes – just for a drive."

"All the way to Fredericton?" Delano smiled. "With Silver Brassaurd?"

"Yes – why not?"

"But it was to see if Karrie could enrol in a course – and go to university – this is what she tells Dora and Emmett on September 7."

"Well – in a way – yes," Michael said, blushing.

"Well, that was kind of you." There was a long pause, perhaps a half a minute. "She went with you on the sailboat – where did you go, to P.E.I. one time?"

"We never went to P.E.I. – to Portage – Island once –"

Michael felt he was being forced into a position of protecting Karrie's lies to her parents about university. He halted and looked at Delano.

"I was hoping she would go to university, you know – I thought she had – so much to offer –"

"So that was on her birthday – and you proposed to her –"

"Proposed?"

"On the sailboat –"

"Who? It wasn't a proposal – friends go on a sailboat – so, you know, friends – don't you have any female friends – as *friends*?"

"So there was no trip to P.E.I.?"

Michael looked about the office.

"I tried to be her friend," he said, shaking his head, and looking deeply hurt.

"Of course – so there was no sexual intercourse? You weren't her friend in *that* way."

"Well – we knew each other – on a sailboat, you know, you see each other –"

"But there was no sexual intercourse?"

"I was very fond of her – I tried my best to protect her – I thought – you know, if she could just be her own person, what a wonderful person she might be. But why can't the police protect someone like this – why was it up to me?"

There was another long pause. Then Delano, taking a sip of coffee, while still looking at his notes, continued.

"Do you know why she was carrying money? Or who she might have been carrying money *for*? It wasn't for you – this money?"

"No – of course not."

"You didn't owe any money on P.E.I.?"

"Why do you keep mentioning Prince Edward Island?"

"The coast guard towed you – one night. Karrie told Dora she went with you to P.E.I."

Here Michael laughed. "No – we never really got there – the old *Renegade* –"

"You didn't owe any money to Professor Becker for some-thing – a course for Karrie perhaps?"

"Of course not. Things aren't done that way."

"Did you ever see a tin box at the Smiths'?"

"What tin box?"

"You are not in any debt?"

"No."

"And you know of no bad drugs sold late August in P.E.I.?"

"No, of course not," Michael said, his voice a whisper.

Two

For a few days Tom and his brother existed in limbo, where nothing was expected of them, and nothing could be done for them. They stayed in the house, which suddenly looked unnatural, with its built-on extra room for Vincent. The little dog stayed outside. The farrier did not come back. But the police were there, taking photos. Twice he had asked them if they'd found the diamond ring he had given to Karrie, and twice they brushed him aside, saying they were looking into it.

The days went on and each day the trees suspended in autumn dew changed colour slightly.

Sometimes everything was extremely lighthearted with Tom and the police officers, and then a police officer would get a call, and come back into the house and address him.

"Vincent's fingerprints are all over Karrie – his footprints are near the murder scene – his prints are on the tin box, he had a bloodied one-hundred-dollar bill in his pocket. Vincent carried her back and laid her in your barn and went to some trouble to try to hide the crime."

Tom wouldn't answer.

"The police will find the man," Vincent kept saying. He said he was going to become a policeman and find the man. He asked Tom to telephone the police station every other hour to ask them if they had found the man.

They sat in the house together, both of them dressed to go to the funeral, as the hearse passed on the road beneath them and turned into the church lane, with its soft gracious trees in the bright sunshine.

"Karrie loved a day like this," Tom said to Constable Matchett, but she looked at him and frowned just slightly, as if for some reason he wasn't allowed to express devotion *now*. As the day wore on, as the moments passed on the small grandfather clock and sunlight flitted over the small dining-room table, Tom felt more and more as if he had caused everything.

"Karrie loved a day like this, boys," Vincent said, nodding at Tom. And that in itself was excruciating to hear.

Line after line of cars passed their front field behind the hearse.

Tom couldn't bear to look. An RCMP constable was taking pictures of the barn once again, and of the oak tree where the tin box was found. The area had been taped off and Tom had to ask permission to leave the house.

He had asked the police permission to go to the funeral that morning, and the last car had turned onto the church lane before anyone seemed to remember this.

There was a shuffle at the door and Constable Delano and Constable Matchett came in. Constable Matchett was looking at some papers in her hand, and leaned against the counter in an easy, callow fashion, her gun on her left side, as if those who owned the house had no right to expect her to stand on ceremony any more.

Constable Delano approached Tom. He advised him quietly not to go to the funeral.

"Why?"

"It's just safer for you," Constable Delano said.

Vincent sat with his photo album on his lap and stared at it, tears streaming down his face. He stared at the picture of him and Tom and Karrie at the picnic. He remembered they had been working in the stall that housed the game of rings, and Everette Hutch, who always tormented Vincent, put a ring on his head, and Tom said: "If you ever touch my brother – I'll kill you."

Then Everette and Tom fought, and toppled the rings; both of them were identical in stature and size, except Mr. Hutch (as Vincent called him) had a scar. Both threw some good punches. But Tom got in the best punch, a hard right uppercut. Then some of the men broke it up.

Later they had the picture taken, and Karrie stood between them. She put her arms around both of them, leaned forward and said: "Here I am between me two men."

And Tom, with a cut lip, said it was still a nice day to have a picnic. Vincent had waited all week and had bothered Tom all that morning about the picnic.

Now, today, with the same childlike insistence, every five or ten minutes Vincent would ask Tom if they had caught the man. The wind blew against their farmhouse in the middle of nowhere.

Vincent said he was going to take the picture of Karrie down to the funeral. But they stopped him, so he did what he had always done: he asked Tom to help him. Just as he had asked Tom to tie his shoes every Sunday morning before they went off to church.

"Vincent, they don't want to hurt you – Vincent, they don't want to hurt you," Tom kept saying.

Later, Vincent sat in his room, smoking his pipe. Tom came in and, sitting on the edge of the bed, he looked at him. At times in his idiocy, Vincent took a stubborn, implacable turn. Now he would say nothing. He only looked out the window as Tom spoke to him. The more Tom asked him about Karrie, the less Vincent would communicate.

"I don't know – ya – okay – but I don't remember," was the only thing Vincent kept saying, puffing dramatically and stoically on his pipe.

"It is my fault, Vincent," Tom finally said, staring at his brother's immense shoulders and large hands. "It's my fault. I drove you to it without even knowing – I caused it all."

$\sim$

Karrie was buried in a grave near her mother close to the bay. Later, Emmett and Dora would have a fight over the stone.

More than four hundred people attended the funeral on September 14. Gail Hutch went, but left her little boy, Brian, at home, in the care of her brother Everette, who said he didn't mind sitting at such a time. The men wore suits and ties; the ties, and Emmett's salt-and-pepper hair, blew in the wind. Emmett was visibly weakened and crying. Michael, one of the pallbearers, looked tired, pale, and confused. Silver Brassaurd was one of the pallbearers also, and, like many working men, looked and moved unnaturally, almost robotically, in his suit. Often he was seen breaking down crying.

Dora followed them, standing beside the Skid family, looking immensely proud and unshaken.

THREE

Four days after the funeral the community was jarred by another event that gave people an unnatural feeling of regret, repentance, and culpability.

The night they finally took Tom in to be interrogated, Vincent ran away from Constable Matchett and, holding on to Maxwell, he escaped into the woods. The little dog had one eye swollen shut because someone had come into the yard and booted it, and then that someone had run back along the fence so that Matchett couldn't get a look at who it was.

Vincent had fed his gerbil, Snowflake, its supper and put on his jacket with the four big buttons. He had attempted to leave a note about going to visit his Aunt Libby. His main intention may have been to hide the dog from people.

As soon as Vincent began to cross the brook he lost his balance and Maxwell fell over the falls, scampering here and there in a circle, its swollen eye unable to open, its two big front paws splashing the water in front of it.

Vincent jumped over the falls after the dog.

For two days men searched everywhere for him and found his dog, drowned, at the mouth of Derrick's stream at nine o'clock the next Wednesday night.

Tom, thin and haggard-looking, was then taken to the Sheppardville Road to join in the search along Arron Brook.

Behind a windblow they found a boot. But for two more days there was no other sign.

And then Bobby and Joyce Taylor discovered the body lying half-hidden in the swirling water only thirty yards from where the dog had been found.

He had been dead four days. His jacket was still buttoned up. His pipe was gone.

Bobby remembered teasing Vincent once when he said he was sweet on Gail Hutch.

"I could protect her," Vincent had said finally. "From Mr. Hutch."

Bobby sat in the wet dirt on his knees, turning around at everyone: "No one will have to send him home now at ten o'clock," he said.

Arron Brook rushed on. And it rained all night.

∾

The police, Constable Delano included, felt they had a weak case against Tom Donnerel. He went to Laura McNair at the prosecutor's office with interviews and documents, and some pictures of Madonna Brassaurd found in Michael's farmhouse. He said he did not know why these pictures were significant, but he had some faint "ongoing objection" to the direction they were taking in the case they were on. The interviews with both Michael and Silver made him feel this way as well.

"Why?" Laura said, glancing at the pictures and looking up at him, completely mystified.

"Perhaps it is this picture here," he said, shuffling through them and handing one to her. It showed Michael Skid on the verandah, leaning against the post, smiling, his long hair braided, a bandanna on his leg. In the corner, on a deck chair beyond the blue wooden table, was a small chocolate-coloured block of hash in tinfoil, and beyond that was Hutch's Harley Sportster.

"Perhaps it's because they believe they are the ones fashionable enough to be crucified," Delano said, finally. "And Karrie wasn't included," he said, fumbling for another picture, this one of Karrie standing on the bow of *The Renegade*, in a dress and carrying a purse.

"Well, Michael was with me – the night of the murder," Laura snapped, noticing neither the hash nor the Sportster, "and he did everything to protect her. More than the police ever do in these matters," she said. "Two hundred women a year are battered to death by their husbands or boyfriends –"

John Delano was taken aback. Not by what was said, but *how* it was said. It was as if Laura felt that *he* was trying to please her or prove himself to her by discrediting her friend. He had been infatuated by her, he had asked her out a half-dozen times – found out when her birthday was and sent her a card. All of this was known, by everyone, and it had made him look and feel ridiculous. But he was not ridiculous enough to be able to promote himself by this.

"Anyway, John, there is no case to solve," she said, more kindly, turning away and taking down her coat to put on.

She added that it was clear that Vincent killed the woman, and certainly Tom put him up to it. Michael Skid had tried to protect the young woman from them. This was becoming more and more evident now.

"I think you are on an entirely different case than we are, John," Laura said, laughing suddenly.

"I think so," John said. Their eyes met in the mild, stuffy air of the back room of the courthouse. Suddenly a dark wave came over the sky, just for a second. And Delano knew by this that everything was over between them, every faint hope he had entertained about being with her.

"All this mystery," Laura said, buttoning her coat and giving an acrimonious smile. "My, my."

Over the next five workdays, the police took statements from Dora and Emmett Smith, and from Madonna Brassaurd, who admitted that since Michael and Karrie had become friends, Tom turned jealous. They were able to verify that Daryll and Everette Hutch were in Chatham the night of the murder, and could find no evidence linking Silver Brassaurd.

The prosecution's office was adamant that they had to charge Tom Donnerel. Laura said that they should enter two charges against him. One for criminal negligence, the other for conspiracy to commit murder, by using his brother. The entire community, and by now the province, wanted Tom, with some justification, to pay. By these charges, the prosecution felt it would throw light upon the whole messy circumstance.

"OUTRAGE ON A VIOLENT RIVER," read the headline in the largest provincial paper.

"Certain cases in our province unite people in outrage and remorse," it stated. "And never has this been more evident than the murder of young Karrie Smith."

"BEST FRIENDS' RIVALRY TURNS DEADLY," read the headline in the other provincial paper.

The reaction to the case caused a certain pressure. And Laura was in fact pleased by this pressure. She had interviewed a bartender and three or four patrons of the bar in Neguac who had seen Tom just after midnight that night, telling people that Karrie would no longer be around to bother him. It was also known that, a month before, he left Vincent and went on a five-day drunk, where it was reported he had turned violent.

The idea now, quite apart from everything else, was that he was like his father – an obstinate, mean, unpredictable, and domineering drunk. And this more than anything inspired antipathy for him by Laura McNair, whose own father was kindly, helpless, and sad.

"He spent the money at the bar," she said. "That's where the money went!"

With small, inquisitive eyes which gave a cute and impish puffiness to her cheeks, she looked up at her mentor, Mr. Tait, who stood by the window overlooking the main street running back through this part of town. She was impish when *not* in court, and liked to tease.

The loss of her heroic brother, Lyle, still evoked a silence in her, which could be seen in the knee-length skirts and heavy brown shoes she wore, which had become her trademark – as much as the sou'wester she wore in the rain.

But the tragedy also gave her a more outgoing posture, for her family's sake. And someone had finally come her way. Michael Skid. They had met as children and had dated as teenagers.

She had always been attracted to him. And John Delano knew this, and she felt that this was the reason he was trying to ruin this case.

"Even on criminal negligence we can press for eight to ten," she said to her boss now, emphasizing *ten* the way people do when it will mean the undoing of others and not of themselves, and to show that she was savvy and knew about ten, as opposed to five or fifteen. She stared at the prosecutor and her eyes glowed, and the cuteness of her face didn't match what she had just said.

The prosecutor, a heavyset man of thirty-eight, who was new to the community, and had the feeling that he was in an area of intangible remoteness because he himself had grown up twenty miles outside Fredericton, said emphatically, while reaching over to tie his shoe: "He's a son of a bitch. I'm sure he was there – I mean, at the scene. He probably told Vincent to run away, hoping he'd get killed. But we'll never get him for conspiracy or anything if he has any kind of lawyer. He's smart enough to get away with it."

The further outraged Laura McNair phoned Tom's defence lawyer on her own initiative.

"Lookit," she said, as she played with the telephone cord without taking her eyes off the notes she had written, "we can take this all the way – let me tell you, we know the son of a bitch was *there*. We'll sit down on this one and prove it. The hundred dollars was found – it was part of the money Tom wanted. What would Vincent know about money?"

It was very strange that she had said, "Sit down on this one," because it was her first murder case, and she had never used that expression before.

There was a long pause, and it seemed longer in the heat of mid-morning. Then Tom's lawyer spoke. His voice came as a whisper, like a distress call from a wounded animal: "I'm getting death threats over this damn thing – what am I s'posed to do if that son of a bitch came to me? My wife is angry – phone calls. I haven't slept in a week. The best thing to do is to get this case behind us –"

"Oh, I know – he's a bugger," she said, and she wrote in her notes: "BIG SCAREDY-CAT!"

Yet Laura came into the office the next morning and found she had a phone call waiting. It was Tom Donnerel's lawyer. He said there was no way to stop his client. Tom had resolved to plead guilty, saying that he had planned everything and had forced his brother to murder.

So, on his own initiative and to the relief of his lawyer, Tom pleaded guilty to the charge of criminal negligence and the further charge of conspiring to commit murder.

"Do you wish to do this?" his lawyer asked, pretending to be concerned, when his only concern, Tom knew, was if Tom said no. So he looked into his lawyer's eyes, with fear and regret, remembering how Vincent had bothered Karrie all summer long, and understood his lawyer's plight.

"It makes no difference now," he said.

"Conspiracy to commit murder – we should fight that all the way, at least – we'll go for the first charge – it'll make a great difference in your life – it might have been criminal negligence, I'll say – but conspiracy?"

Tom said no. He had, he said, led Vincent astray. And saying this, he remembered his brother's huge lumbering hands. "If it weren't for me, Vincent wouldn't have done what he did."

"Well – a terrible thing – a terrible thing," his lawyer said.

FOUR

Three weeks later Tom stood in the dock, in that brown suit he was going to wear to his parents' funeral. There were many derisive cries: "Hang him!"

There was an audible grumble of disbelief from Mr. Jessop. And then there was nervous laughter.

Judge Skid, his face flushed and clean-shaven, with white, dried-out, lifeless hair and small red lines on his white cheeks, which indicated his drinking bouts, looked about as if counting the people in the room.

"The whole community has been outraged over this affair," he said.

"Yes, sir," Tommie Donnerel whispered. He kept looking around, as if he wanted to be certain that it *was* the entire community or even if it was he they were outraged by. He began to shake uncontrollably, which caused Judge Skid to frown in disgust.

He then spoke with great affection for Karrie Smith, a young woman whom the community downriver loved and whom he wished he had met. Then he looked over at the parents and nodded, and both of them seemed pleased.

Then he looked at Laura McNair.

Ms. McNair gave her summation. She did not speak of the murder for more than a few moments.

She spoke of Karrie and her dreams washed away in her blood. And then she spoke of Vincent. She spoke of his childhood. She spoke of his dog, Maxwell. And she introduced the report, from a day in the early 1950s, when Vincent, in stopping his baby brother, Tom, from falling off Burnt Church wharf, fell himself, causing the massive head wound that left him mentally like a child of four. This was something that Tom hadn't known until that moment. Something that his parents had always hidden from him, something that now made him clutch the dock so he wouldn't fall.

"FAMILY OUTING TURNS TRAGIC," read the headline in the old and distant yellowed paper. It was one of the provincial papers and the story appeared on page six. Ms. McNair lifted it up triumphantly. Then, putting the paper down, she went around to the front of the prosecution's table and suddenly turned and glared at Tommie Donnerel, her nostrils flaring out.

"And this was how he was repaid, in part tortured himself, because of his brother's cowardice and jealousy, not responsible for his actions, and yet driven to protect his baby brother to the end. And who was there with him, Tommie Donnerel – if not in person – by proxy. But you couldn't do it yourself, could you –?" Here she shrugged and, at the same moment as she turned away, said, "So get Vincent."

Which left a deep impression on everyone.

For a moment there was silence. They all looked at Tommie, who could not stop shaking. She walked around to her side of the table and, without looking at him again, said, in disgust.

"And here he stands shaking like a leaf, a coward in a brown suit, in front of us." But this comment brought comic relief to everyone, and they burst out laughing. Tom too, looked around and smiled. Only old Mr. Jessop, seated near the front, looked too saddened to smile.

"Hang him!" someone shouted.

"Enough," Judge Skid said.

Tom Donnerel's lawyer, impressed by Ms. McNair, whom he'd been told to keep an eye on, kept trying to adjust his glasses, and, shaking as much as Tom, asked for mercy, said two lives were already destroyed here – show leniency towards the third. Then he nodded and sat down.

It was quiet again.

And then Judge Skid spoke: "If there were law enough to hang you, sir, I would. You have disgraced yourself in the eyes of man and God – I sentence you now to twelve years."

A displeased murmur went up in the crowd. Then in the balcony and out in the foyer, the murmur spread.

"Only twelve years – only twelve years."

"Yes, but they didn't prove it, he confessed."

"So – so what – only twelve years."

Tom could not stop being afraid. He kept hoping that someone, anyone, would look at him in kindness. He wanted someone to tell him how it had all come about, wanted someone to tell him how things had got so bad. He kept looking for Michael's face amid all the other faces, but Michael wasn't there. In the end, he tried to speak about the mare, and little Snowflake. Who would take care of them now?

FIVE

Tom wrote Judge Skid a long letter of apology from prison. In it was the testimony of a man trying to reorder his life and to gain back his self-respect.

"I asere you, sir," he wrote, misspelling the word *assure*, but liking the word because it was one Karrie had used when she spoke to him of her love, "that I will do everything in my power to change my life and be a decent human beink. That I have wronged others I am awere of, but I will never harm a soul no more. I didn't know this about poor Vincent – how he fell off the wherf – it was a brave thing he done for me. Now I will member that as long as I live – and member that whenever anything is done to me, even if I was hit, I cannot do nothin to them. I will member that to the end of my days. I wish God to bless you – sir. And hole no grudge."

The judge wrote a formal reply where he spoke of mercy as being in the hands of God, and that the judge was simply the instrument of the law. He said he was pleased that a man like Tom Donnerel might consider reforming. But he added that at this moment he had no kind words of encouragement to give.

"It was a case – so sorrowfully senseless and brutal, one of the most difficult I've ever had to sit before. That my own son was involved in a minor way in trying to help this young woman seemed to make some conflict upon my sitting, but I was and am the principal provincial court appointee and regarded it as duty. As regards your property, it was burned, and is in the hands of the law. So I suppose if there was money hidden it is now destroyed.

"I take no pleasure in informing you about this, and you can be guaranteed it will be investigated to the fullest extent."

Then, pleased with this note, he mailed it on, but couldn't help telling the postal clerk what it contained.

The postal clerk nodded gravely, and stamped it accordingly. He felt a twinge of happiness, because the judge had confided in him, and because he himself had known Tommie Donnerel, and had taken Karrie Smith to the high-school prom, where she had treated him meanly.

His life had turned out well compared to theirs. And then he thought of Karrie, and how her body had been found nude. And as he remembered how attractive she was in high school, with the wonderfully suggestive and still innocent sway of her hips in her pleated skirt one day running down the hallway, a sudden obscene pleasure took hold of him, which he felt in his groin, and which he tried to dismiss.

~

For a while the judge was bothered by Mr. and Mrs. Smith, who had taken comfort in his words at court, and believed them all, and began visiting Michael at the house. Dora, wearing a black dress with a lace front, which made her white breastbone look like it was marked by blue ink, sat in the large chair drinking tea out of the best china, holding a Kleenex up to her nose.

"My, what a fine, grand house – this musta cost somethin now," she would say, with humiliating graciousness.

She talked nonstop about Karrie to Michael's mother, who soon had the habit of sitting on the far side of the room, continually glancing out at the street.

Once when Judge Skid said he was sorry she was robbed, she answered: "Yes, my money is gone, let alone Karrie."

She brought some things over that Michael might want as souvenirs – the brooch of a sailboat, with the name *Karrie* engraved under it, and, again, the book of Robert Frost's poems. It had come back to Mrs. Smith by way of Madonna, who had been given the duty of cleaning the sailboat before it was housed for the winter, making sure that the remnants of the fatal summer were removed forever.

Michael took this book and opened it while they were there. His own responsibility was measured in the fact that he had not done enough, he said suddenly to them. And he suddenly felt this to be absolutely true. That he had known Tom Donnerel and had seen all the signs but had done nothing about it. The Smiths both protested, Dora especially.

But more than this, Michael was burdened by an agitated remembrance of Karrie's strangely sad smile when she spoke of her parents one afternoon. He could not forget it. She had looked at him in a wistful way and had said, "Oh, Dora" so plaintively that it still haunted him.

It seemed for a while that Michael could not get rid of her parents, and had a dreary time during these prolonged visits, which happened with annoying regularity. He began to be able to distinguish the sound of their car from all the others driving down his street that fall, and to go upstairs and sit in his room, waiting for their visits to end.

Karrie's book he gave to the Salvation Army, along with the old brooch and other things, because it reminded him of those forlorn events. And his father thought that this was a reasonable thing to do.

As it happened he felt guilty about these events, even though he was unaware. In a way he felt responsible for Tom, and hadn't been able to go to the courtroom to watch the trial of his friend. And even though no one bothered him now, and he was free of the summer, he still felt these things. He felt guilty because of Karrie's smile. This disturbed him more than he had initially thought it would.

The autumn faded. And cold weather came. Quite suddenly everything about the summer seemed over. The wind blew cold, and children were back at school.

Michael then played his trump card. He finally finished the long article on his private school near Sackville, which he had been working on for over two years, and which would be published in the *Moncton Times*. It contained interviews with certain students and made accusations against the drama teacher, who had various relationships with his students. It would not have been published had he not been *the* Michael Skid, associated with *the* Karrie Smith.

Yet because it was published, the article caused Michael's name to be spoken about, and his old drama teacher, Mr. Love, was forced to resign. Suddenly, all the dark corners, the small mean suppers, the warped floors, the old back buildings, took on a different, more odious slant. And the world of this particular provincial private school with its subterranean values was exposed.

That he had been working on this, quietly and without giving any hints, seemed remarkable to his chagrined parents in the cold days of late autumn.

Michael was then offered a contract by a publishing house in Toronto to write a book on Karrie Smith, the events of the summer, which had briefly made the national news and pricked something in the national consciousness. He said yes, and set about, he felt, to tell the truth as best he could about the murder. Not to spare anyone and to ultimately show that *his* values – the values of the new man – were much superior, say, to the values of his old friend Tom Donnerel. He felt that he was a moral representative of his age group. There were those young men and women who were liberal and believed in what had to be done to secure equality for everyone and there were those who still clung tenaciously to the repressive dogma of a former time, of community and church. Michael believed more than ever that he belonged to the former group, the best group, the more inclusive group.

One night in early November he went for a walk after working all day on the first part of the first draft of his book. A young woman came out of the side door of the courthouse and moved ahead of him in the rain. She wore a yellow sou'wester and a matching rain jacket. He walked behind her for some time, and suddenly realized who it was. He had not seen her since the trial.

"Laura," he said, and she turned and gave a quick smile. "Oh, Laura," he said. "It's – you."

"Oh, my God," she said, "I was just thinking that you might have gone away, now that you're famous, and I wouldn't get to see you again. I was going to phone and ask you up, but you just lost your friend Karrie – and it's horrible about Tom. Then I waited for you one night at the theatre – but you must have gone out another door."

A car passed and its lights shone on her startled childlike face.

And for some reason she started to cry. And he went over and hugged her.

In a way, all that autumn at home, Michael was treated like a hero by his apologetic and relieved parents. And he was very relieved too.

Soon he and Laura were inseparable, and then impulsively, because Michael was always impulsive, engaged to be married. And everything had turned out for him as well.

SIX

Nora Battersoil had gone to work in grade ten at the small bowling alley in town. She was a thin, nervous girl and felt she was homely and would not be loved.

She met Michael Skid and fell in love and had a son out of wedlock in 1969, whom she named Owen after her grandfather. Michael did not know about this son, and she did not tell him, because he was wild. She did not want to burden him with what she considered an unnecessary request for sponsorship.

She felt that this was a brave decision on her part, because she did love him.

She had to tell her family she was pregnant but would not name the father, so her father blamed everything on her, and said terrible things she could never forget. So she left home. And, except for her little sister, Amy, who sometimes took care of the child when Nora visited the house once or twice a year, she never communicated very much with the rest of her family.

So much so that in the fall of 1973 she quit her own Catholic church and joined the Salvation Army, as a member and a volunteer.

She helped take care of drives for food, fundraising for events, and, in 1974, books for the prison library.

One day in November 1974 she was given a box that had been sent down by Mrs. Fewella Skid. In this she found a brooch of a sailboat with the name *Karrie* on it. And at the bottom of the box was a small volume of poetry by Robert Frost.

Mrs. Skid, when sending these things along that particular day, did not have any idea who she was sending them to.

For Nora it brought back painful memories and desires, and the kind of self-incrimination she'd always felt because her father had refused to stand up for her, threatened her with the belt, and called her a whore.

Karrie Smith had been her first-cousin, but she had lost contact with her after Karrie's mother died. She remembered Karrie one afternoon, the last year of high school, as she ran down the hall, touching the lockers with her hands. She had been so happy at that moment. But Nora did not see Karrie again.

Twice that fall she had seen Michael Skid in town, walking arm in arm with Laura McNair. On both occasions Michael, his thick black hair falling to his shoulders, his piercing eyes as brilliant as ever, did not see her himself. Now he was writing a book on Karrie and seemed to be talked about, however grudgingly, as a very heroic man. And she was happy for him.

Thinking of this she placed the brooch in her pocket, and sent the volume of poetry to the prison library in the centre of the province.

Then she went out, on a cold snowy day towards the end of November, to ring her Salvation Army bell at the grey liquor store near the corner.

A week later she received a letter from a man at the prison. That man was Tommie Donnerel.

Dear Miss Battersoil:

I got your name from the libary here who sent on the poetry. Because of the writin on the cover I felt it was for me from Karrie Smith – when I was gonna go to do my upgrading. But she didn't have no chance to give it to me. How I want to thank you for this here book. Have you read the Apple Picker – I have never read a thing as good! It makes me think that all things will turn out someday. I want to thank you for Karrie's book to me!

Tommie Donnerel

P.S. I like the book!

Nora Battersoil didn't answer. But a few days later, with the smell of cold snow mingled with ice and the sunlight frozen across the tin roof with its rusted rivets, she received another letter from him.

It was a letter wishing her a Merry Christmas. He never mentioned his time, except to say that he could do two lifetimes if he could only be sure Karrie had not suffered. And he was now reading Stephen Crane.

This letter begged an answer more than the first, so she replied, somewhat sternly. She told him that though she too prayed that Karrie had not suffered, it was unconscionable to think that she had not. She added that she hoped he was in good health, but that he should read the Bible more and literature less, and added that she knew Vincent was not responsible for his actions and therefore was at peace.

Tommie Donnerel received the letter on December 11, his second full month in prison.

The day after he received this letter he was down in the small barren gym watching some men play basketball. He kept looking out the window at snow falling against the mesh, and trying to see as much of the sky as he could. He was wondering if Nora was the same woman Michael Skid knew a number of years before, and he was also thinking that he would be allowed TV privileges this night to watch the Christmas special.

As he stood there a man walked by him with his arms folded. Then looking up at him and smiling he shoved a homemade shiv into his chest.

"Here, this is a treat for you," he said, his face twisted in raw glee. The handle had a piece of rubber attached to it, and it vibrated slightly as it stuck in. The hope, of course, was that it would break off in Tommie's chest. He was Everette Hutch's friend, the man Laura McNair had prosecuted for the rape of the young woman. He was doing this as a favour for Everette, who would now, he believed, be obligated to kill Laura McNair for him.

Tommie dropped backwards, hit his head, and everyone started whistling, clapping, laughing. The man stood over him, giving the knife a tug sideways and trying to break the blade off. "I can't get it," he said.

Then he went to the other side of the gym, furtively, and stood with the group. He went out onto the court alone, took the basketball and tried to throw a basket from the key, as if this would increase his popularity, and Tommie's blood ran onto the floor.

Seven

Tom awoke in the hospital in Moncton. The shiv had missed his heart but had punctured a lung. Both the doctors and nurses, though they did everything they could to save him, maintained a dismissive attitude towards him.

In the seven nights he spent in hospital he received two get-well cards, one from Nora Battersoil, the other from Madonna Brassaurd.

The first night, when he was on morphine, he had a dream. And then another almost exactly the same three nights later after they had taken him off the morphine drip.

In the first dream Vincent was standing on the far side of the room. He was not Vincent as Tom had known him, but Vincent as he might have been. He approached Tom smiling and he bent down and showed Tom his head. There was no wound there any more.

"The doctor I have knows how to cure it," Vincent seemed to say.

Then he showed him his pipe, which was not nibbled at on the stem like it had been, but was silver, and bubbles came from it and disappeared into the wide, blue sky above him.

"I like your pipe – did you get it at the gas bar?"

"No – you can't get a pipe like this at the gas bar – but I want to show you something."

Suddenly Vincent became solemn, and he turned about. Someone spoke to him and said: "Not now."

And Vincent smiled and nodded, and disappeared.

There was some incident in this first dream that Tom tried desperately to remember. But as long as the pain was severe and he was kept on morphine he couldn't.

Then, on the night after they had taken him off the morphine drip, he had the second dream.

In this dream, Vincent came into the room. He was wearing his jacket. He took out a picture of Karrie and him at the picnic. It wasn't the picnic they had gone to with Tom. Karrie was wearing the pantsuit Tom last saw her wearing. She and Vincent were smiling, looking up at someone.

"Look into the picture," Vincent said, as if this was most important. "Tom you *must* look into the picture – see? Not like in my room – it's quite a different picture."

"Will he *know*?" came the voice on the other side of his bed.

In the dream Tom felt terrified. For a moment he looked at the picture as Vincent had asked him to do. And then he turned. Sitting on the chair to his left was Karrie. He knew it was her, but he couldn't recognize her. He only saw her smile, which caused a light to glow in front of her face.

"You must not ever worry, Tommie – I am to inform you that the clutch is fixed. You must tell Madonna to find the distributor cap for you. You must tell Michael to spend his time now to search for the good answer, and he will find it helping those he does not yet know. You must wait for Nora Battersoil at the window of the bus." And she smiled in angelic delight.

When he turned back Vincent was gone. And he awoke.

For two days he didn't understand the dream. The hospital was grey and hot, filled with weak and smiling clerics, and he began to run a fever. They were worried about infection and changed his bandages three times a day.

On the third day a nurse named Sally came in to change his bandages at four in the afternoon. He was sitting up, looking about morosely as she unwrapped him.

"No spots of blood today," she said as she crumpled the soiled bandage in her hands. He came awake and looked at her.

"Yes," he said, quietly. "Yes, yes – yes, yes!"

She looked at him curiously, and then wrote on her clipboard and left the room promptly, her white uniform hugging her hips so that he could see the outline of her slip.

Tom kept looking about for someone to talk to. But then he never spoke to a soul. He waited vainly for another dream so he could tell Karrie and Vincent that he understood. But there would be no more dreams of them. He was transferred back to the prison, along the old back road on a sunless day. It was now December 18. Snow and dirt crowded the ditches, the air was sharp and metallic. He sat in the back seat, handcuffed and staring at the white ice of the strait, and the white formless houses that they passed.

In the picture, in his dream, Karrie and Vincent were looking up at someone in mesmerized joy. And Vincent's hands were glowing, resting on the cane stand. There were no spots of blood.

PART FOUR

ONE

After Karrie's funeral, things happened as always. As always, laughter and life returned.

Everette Hutch still kept his bike in the back room of Gail Hutch's shack, the crankshaft sitting in oil and lubricant, with white rags in the cylinder heads. He still took morphine for the burns he had suffered and the doctors were still frightened of him, and turned their backs when he rustled pills from their cabinets. He still wondered why things never worked out for him, still threatened people, still played cards, and his uncles still ran errands for him, the old aunt still laughing at them when they did.

Dora Smith and her husband still slept in separate parts of the house, and each night, as always, she made her way over to the gas bar after supper to flirt with certain young men.

The young men still came, even though it was not the same. Vincent was no longer there, as a comforting person to graciously tease, and Karrie was no longer there, as a young woman to look at and admire, though the pair of gloves that she liked to wear to church sat on the inside window sill near some old bottles of fly dope and mosquito repellent.

The worry over where the money had gone, the feeling she had that the police were suspicious, the worry that Emmett wanted to confess because of remorse, aggravated the skin condition on her hands, and made Dora's life miserable. And that was why Karrie's gloves were on the inside window sill.

By Thanksgiving John Delano had forgotten about Laura McNair.

But he had not given up on the case, which had too many unanswered questions. He was puzzled by the robbery. And he was puzzled by Michael Skid's trip to Fredericton. No one else was. Yet one day when he had to drive over to the main office in Fredericton he decided to see Professor Becker. Constable Deborah Matchett thought it ridiculous and petty for Delano to keep at it, but he could not help himself, and so he met with the professor for over an hour.

A few days later, on Thanksgiving Saturday, John went downriver and walked the path. Some partridge hunters were in the field, and the air was warm. He could hear a little brook running, and the sky was blue. The trees trembled, their leaves gone red. He came to where Karrie Smith was murdered. He was a methodical, careful man. He understood houses like Karrie's, and meanness over nothing at all.

He stood, brushed his pants off, and walked towards the Smiths' yellow house at midday, and remembered Karrie when she was in grade nine.

Dora was standing in the gas bar in the mild yellow sunlight.

She stood behind the counter waiting on two customers, and did not look his way. He wanted to ask her about the money and about what she had heard that night, so after the customers left he approached her.

"Oh, there wasn't much money," she said as she took a breath. "I'd already said all that, my, my –"

"Are you sure there wasn't much money?" he said. "Perhaps there might have been some *other* money – I'll confide in you, I think money was used to pay off a debt – I mean a lot of money – Would Karrie have any reason to have a lot of money on her – was she going away? I mean, if there was a lot of money it might just change the complexion of the case – Vincent was not really a thief, was he? I don't care *where* the money came from. My concern is to help get Tom Donnerel out of jail."

Dora smiled. There was a hesitation, as she looked towards the back of the store, where Emmett stood in a kind of acute resignation.

"Get Tom Donnerel out of jail – get Tom Donnerel out of jail," she said in an almost pleasurable, catatonic way. "You know Judge Skid is a friend of mine. I'm up their place all the time –"

So John left these questions unanswered. But he asked, "Did you hear anything?"

She thought a long moment and then nodded.

"Something – a door – I was tired, it was after midnight – I said 'Karrie – get in this house.' Yes – I do remember that."

He went out into the flat parking lot, looked at the penned-in tires, all of this vista having an uncrowded mild despair, and glanced up at the window over the porch. It was as if he could see Karrie leaning there one summer night.

He glanced at the pumps, and walked over to them, looked back to see Emmett staring out the window. Then he turned and walked sanguinely back down the path and to his car.

Far across two fields and a fence, near the dry autumn inlet, the large old farmhouse that Michael had rented was boarded-up and empty. John sat in his car, with the door opened to a gentle autumn breeze, the scent of fall musk-like and sexual on the warm, fading yellow grass. The arm of the bay moved dark and full. He read over his notes, flipping through the pages as if angered by them.

"Carried money next to skin, under panties – robbed gas bar – tin box, robbed for who –"

He had written this line sometime during the day of September 10 when everyone was in a rush.

Now, in red pencil, while the fall wind came up and gently buffeted the car, he wrote, "Someone in house – murderer? Two robberies – Karrie's and ??? –"

He then took a walk across the field and went onto the verandah of the old farmhouse. The wind had picked up. The porch was saddened by vacancy, the window ledges glutted with fallen leaves. He thought of all Karrie's eager laughter frozen in time as he looked across the shore. He stood a minute and walked away, and as an afterthought turned and walked towards the barn.

It was already the middle of the day. A shotgun sounded in the distance. It seemed to John that he was visiting ghosts in this autumn wind. He tried to open the barn door to go inside, and found that the door was blocked by the dinghy they had used to travel to and from *The Renegade*. He moved it as he came in and set it against the cord of yellow birch. *The Renegade*, its bow showing the beating of summer, was also housed here. John leaned against the woodpile and shone his flashlight at the sailboat.

Now the barn door banged open and closed. He started to leave, and as he stood he heard something almost weightless drop from underneath the dinghy's rear seat and land against his left shoe. He lit a cigarette and waited, five minutes, maybe longer, and then he reached down and picked it up. It was a small plastic bag.

The next day – Thanksgiving Sunday – John took the bag of mescaline and went to see Laura again. She was just leaving the house to go to Michael's parents', and she looked at him like one does when they expect never to see someone again. He recognized in her eyes the soft beat of instant dislike.

"Do you remember the mescaline that made those Ingersol kids sick on the Island?" he said. "I might have found that mescaline, or some of the same, downriver. I'm sending it to the lab, but it will probably take weeks." He looked at her, as if wondering what she might know, and this bothered him.

She nodded, said she vaguely remembered something about it, but seemed distracted.

"Do you know a Professor Becker?" he asked.

Her face suddenly blanched. And he noticed that she was wearing a diamond.

"He's to be Michael's best man – why, is he hurt? Has there been an accident?"

"No, no – he's fine –"

So John, with a sense of chivalry, kept the bag of mescaline in his pocket. For her sake he would not use it against her fiancé if he could find some other explanation.

And this was something of that secret summer no one else knew.

Two

As time went by, rumours spread about where the money was. Rumours spread about how much money it was. Rumours also spread, almost with a kind of gaiety, that someone else must have killed Karrie Smith.

Dora couldn't sleep, thinking of this money, and as a by-product of this thinking how much she had always disliked the Donnerels. At first she felt the money had to be at Donnerel's house, and though she had no part in the burning of Tom's property, she had searched the ruins. There was no money found. Now she felt someone else had it.

Emmett began to have trouble with his stomach. He took pills, and his hands, brown with hairy wrists, began to shake. He came to her on the morning of December 11, and said timidly: "It couldn't have been Tom."

"Why in hell not?"

"Because he wasn't found guilty – he *pleaded* guilty – Why wouldn't he tell where the money was? He has no knowledge of our money –" And for the first time in his life he grabbed her aggressively by the shoulders. "This is our fault," he said. "All of it."

For the first time Dora looked at him, confused. But she hated what she was hearing.

"I can't do anything about *him* – what do you want me to do – save the man who killed your girl? You weakling – you weakling – you weakling – you keep your mouth shut."

And she smiled because he dropped his hands.

Emmett sat on the couch and looked about, distracted, shaking his head in dignity.

They were now enemies. She, herself, with great pride, refused to go to the graveyard and was fighting over the price of Karrie's stone.

At night, Dora tossed and turned. She wanted one thing: to find the money and move away to Moncton to live with her sister, where no one would bother her again.

She then asked someone to look for this money – for a 5-percent finder's fee. Someone whom she could count on. Gail Hutch.

So on the afternoon of December 16, suffering from a heavy cough, wearing a pair of men's rubber boots, the road she walked trailing off long and broken and barren, Gail came to the house. They sat in the porch overlooking the back field.

"I might be able to find it," Gail said. "I could ask people at church or I could put up posters about it. How much was there?"

"I can't tell you because I don't know," Dora said. "But don't put up posters – just keep this quiet. The only thing I can tell you is if you do find it it might have "D" marked on the bills – have you seen any bills like that? Did Karrie ever give you one?"

Gail tucked Brian's shirt in, and then took a puff of air, from her inhaler, and looked perplexed.

"Comme ah sa va – da diddly poop," Dora said suddenly, looking at the boy. Dora's victories were always over other people – children and the brokenhearted especially – and she laughed a short presumptuous laugh.

"The money might be all gone by now, Mrs. Smith," Gail said. "It could all be spent."

"Yes," said Dora. "It might – but I have a feeling it is not."

Wind blew over the field, blew snow over the paths, and down against the old crab-apple tree and over the graveyard on the left where Karrie's grave was already a sunken mound, against the brittle salt air.

"Karrie didn't say nothin to you?" Dora asked. "You were so close to her – she didn't say nothin to your son about getting money for you?"

"Mrs. Smith," Gail said," Karrie was kindest ta us – all summer – except for you." She shook her head rapidly and shifted her gaze, and then breathed a sigh, and then popped the inhaler in her mouth and took a breath. Her thin legs seemed to grow out of her rubber boots like twigs out of a pot, and she moved them back and forth, touching her toes together in the chill afternoon air.

"Well, I know she liked you. I don't know what could have happened to all me money," Dora said.

∾

Gail and Brian went back to the small shack and sat on the bed, looking at Brian's toys, and the wind blew snow off the pines and spruces and lifted the snow from the ground. At twilight, everything was black except this wind, which had the reddish tint of the sun. All day that sun hung over the rivets on the tin roof and the one window, and splashed on Gail's straw-like hair. All day the boy tried to put the blanket against the holes to keep the wind out.

"A flat wind," Gail called it, as she coughed, fumbling with the damper on the stove. A small yellow plume of smoke rose in the raw air outside. The little boy went to the door, opened it an inch or so to let the smoke out, and came back and sat on the bed, where he too began to cough.

He and his mother were filled with plans, and some of them were wonderful. His mother planned to have his birthday party before Christmas and said she would get party hats. And Brian was hoping to go to the store for them the next afternoon.

The boy had witnessed many things. They tried to get Everette to go away, and once Brian tried to lock the door when he came.

Gail had often been struck and bullied.

Once, after Everette had gotten out of the hospital, she had been hauled all the way down the wood path by her feet, so her head hit all the bumps.

"You are going to hurt her head! You are going to hurt my mommy's head!" Brian kept shouting, astonished. But Everette said he would make Gail take off her clothes, and he would strap her legs apart on the bed and let his friends come and do it to her if she didn't smarten up. And that's how he would get back all the money. And then, after swearing about this, he got Gail to make him a Pizza Pop.

Whenever Brian remembered these things, he would sit in the shack in a kind of startled agony with a small apocalyptic smile on his face.

Brian had tried to protect his mother, but he was too little.

And though they were broke, had nothing, their nights were tortured by the thought of what they owed. The little boy would count up all his toys, and think of how much he could get if he sold them.

Gail looked towards the window. She was waiting for word from Social Services about a piece of paper coming from Quebec that would ensure her child's welfare. Then she might be able to get some kind of job, perhaps at the fish plant in Neguac.

Every week they went to the road and hiked to town for a stipend of money. But they got little else. The local Social Services took a cursory interest in anyone who demanded nothing. And they would stand at the corner and hike home again.

"What would you do if you found Dora's money and we got the reward?" she asked Brian, moving her fingers through his hair.

He sat on the bed beside her and smiled as light beyond the plastic on the window came in, and washed his face.

"We would pay back the business loan," he said, for that's what Everette had always called anything he had loaned them, "and move into a big house," he said, "for my birthday is what I would want, with heavy locks on the door that no one could kick at –"

"A house," she said.

"Yes – where you would have your own room," he said. "And we would have our own stuff. And go on a trip. I would take you on a trip. That would be my present at my birthday party, if I had money."

They talked about what they would have in their house. And then she tucked him into bed, even though it was early, and turned off the light.

She had no idea that all that money – all those thousands of dollars – had been hidden by her brother the day she was at Karrie's funeral. That this money was hidden almost directly under her feet, as she tapped them together, hauled on her inhaler, and sang a Christmas song.

THREE

That same night Silver waited for Madonna to come in from town, where she was taking a secretarial course she had started in late September. He paced back and forth with his hands behind his back, his right hand holding on to the index finger of his left hand.

The course Madonna was taking in shorthand and typing, given in a small, red building that had been turned into an improvised schoolhouse at the height of the baby boom, was a course that by the very nature of the world would mean nothing in ten years.

Madonna was the oldest in her class and would be in town at ten minutes to eight every morning. The woman who taught her was perhaps the first woman who was not frightened of or mortified by her: Nora Battersoil.

Madonna came home that night at six o'clock. She made a supper of beans and wieners and brown bread left over from the evening before. Tomorrow was the last day of classes until after the holiday, and she was happy because she had made 85 per cent on her shorthand test.

Silver came downstairs and sat at the table, looked at her, and when she looked at him he put his head down as she said grace. He had just been asked by Everette Hutch to go into town to get Michael Skid. He was worried, and couldn't think straight.

"Have you stopped screwing?" he asked her.

She looked up, blessed herself, and smiled.

"Are we going to get a tree?" she said. "Let's get a tree this year."

"Maybe – I dunno," he said. He said he wanted to go to Ontario. He was worried. "I wish you was the way you was," he said finally.

"Why?" she asked. "That was no way to be or to live."

"Why not?"

"I caused so many trouble."

"Ahhh," he said in disgust.

She looked shy now. The way she had been was better. For instance, she had gone on a date with that businessman Everette had set up. Mr. Jupe, who had come to Hutch's looking for a bottle of moonshine.

He was on his way to Tracadie, and was pleased with himself, pleased by his own plump nature, and the nature of his business, which was fish, and had a gold chain about his thick, brown neck, wore three rings and a watch which he said he had bought in Boston. Though married, he flirted with Madonna for weeks, encouraged because no one in the shack said anything to discourage him.

One afternoon, they did a lot of hash together. Then hugging her about the waist and cupping her breast he walked her to the car.

She drove with him down a dirt road, hit him over the head with a wine bottle, removed those rings, tied his hands behind his back, put him in the trunk of his car, which she drove to the dump, stripped him naked, kissing and fondling him so he begged her to make him come, stole his watch and wallet with four hundred dollars in it, and went on a three-day wine-and-bennie drunk, ending up at Hutch's with a completely different man, and wearing the bathing suit Tommie Donnerel saw her wearing two months later.

She was no longer that girl. And Silver worried about it.

However, other things now occupied Madonna's mind. In a dream the night of the murder, at about three in the morning, Karrie appeared and hugged her, and handed her a present. This present was a small brooch in the shape of the sailboat with words upon it, and these words said: *Pick up your cross and follow me.*

In this dream Madonna had cried and said, "I don't deserve none of this."

But Karrie just smiled and hugged her again.

It would have been less extraordinary if she had known at the time that Karrie had been murdered.

"Poor Vincent," Madonna said now. She had hardly eaten in a month and her body was thin, her face drawn.

"Deserved what he got –" Silver said, yawning. "Tom too. It's sad – but eye for a eye Bible says." He nodded at her again and wiped up some beans with his bread.

"I s'pose yer right," Madonna said.

"A course I is right –" Silver said. "I mean, we knew that girl. We was friends with her!" Then, agitated, he left the room.

She turned and he was looking at her from the living room, which was dark and cold and had but one small couch and chair. The kitchen light shone on his hands, but she couldn't see his face because no light shone there.

"You must stop at this conjecture – you must know Tom is guilty. You must forget Nora Battersoil and her prying around you. You must stop hiding my distributor cap every time I get drunk. You must stop taking the bus back and forth every day to that damn course – you must stop thinking there is ever a good answer. And be the way you was. The way you was was better!"

Then, sad and alone, he walked upstairs to his room with tears flooding his eyes. If only they knew how sorry he was, they would be sorry and love him. Even Karrie.

His room had nothing except a picture of the *Bismarck* and some toy soldiers. The strange position he and Madonna had been forced into by their terrible fear of Everette Hutch had changed both of them radically and forever – but it was up to both how this change would finally manifest itself.

It was now nearing seven o'clock. Madonna sat at the table. Her beautiful eyes roamed the desperate little place. It had taken her a while to begin to think she could change, to find the new and wonderful life she was seeking on her own terms. When she cleaned the sailboat of its mescaline dust and hash, of its cups and saucers, she had been too frightened to go into the cutty because of how she and all of them had made fun of Karrie during that night trip to the Island. But finally she did. She rushed down the teakwood stairs and saw the poems of Robert Frost forgotten on the couch. It was at that moment, that very moment, the process of change began in her. It was a change that did not include that brilliant life she had once dreamed about when she had looked through the old glamour magazines over at the gas bar. The tight-waisted garments, the fashionable cosmetics that she felt must adorn a woman's life. No. It was a very different life. A life she never ever thought, for a moment, until *that* moment, she would seek. But now she sought it. And now, her past life seemed a distorted jumble of drugs and sex and men, and was foreign to her.

Tonight, after cleaning the table, she went out to church. She had to decide something very quickly, and it was imperative that the decision be the right one. Time was running out. She had been procrastinating for over two months, and this was probably the reason Silver and Michael were both still alive.

The pews were dark and the candles fluttered and sputtered in their grates on the side of the altar. An altar girl carried the book out to the table, and the priest, his face white, and coarse with wrinkles, spat into his handkerchief and looked out the vestry door to spy the mean, sad congregation. He was the same priest who had said Karrie's funeral Mass to that huge assembly that day, when he spoke of redemption and healing.

Madonna blessed herself and knelt and bowed her head. She smelled the worn pew and imagined the thousand thousand hands that had touched this pew since the church was built in 1853. The hands of tiny children or severe old ladies, soldiers, thieves, and citizens of the great world, gone. All gone in little frocks or old shawls, as distant with age as was Karrie.

She remembered the look she had given Karrie on the sailboat, and the time she had smiled and said: "Well, look at it this way – you no longer have a tight little cunt." And Karrie had hung her head.

She did not know why she had said that. But it was a part of everything that summer, a way to get back at someone for something.

She had been going to church off and on since the murder, but All Saints' Day was different. That day, her culpability in the summer struck her with a terrible force, suddenly and overwhelmingly. And when it did, as she knelt in the pew, it made *her* body seem dead. Awful enough by pride and arrogance, for her own body, to the wilful disregard of a young girl's life, and the robbery of a pompous, sorrowful man.

And this is what flooded up from her breast over the sputtering of candles that day. And as soon as it – and it did seem to – spewed from her, she heard Vincent's voice, as clear as a bell: "Karrie loves you, Madonna."

And with tears of hope flooding her eyes, Madonna knew she would never be the same.

The vision of Karrie never came back after the first night, and had in effect evaporated.

That same night Silver visited Michael Skid. It was just before Michael was to go to the McNair house, for the party celebrating the upcoming wedding. The night was cold and airy, the sky filled with bright stars, the snow powdery on the streets, and the alley-ways between the old houses looked warm with newly fallen snow.

Michael had laid out his suit – the one Tommie Donnerel had sent back to him – upon the bed, and was looking at his collection of silver cufflinks. It was a moment when he had let his guard down, the one moment when he was not thinking of the past.

It was anticipated by everyone, up until this moment, that it would be a great, if impulsive, wedding.

Silver hadn't seen Michael since the funeral and stood inside the door looking small and remorseful. He breathed heavily, smiled glumly, and came to the task at hand. He gave Michael the message Everette had told him to bring. That Michael was instructed – and he used the word "instructed" – to go down-river and wait for Everette to come and see him at the farm.

"I can't go now," Michael said. "I won't go."

"If you don't, it'll all come out in the open," Silver said, and he looked up at Michael. "I've tried to stop him – he'll just come up and see your father with the tape."

"What tape?"

"A tape he has made on you talking – over a whole month –" Silver shook his head like a little boy. "I listened to it. It'll put us both in prison. One day on the sailboat – tons of things we said and did about the mescaline. He told me he just did it as a joke – but now he realizes how much he could get for it. That maybe he could sell it to your father – and he is ready to do that. He is thinking all kinds of fuckin things – Daryll is lookin for him – and so is that guy you met in New Carlisle. So he's scared to go to Gail's shack and I never know when or where he is going to show up. He's like a fuckin ghost."

Silver shrugged, and a sad smile formed just slightly on his lips. Michael was too sickened to answer him. He looked away quickly, as if he had just been punched, and stared at the couch. The couch seemed to mock him, and his eyes blurred.

They were in the small apartment Michael had taken in October. Books surrounded them, and a typewriter sat on the table. His article on local politicians had just been published in the local paper.

Until a short moment ago, Michael had been pleased with the jabs he had made at the mayor and the town council, pleased with everything that had come his way in the last three months. And now – in a second – everything was as petered-out and as cold as the ash he had seen one day falling from a chimney in a snowstorm.

"Can you help me?" Michael asked. "Can't you get the tape – or tell him to wait?"

"I already asked – for you. He said no. So go down to him – if you don't do as he says, he can accomplish it –"

"What? Accomplish?"

"He can finally get back at everyone who put him in jail – your dad, Laura – that's what his real intention always was – it was underneath everything else." Then Silver paused and thought. "You have never been on your own – he has been on his own from the time he was eight. You care about what people say and think of you. He don't care what people think – it's not in his nature. He don't care if the police are chasing him – or if others think he is kind. He don't. You do. He has real power. You don't."

Michael listened to this, but said nothing else. He waited until Silver left. He poured a glass of red wine and drank it down.

Then he made a phone call to Laura's house. He could hear all the celebratory noise in the background, and hung up without speaking. He took more wine. The article in the paper, on the town council, sat on his small table. He picked it up and lit a match and burned it until it crinkled in his hand.

Then he got in his car and drove back downriver to the cold deserted farmhouse on the bay, took his hunting knife that he had bought for his one hunting trip with Tom Donnerel and put it in his belt.

He's dead, he thought.

He smoked Craven A cigarettes and waited. No one came. He lay awake all night, furious that he had missed the engagement party on a whim of Silver Brassaurd, and fell asleep at dawn.

At noon the next day, December 17, he woke with a slight fever. Sick of waiting, he found an old pair of snowshoes, and set out in the direction of the gas bar. After a while he came to the spot where Karrie was killed. The path that ran down to his house and the path that ran up to Donnerel's formed a cross in the middle of the dry wood and, except for the chattering of a squirrel and the queer clean sound of snow whispering over snow, the day was soundless. The trees were muted and caught golden rays of sun on their frozen bald tips.

Why would she be running back *towards Tom*, he thought, *if Tom was such a part of the murder?* The question was strangely impressed upon him at that moment, and he shuddered. He turned towards the gas bar and red sunlight touched the snow. As he came behind the propane tank, which was also crusted with snow, he saw Emmett in the window serving Gail Hutch and her son.

Across the road the potato field stretched furrowed and rutted, near where Karrie and he had once walked. And far down at the turn he could make out the stovepipe stack of the Brassaurds'.

For just a second of *déjà vu* he felt he had entered the past world again, and Karrie would turn and smile at him. In fact, he longed for her smile one more time.

He did not go into the gas bar but waited until Gail Hutch, with her tiny son, came out and started home.

"Brian," he said, and the little boy turned. He had on a jacket with a worn American flag on its arm. Gail carried a tin of beans in her hand.

"You want to buy a treat?" he asked, and he handed the boy a dollar. He saw his own hands the way a condemned man might, and he thought of the knife in his belt.

The boy had some coloured paper to cut out Santas to paste over the back window. But the store did not have any party hats for his birthday, which was on December 19.

"Where's Everette," he asked.

Gail said she hadn't seen him, but she thought the police were looking *for* him.

"Why is that," Michael asked.

"Because he tried to hurt Laura McNair."

"When in Christ did this happen?"

"Last night –" Gail stopped speaking and looked up at the sky, where thin, rice-like snow began to fall. "Its been on the radio today – Constable Delano on the radio – we heard it at lunch –" Gail rubbed her nose, coughed a short, hot cough, and began to tremble slightly.

Michael found himself inside the store, standing in front of Emmett, asking for the phone.

"You're down here to do research for the book," Emmett said, and smiled.

The door opened as Emmett handed him the phone. The bell tinkled and Michael felt suddenly that the day was too bright, and he shuddered.

He didn't remember dialling Laura's number. But the line was busy and remained busy for twenty minutes. Finally, with people coming into the store and staring at him, and seeing old Mr. Jessop pull up in his truck, Michael decided it was time to go.

He crossed the yard quickly, back onto the path, down past the scene of Karrie's death – turning this way and that through the naked birches, feeling constantly as if he were being watched, and came out behind the farmhouse.

The accord he had paid to high frivolity and rebellious youth now seemed like paste in his mouth. He tried to start his car and couldn't, and he found himself, after agonizing about what to do, in the barn.

The barn had a few cords of wood, the dinghy rested against it. *The Renegade* was wintered there, resting on sawhorses and blocks. The small river that ran behind the property was frozen, with traces of thin white and yellow ice.

The inlet was frozen solid, and he could see puffs of smoke far off.

He spent the late afternoon trying to get his car started. He took the manifold off and checked the carburetor. He was doing work as Tom had taught him. The problem was that he had known all along Everette would attack Laura. And it was clear that the attack on Tom, which he had heard about as soon as it had happened, and the attack on Laura were linked.

He spent four hours in the cold, trying to start his car, and finally, exhausted, he went back into the house.

"I will hitchhike up in a minute," he thought. But then a feeling overcame him that he would wait for Everette – that he would have to settle with Everette now, before he could possibly go on.

He sat in the kitchen, with its windows low to the floor, with a blanket over him. It was an hour later, and he had fallen asleep in his chair.

He awoke with someone talking to him.

"How's it going?" the voice said from the far, deep side of the room.

The man was sitting by the stove. It was Everette Hutch. He looked ragged and filled with energy like a man on the run. His thick legs were wrapped in snowpants strapped to his boots. His boots were caked with snow, his Ski-doo suit unzippered at the chest.

"I have been sneakin around. Daryll don't trust me no more – I never cared for him no how," Everette whispered hoarsely, as he had since his motorcycle accident. "They want to arrest me. And the police have already been at Gail's, so don't you fuckin say you've seen me. So I want you to get me some tickets – train tickets – I can't chance going up there again – you'll have to do it. Have them made out for a Gary and Susan Jones. I always liked the name Gary."

"What tickets?"

"Go away with – get rid of Daryll Hutch – get away from him for a while. You go to your old man – tell him I have a tape that will put you away – he'll give you five thousand for it – no problem. If your old man wants to turn me in, then he'll turn you in. That's the chance I'll take. Then buy two tickets first-class on the train for me – go to B.C."

Everette sat back and looked at him, and took an envelope from the inside of his heavy jacket.

"Who for?" Michael asked.

"For me and someone – *you* don't need to know that." Then he paused. "If you do this it'll be the last thing I ask. You and your father can pretend you have done nothin wrong – and you can go on with your weddin."

He took a tape recorder from the envelope and pressed the play button. He seemed as curious as Michael to hear what it had to say. Michael saw a small red light, and heard his voice. He didn't recognize his own voice at first – but as the tape moved, it became clearer.

"Make the tickets for December 20 – the evening train – and meet me at Tom Donnerel's tomorrow night – not leaving from here, mind you – from Campbellton," Everette said. Then he sniffed, satisfied with himself, and nodded to no one in particular. Dante had said betrayal was the worst, the most private sin, Michael had learned studying the classics. It flitted through his mind that he too had betrayed.

"What happened to Laura?" Michael said, and he slowly moved his hand towards the knife.

"Quiet. Nothin happened – but don't worry about her until you worry about me –"

"I swear to fuck if you dare go near her again –"

Michael lunged at him, the knife in his hand, and found himself a second later sprawled on the floor against the stove.

He heard Everette leave as he regained his feet and stumbled, himself, towards the door.

It was now after eight at night. Far away, up on the highway, a remote light twinkled and a car passed on in a drift of snow.

Michael needed to find a phone to call Laura.

Again he went to the gas bar, and this time Karrie's aunt was there. Again he asked to use the phone. This time Laura picked up.

"Michael," she whispered. "Where are you? What has happened?"

"I am downriver doing research and my car couldn't start – and no one was here to drive me – I'm sorry."

"Michael," Laura said again, in a fearful voice, "Michael –"

"Everything will be fine – everything – I've just got to be by myself another day. How are you – how –?"

"Michael," Laura said again, "Michael – I'm fine – everyone is being so kind to me – I've – got my passport photos done –"
Here she laughed. "I look like a criminal – I –"

"Yes," Michael said, "I know – we always do."

He placed the phone down and turning, his eyes looking so frightful that Karrie's aunt backed away from him, he once again found himself on the road. He turned impulsively towards Gail Hutch's.

The moon was high, the river glassy, the bay black as stone, and everything outside looked serene. The temperature had dropped to minus-twenty. And yet Michael didn't close his red coat.

The lights of stars were far away, behind the moon. Somewhere up the road, Christmas music played.

As he walked, with every thud of his heavy boots, he thought of the wedding.

Now, just when it seemed impossible, Michael wanted to be married, wanted a small house, children, even have a minor, nondescript job. And he still could. That is, everything was settled except for this.

By the time Michael got to the shack, Gail and her son were asleep, but he went to the door and knocked anyway. There was a shuffle inside.

The little boy opened the door, and looked up, seeing a man with long dark hair and brilliant black eyes.

"Can I come in for a minute?" Michael asked, remembering that innocent smile from months before. "I need to speak to your mom."

Gail lifted herself from the bed and snapped on the light. Wearing long underwear and a woollen sweater to bed, like her son.

The fire had burned down and it was icy, her breath was pale. There was plastic over the window and plastic up the wall behind the bed. Michael kicked off his boots at the door and entered. He took a cup and poured some moonshine, and drank it down.

She went to work lighting the stove and he watched her.

"Everette's not here," she said, jabbing at the half-burned and still-damp wood. "The police was here earlier asking about him."

"That's okay – I didn't come to see Everette," he said. "I came to see you."

"Why?" she smiled, looking over her shoulder.

"How much wood do you have?"

"We have six pieces a day till February 4," she said. "Or we have five pieces a day till March 21 –"

"How much have you been burning?"

"I been burning nine or ten pieces some days," Gail said, rubbing her thighs with her hands to warm herself.

"And what do you plan to do?"

"Burn garbage," Brian said. "There's lots at the dump."

Michael looked at Gail's straw-like hair, and her crinkly soft smile. She rubbed her nose, and stood.

"I'm going to leave you some money," he said. "Karrie would want me to." And he took from his wallet three crisp, brand-new twenty-dollar bills and placed them before her.

She objected by saying she was sure things would be very different by the New Year because she would have another cheque, and by next fall she was sure to have a job at the fish plant.

"No, you must keep the money," he said. He looked at her squarely as he spoke, and bolted back another cup of moonshine. "But there is something you can do – Everette has a tape, and I need it back," he said. "Can you help me?"

Gail came and sat down and said with some urgency: "Everette has a tape on everyone. On Silver – and all his transactions. On Madonna and the robbery of Mr. Jupe. Even on me," she said. "All them times when you were laughing and talking – when Madonna burned the picture of the Virgin – when you laughed – the night you came down and Everette talked about pooling all the resources to make it a family – Do you remember in the hospital when I prayed? I –"

Michael waved his hand at this but Gail screwed up her nose and then put her head down. "I'm sorry."

Michael thought this a profound act of cowardice, on Everette's part – but he didn't say so. And it was too late now. He only realized that he had not used sound judgement in any of his dealings. And that he was dealing not with bodies but with souls. And the souls of men and women lived inside those bodies and flitted in and out of consciousness.

It was in the soul where everything was determined. And this is what people must have recognized in their dealings with *him*.

"It's not your fault," Michael said softly. "I'll make out okay – no matter what comes out of this or what they say about me. They cannot take my spirit – only I can take that – only I can get it back – no one else. That's God's plan."

Gail found it strange that this man who teased her so much about religion would mention God. There was a long silence.

"It's too late," Gail said, after a time. "I guess we're all in the same boat. I'll probably go to jail too."

"Why would you go – to jail?"

"I stole two jelly rolls – for Brian and me – and I told Everette –"

"God, Gail – you can't go to jail for that –"

She smiled, and the little boy smiled, as if both of them were suddenly relieved to hear this. That both of them had worried about the jelly rolls.

"We're all in the same boat," she said. "Everyone suffers the same amount, I guess."

Suddenly Gail began to cough and the boy began to pat her back. Then he ran over to the counter to get her inhaler. The inhaler, shaped like a squirt gun, with yellow tape about the handle, looked in part as if its function was to be a poignant reminder of Gail Hutch's humanity, a humanity, when looked upon, as glorious as any other.

And seeing this, Michael realized that he did not want to suffer as she did. Or as Mr. Love, his old drama teacher who had taken an overdose of sleeping pills after Michael's article came out, was suffering. Or as Karrie must have suffered that last moment.

As Gail coughed, he looked about the room. He spied on their mat two pairs of rubber boots – a large pair and a little pair. Each boot had a woollen sock sticking out of it. There was a small candy cane hanging from the door handle for Christmas.

The wind howled outside. The light bulb shook. Suddenly he was desperately ashamed of himself. But had no idea why.

His visit initiated one event neither of them would ever know about.

A medium-sized rat with a slick, black face, which had smelled the blood on the money beneath the floorboard, had come down from the dump that afternoon. It had come up inside the shack that night when it smelled the tin of beans cooking. It was behind the stove and made a dash for the door when the boy opened it for Michael. It found itself outside. It turned, trying to find a way back in, lifting itself on its hind feet in the moonlight, and then, fearing the white sky, it scampered over the snow to the back of the shack. There it found the open cement pipe that followed the road, and began to move inside it.

In a little over an hour, it caught the almost indiscernible scent of maggots and blood and, moving to its right, hopped like a dark spectre across the frozen, windswept field to the back of the Brassaurds' shed. Clawing its way down, it found two other rats and a nest of young. There it settled, squeaking its own brand of power, upon the pants and scarf that Silver had hidden three months before, until it was pushed out by the other male into the inside of the shed, and sat on the back counter near the tool board, under the rafter where Madonna had hung the buck.

Everette Hutch was waiting near the Brassaurds' shed at that moment. He was scared of Madonna for the first time, for she had something that she could refuse him. And that something was *her*.
The night before, he had waited for Michael to come downriver and then he had gone to town. All the lights were on at the McNair house, cars were in the yard and parked on either side of the cul-de-sac. He waited near the front of the garage. And he had a piece of luck. Laura ran outside thinking Michael had arrived. She stood very close to him, calling Michael's name. Then Everette made a lunge. But at the very second he lunged she moved, and he slipped on some ice, and lost hold of her. He snarled when she kicked out at him, and she screamed. Then people came running out of the house to protect her, and he ran.

He had been hiding in thickets all this day, making his way back downriver, through drifts of frozen snow. Everette had done this deed for his friend in jail – the one who had stabbed Tom Donnerel for *him*. But like most events in his life, it was a halfhearted try. She got away. The man in prison was angry. And Daryll Hutch, his cousin, whom he feared, said he wanted the money that he was owed before Christmas Eve. Everette had told Daryll nothing. He had neglected to tell him that Silver had already brought him all of the money early on the morning of September 10.

"And if I can't get the money?" Everette had asked his cousin yesterday. "What can I do? They screwed both of us, not just you."

Daryll had looked at him with a sideways glance, and sniffed. "Kill Michael Skid." He had smiled. "That'd be a good, good thing."

Then Daryll, complaining that the prices of everything were going up year by year, had said Christmas was not the same as it used to be.

When Everette saw Madonna's upstairs light go on, he crossed the yard and went into the house. He climbed the stairs and opened her door. She had just finished putting on her night-gown and was ready to turn off the light.

She was sitting on the bed with the light-string in her hand when he entered. Two books she had been studying sat open near her pillows.

"So," she said coolly, "don't you ever knock?"

"Have you thought over what I asked you?" he asked.

"Yes," she said. "Every day for a month."

"And?" He looked at her expectantly, with his eyes half-closed. She was silent.

"And?" he asked again.

He had asked her to go away with him, to British Columbia. He had not been able to touch her yet, and this was a game she had played for thirteen months. Always using her body, as a chess piece, as a queen that could move in any direction and con-found him, to protect her life and the life of others.

"I will go," she said, "under two conditions." She smiled almost as if it were a joke. Sadly, it was the only joke she would be able to play.

"What conditions?" he said.

His bald head made him look impressive. The scar on his cheek added to the darkness of his wide eyes. His life had trailed in a vacuum of petty hopes and disillusions. His voice, like the voices of all the powerful, contained nothing special in its vocab-ulary, but rather rested only on how things were said.

"You must do two things," she said.

The wind blew.

"What?"

"You must never see Gail or Brian again – you've beaten her enough."

"But Gail is my sister – the little boy – I care for him. I can't –"

She was silent. The room seemed possessed by great weight and determination. In his eyes Madonna saw the slight, unmasked look of confusion. He scratched at his head quickly.

"Fine," he said. "They're not important, but I have to go back once more. To get something."

"I said never." Her voice turned so cold, and yet such fire came from it, that he nodded. Her voice held in its sound the age-old fire of singlemindedness, of suffering and mortification, that the poor and the elderly have.

"But it's the money we'll need – I took a chance in hiding it where I did –"

There was a slight start to her eyes.

"I said never go back," she repeated. "I will find out if you do – and you will never get to touch me!"

"All right, never," he said. "What else?"

"You must never harm anyone again – in any way – especially Laura McNair – or ever come back here once we leave. You must give Michael Skid that tape, because it will destroy his life – and ruin his chance at getting married – and it is a cowardly thing to do. And if you promise *this*, I will leave with you – you can do me every day. But that is my conditions."

"I don't harm anybody." And he firmly believed this. All his problems came, in his mind, only because of others.

But she stared at him, in the simplicity of truth and justice and determination, and he felt his hands tremble just slightly when her remarkable eyes were upon him.

"Okay. It's just a joke. I like joking people. I wasn't going to hurt her." Then he became relaxed and reflective. "Why did Michael throw all that mescaline away? I owed people too –"

"You're frightened of Daryll, aren't you?"

"No, I'm not," he said.

"What if Daryll found out you had the money you owe him – that you hid it instead of giving it to him?"

He looked at her, trying to understand her.

"You'll never pay them – you're a thief, and will steal even from Daryll," she said, and smiled. "That's why you want to go to B.C. You are only running away from the evil you have created. But it can't be run away from." She made this last phrase in a taunting sing-song voice.

Everette paused and looked at her. He shrugged. Then he moved so quickly she didn't have time to flinch.

"Look at me," he said, holding her chin and mouth. "If I went and killed Michael Skid – Daryll would take that as all the payment he'd ever need. Judge Skid's son. I'd owe him nothing."

He let go of Madonna's head as if he had told her something she did not already know. She shrugged.

"No, he would never be satisfied," she said. "He is like you. Neither of you will be satisfied until you kill one another – that's the secret."

"I have been keeping the money for us," he said glumly. "What is so wrong about that?"

"It doesn't matter," Madonna said. "No one cares if a person is guilty or not – they care only for the way they can excuse themselves by letting others suffer for them."

She said this not because of him, but because of Tom Donnerel and of the mob reaction against him. She too had initially thought he was guilty. She too had thought what others thought, that the evidence proved Vincent and Tom guilty. And she had been bitter and depressed about it. Now, she wondered if it wasn't someone else. So she had sent Tom a get-well card, and drew a happy face, which said: "This is the face of Madonna now."

But Everette was very pleased she had made this statement about *him*. It was what he had believed about himself for years and years. He sniffed happily and then thought of something.

"He's come back to the farm."

"Who?"

"Michael. If I go there – just to pay him back – not for Daryll, but for you. Look how he treated *you*."

Here she put her hand over his mouth and smiled.

"Don't be jealous," she whispered. "It's over – let him go – he's not important –"

"After we get married – I'll give you your tape back too," he said.

"If you do I'll just hand it over to the police," she said.

"You will what?"

"I will hand it over to the police – what does it matter?"

He laughed loudly at this and then, half-genuflecting and half-shaking, he hauled out a diamond and slipped it on her finger, standing quickly as if afraid of being on his knees.

"Here," he said, proudly. "I been waiting a long time to give the right woman this! Hold her up, and look at it under the light."

She had seen this diamond before. It was the same diamond Tom had tried to give her four months ago, when he was drunk. Same diamond. A woman knows.

"Why are you trembling?" he asked.

"I'm not at all," she said.

"You have nothing to fear now. I got the money – but your heart is beating like a rabbit in a snare," he said, holding his hand over her breast.

"It's just exciting to be with you." She smiled.

"Well there now – give me – a look," he said, trying to lift her nightgown.

"Tomorrow," she said, as a woman can say, without any thought at all, and she looked over his head, as he lay it against her chest. Then for some reason she sang to him, as if she were singing to a child.

Silver came in later. The downstairs was cold, especially the kitchen, so he lit a large fire and sat at the table, smoking. He was very drunk and fell asleep, and the cigarette burned down to his fingers, while the snow on his boots melted, and there was an unpleasant scent of warm wool. He would take a drag, push the cigarette ahead to keep his fingers from burning, look about, and fall asleep again, with his old woollen hat still on.

It was after two in the morning when he was shaken awake.

"I want you to help me," Everette said. He had always thought of Silver as simpleminded. And he liked the way he had been able to bully him, tease him, and hold him up to ridicule in front of people like his cousin Daryll, whom he truly did fear.

He sat down across from Silver now, and poured a glass of red sherry. He was bare-chested, and Silver could see the man's half-dozen blue pen tattoos on his white body. He tipped the wine up.

"I'll tell you where the money is – you go get it – you give Gail two thousand – you bring me a note from Gail that says she has the two thousand – and I will give you a thousand. Fair?"

Silver nodded. But he was too drunk to really understand and had to be told again. Then he stood, washed his face at the kitchen sink, and lit another cigarette.

"Where is it?" Silver asked.

Everette turned and hesitated. He was mulling something over.

"If you do not help me," Everette said, "things will not be so good for you – everyone will want to know who dealt the bad mescaline – no one will give up looking for who did that."

At this moment Everette looked like his sister. A part of his family portrait. Yet where the same look in his sister was gentle and good, in Everette it was cold and distant.

"But if you bring me the money – Silver, listen – if you bring me the money, I'll give you the tape, and have no more evidence on you. We'll be all square and count it as a learning experience." He shrugged to show his affable side. "That's what I'm willing to do."

Silver said nothing. But his body felt suddenly as if it had turned to lead.

"What if the money isn't there – and I'm blamed for stealing it, just like I was blamed for losing the drugs?" For Silver was always thinking of a trick now. He had lived in the world of tricks so long.

"Well then, you come and see me anyway and we'll figure something else out. I'm not joking," Everette said. "The world beat and hated me long before I hated it. I kept asking it not to hate me and begged it not to hate me and my sister – but it wouldn't listen."

"I know exactly how you feel," Silver said without any emotion at all.

Madonna lay awake, listening to the men talk, smoking and listening to the wind. At 3:30 in the morning, she heard Everette leave. She felt the diamond on her finger grow heavy and could not sleep. But she now understood something very important. It was still up to her to protect Michael Skid and his fiancée. That they had not protected or cared for her or her brother did not matter.

This realization kept her awake, tossing and turning, until dawn. Finally she sat up in bed. The back of her head was pounding. She looked about her room – the busted chair, the small dead flower she had taken from her mother's casket, still in its plastic, the cardboard box in her closet filled with bits and pieces of clothing. A small painting of Arron Brook bridge she thought looked nice and had bought for thirty dollars three years ago at the church picnic. For a while, every time she looked at it, it had made her feel glad. Now it no longer moved her. She thought of Laura McNair, remembered being interviewed by her, remembered her tweed suit, her small expensive wristwatch, and the sound of her shoes when she walked.

"Well, for her sake, if not mine." Madonna smiled.

She got up, dressed, put the diamond in her pocket with the intention of throwing it away in Arron Brook, and went downstairs. Silver was lying on the couch, with his shirt and pants undone. His face looked quiet and sad in the early morning. His lighter, with its picture of an alley cat, rested on the small coffee table. Even in that fake glamour and virility there was poverty and useless hope. She looked at him for a long time, and began to cry. Then, she kissed him. He moved slightly, looked at her and smiled.

"Madonna," he whispered, almost as a plea, and then fell back to sleep.

She threw a coat over him, then a coat around herself, and went outside, crossed the yard to the shed. Above the tool board was the distributor cap she had hidden the night before.

When she switched on the light she saw a rat, with a slick, black face, staring at her. It squeaked, turned, and scurried down the wall and behind the tool board, to the clamour and squeaking of other rats.

Madonna picked up the handle of the rake, began to poke at them. She lifted their nest up, and started to haul it away.

FOUR

That morning, Michael went to town and bought two train tickets from Campbellton to Vancouver. The clerk looked at him, smiled as Michael sat in stupefied agitation. The clerk had once dated Laura McNair in high school. He was still upset to think that she would impulsively get engaged to someone she had known only a few weeks, after he himself had agonized over how to approach her and invite her out. So he thought of Michael as a trickster, and looked upon him as such. He didn't like how Michael reported about the town in the paper, for he was the mayor's brother.

"So, who are you going away with this time – Laura?" he said, and, being a part of the small community and wearing a pink shirt with a wide tie, his statement gave him a feeling of moral comfort.

Michael stared at him, the way he had learned to do when he was being bullied in private school. He would never be bullied again.

"They're for Gary and Susan Jones."

The clerk coughed and said nothing more. He filled out the tickets by hand – made a mistake on the second ticket and had to start that one again, and then put the price of 426 dollars on the bottom.

This transaction only increased the clerk's appetite for the scandal. It was all over town how Michael hadn't shown up for the party. The clerk could not wait for Michael to go, so he could start telling people he was trying to run away. And he hoped Laura McNair would feel as hurt over Michael as he once had felt over her.

"He knocked up that little Battersoil one – oh, he doesn't know that, but most people do – and now he's running away with Madonna Brassaurd," he said, because it was the only woman he could think of at the moment. "Yes, that slut – I've just made up their tickets –" And he felt himself grin selfishly at the moment he said this.

With the tickets in his pocket Michael went to Laura's house to apologize.

He felt as if a giant hoax had been self-inflicted, or inflicted upon him by the simple judicious reasoning of the universe.

There was no way for him to stop real life from playing itself out. For life was unconcerned with what Michael said about truth and justice.

Life was only concerned with the impeccable minutiae of our vice that passed for virtue, and for virtue to be manifest in the end. Once the action was over it was irrevocable. And this is what life managed to say: "Ah, but it is irrevocable. Karrie's smile – is irrevocable."

He parked his car near the McNair house and went uneasily to the door.

Laura's father looked dissociated from the world and from him. Mr. McNair spoke about the attack on Laura in the incredulous way that children sometimes do. Then he just shook his head.

So whatever Michael did or did not say would be fine. If he made up any excuse about not coming to their party with thirty guests and salmon brought in and lobster brought up all the way from the wharf at Saint John, that would be fine as well. That Michael hadn't seen Laura in her velvet dress that she had spent a month making was fine. It was in retrospect all horrible.

"Oh, the party went on – the party went on," Mr. McNair kept saying. "He's just a hoodlum – you'll have to get used to that, Michael – there are some hoodlums here." And he laughed.

Instead of hurling insults at him, Mr. McNair asked Michael to come in, shook his hand, as if Michael had been ill.

"Where's Laura?" Michael asked.

"Down in Moncton to pick up her dress."

Mr. McNair teetered a little and caught himself. He had been in the den looking at pictures of his son, and his eyes were wide with bright tears as the wind blew through the cold breezeway.

"I'm sorry," Michael said, "for all of this."

"I understand – it's just the women, you know," Mr. McNair whispered, not believing at all what he himself was saying, but saying it because he thought that this was what *men* should say. He then nudged Michael as if it were a private joke, which showed how far outside the circles of people and of social events he had always been.

"I can't be forgiven about this – but I had things to do."

Mr. McNair nodded. The whole house was quiet and soundless, as if it were waiting for his boy, Lyle, to come home, to rush in from school. Laura's passport photos were lying on top of a small envelope on the side table. She was to send away for her passport because they were to go to Spain.

"It's just the women, you see," Mr. McNair said again, his bright black suit-pants belt-high on his waist. And Michael, looking at these photos, trembled and nodded.

"Your son was very, very brave – really," Michael said, his voice suddenly filled with emotion. "You must be very proud of him."

"Yes, proud," Mr. McNair said, in a whisper. "He was good – that's the difference. I wish he were here, because good people can always help. Yes sirree – things would be different if Lyle was here –" And he rose on his toes, as if to stretch, and then coughed into his hand.

Michael left. He did not wait for Laura, who had gone to LeClairs in Moncton to get her dress.

He did not know what to do. He smelled in the air the ash from a wood stove, and left to go back downriver once again, collecting his mail at his small apartment downtown before he did.

It did not matter that he himself did not know half of what went on that summer. That after the first loss of mescaline Silver and Madonna had been forced by Everette's cousin Daryll to sell drugs, which made a dozen kids sick and sent three to hospital, one with severe epileptic seizures, which would put Michael himself in prison.

It did not matter that that very afternoon Michael had received the advance for his book, with a note of godspeed from the publisher.

It only mattered that he was now carrying a hunting knife, hoping to kill Everette Hutch.

FIVE

That afternoon, when Madonna got home from her final day, Silver was preparing to go out. He wore his heavy boots and a thick black belt, with a cowboy hat on the buckle, shiny and meaningless, since he had never been near a horse or even liked them very much. Madonna came in with a first-prize pen she had won for shorthand, and set it on the fridge. The pen had the emblem of the high school engraved on it, and the year 1974.

All life can change, this emblem seemed to say. It is just that the farther down a road a person goes, the farther she has to come back. Like finding yourself on an unsafe street in an unfamiliar city, and turning in the dark to find a street that is lighted once again.

It was five o'clock. Silver looked up at her and smiled, as he had that morning.

"Madonna," he said.

"Where are you going?" she asked.

He told her, without looking her way, that he knew how to make some money for them, a lot of it, and this is why he had to go out. But he would be back for her. Then they would go far, far away. He spoke of the house they would have, the rooms all their own, the new car he might get.

"We'll have it made," he said, "if I do it right."

"Are you afraid, Silver?" she whispered. "Are you afraid of our poverty, of how we were treated? Are you afraid that night you went to the Island – it's in the paper how those kids got sick – are you afraid it's from the drugs you used to replace the drugs Michael threw away?"

"Never," he said. He sniffed, looking at her and lifting a cup of scalding tea to his mouth. He then glanced at the floor to her right.

"Well, then, why can't you look at me?" she said.

"I look at you all the time –"

She took a deep breath.

"Why can't you look at me in my panties? You always used to."

"Yer my sister," he said. "What are you talking about?"

She took another breath.

"Why are you now revolted? You can't even touch me."

"I-I-I – yer talking stupid," he said.

"Here," she smiled, as if it was a joke. "Take your hand and touch me."

She reached for his hand, took it, and brought it towards her lips. But suddenly, as if frightened of being burned, he hauled it away.

"Why are you in hell?" she said. "What have you done?"

"There is no hell," he said. But he said this so eagerly she knew he had been thinking about it for months.

"Things are not the same as they were last summer, are they?" Madonna said.

She sat in the chair between the door and the old washing machine that looked like an enamel tub.

"They certainly are not," he said. He sniffed as if he were very aware of this.

"But why aren't they?" Madonna asked.

"Well, they are all quite different, aren't they?" Silver said, and he lit a cigarette. "Just as you said – so don't play the cunt."

"I'm not," she said. "I just want you to tell me."

He sat down on the chair and looked at her, and shrugged.

"I never had a bicycle," he said. "All my life – in the summer – and once Emmett brought Karrie home a new bicycle – do you remember? We were about eight or nine after her mom died. Her old bicycle was still there – a girl's bike, pink – you remember – and we thought Emmett would give it to you – and that you and I would have one. We ran down to see them – ran all the way down. But Dora said *no* – do you remember? – that she could sell it – and then you and I ran about all night to try to find fifteen dollars – we asked everyone, we searched in the ditches for bottles. And then we went to the priest – the priest told us to go back home, that we were ungrateful for what God had given us.

"So we walked up the lane all by ourselves. That night we collected bottles, walked as far as Oak Point – and the next morning we ran to the store again, with fourteen dollars and twenty-six cents. But still Dora wouldn't give it to us."

"I remember," Madonna said. "It hurt very bad – and I had hated Karrie for it – but no more –"

"Ya," Silver said. "Well, I remember too."

He shrugged and tucked his shirt under the large belt as if he were suddenly vindicated.

"That is nothing," Madonna said. "The bike is gone forever – it went to the dump in 1965 – it was the little bike Nora Battersoil bought, so good for her. It was the only bike she had too. And she was Karrie's cousin."

He stared at her and said nothing but there were tears in his eyes.

"So then –" she said kindly, and somehow helplessly, "that is not worth murder – neither are the hits in the head you took from dad – remember how we used to fight back? We fought back all the time then – you and I – we were brave, we fought back – that's what we have to remember. But we didn't murder."

"What are you talking – murder?" he said.

There was a pause. The wind blew down the flue of the stove, and the fridge started up with a crack and a hum so suddenly he jumped.

"Do you want to go to take the Eucharist?"

"The what?"

"Take the host at Communion?"

"No, no –"

"Everette has figured things out – the money – he'll use it to destroy you – so destroy yourself first, and become something new. Destroy what you were and become something brand new. Put on the new vestments. Not bad drugs and blood that you've been living with for four months, and I've been living with, but the new vestments. Before you are destroyed."

"What do you mean? Nothing can destroy me," Silver said.

She looked at him, and took the diamond slowly from her pocket and put it on the table. It was as if he had just been slapped. He turned his head sideways.

He stood and moved away from her, almost ran to the counter.

"I'm not blaming you," she said. "Half of it was done because you wanted to protect Michael – but I want you to come to church – and then go see John Delano tomorrow morning. If you do, we might be able to begin again."

Here Silver laughed, shook his head, bent over and took a drag of her cigarette, but he wouldn't look at her. There was an ooze of broken dreams that seemed to collect on his skin, on his breath – she could tell there was the energy of deceit and malice trying to break away and fall down into the eons of history.

It was now 5:25.

"You would have to go to confession – there is still time – we could both go. I will stand beside you – if you do twenty-five years, you'll still be in your forties. I promise I will wait for you – we will have our own place, and cause no one trouble. Just come with me to church."

His body looked distant. His eyes glittered, and his fingers were sweating.

"It's good theatre," he said, because he had heard Michael say this one Sunday afternoon and he suddenly felt very sharp repeating this. He laughed at her.

"I don't believe in the church," she whispered. "I don't believe in the cardinals with their red hats and pomposity, or the priests. But I do believe in the faith. I believe in our Virgin Mary – our immaculate conception, the body and blood of Jesus Christ."

"But you burned a picture of her," he said. And he gave a laugh. "You'll burn in hell forever now – even if Everette made you do it."

She lowered her eyes, and said nothing for a moment.

"He made us do nothing – we did it by ourselves," she said finally, looking up, her eyes warm and forgiving and bright.

"He'll pay," Silver said, gritting his teeth. And then, remembering that this was the very last thing Karrie had said to him, gave a sob, and closed his eyes.

Madonna left the house shortly after, and made her way towards the farm.

SIX

By now, 5:40 on his watch, Michael saw himself as another person. Simple and filled with vanity. He couldn't even protect his fiancée from Everette Hutch. And the one who might know this was a man he once thought he despised, John Delano.

He didn't mind that John had been in love with Laura for that brief moment. It seemed that, in a small town, things could happen like that, so you could keep in contact with someone you once loved for years. It was that twice he had met Delano, and both times the man had exercised a simple moral pre-eminence over him. And Michael was twisting about trying to change their position. Now he would not be able to.

He came up to the verandah and hurried along to the door, thinking only of the tape, and frightened about what it contained and wondering how to get it back before it fell into John Delano's hands.

Well, this time next year it will all be over, he thought.

As he opened the door he saw Madonna. She was sitting in the chair in the corner and startled him with how she looked.

She was wearing a heavy coat over a pair of pants. A black purse was slung on a long strap over her shoulder and a plastic bag was resting on the floor beside her, as the wind blew outside and seemed to move the wall.

The air was bone-dry, the sky cold, and night was upon her. She sat in dusky solitary at the far end of the main room, near those chimes of sailboats Karrie had bought the previous July.

Her face looked drawn, though as beautiful as always.

She lit a cigarette and looked out the window, so he could see her face in relief and desire the fullness of her mouth.

"You have the most beautiful eyes I've ever seen," he said.

The wonder of Madonna's eyes was that they were two different colours – one was slightly blue the other slightly green. It was like looking into a kaleidoscope. When she stared at anyone she startled them with her mystery. They held in them, those eyes, sunlight and a mirror of a glazed highway. Her voice echoed with them, and her body seemed translucent as rolling summer waves.

She answered him as the Brassaurds always did, quick and without posture.

"I don't know what I'll ever do if anyone ever says that to me again," she said. "My eyes have been my curse – been my curse more than my cunt. I have drownded men in my eyes – like that poor businessman from Neguac – and have gone to the Virgin to pray. Yet the same things happen. Everette Hutch is now in love with these eyes, and it is remarkable to me how I even met him –" She laughed. "And how I've been able to hold him off for a year."

He suddenly realized that if she had had half a chance in life – like the chance Mr. Jessop asked Michael himself to give her – her eyes would never have been her curse.

She raised her head boldly and proudly.

The chimes moved, the radio station played, and the kitchen tap dripped solidly and at a regular interval.

"We put too much pressure on Silver – he was always running about for us – and he was just a kid." Here she paused, took a drag, and looked behind her at the bookshelf, as if the bookshelf were impeding her thought, and turned back to face him.

"He got off his medicine, started sniffing glue. In the end he thought you betrayed us, and he cannot bear to mention your name. We lived in such dirt-poverty you could not even begin to imagine. So he wouldn't be able to step into your father's house, even if he got the invitation he was sure you were going to send us – the invitation to your wedding."

She smiled.

"Silver wanted to take a course somewhere. He got the application forms. Then we came down to see you and ask you about it. Remember? He had me dress up, he wore a sports jacket – he was going to get you to take him to Moncton to enrol. Then we were going to take you out to dinner as a treat. You told us to wait. And we waited. And then you went back to town. We waited. Silver phoned you every day. And when you did finally come back, that's when Everette was planning the robbery and wanted me to help him. I don't know what became of his application form," she said.

"I'm sorry," he said. "I'm so sorry."

"Ahh," she said waving her hand, as if startled by her own vulnerability. "Every time I went to church I was told that Silver and I were made in the image of Christ. Our father beat the snot out of us but I was still told that. We were chased out of yards and houses and stores, and children were not allowed to play with us, but I was still told that. And do you know, I hated to be told that. Then, when I was fifteen, I started getting fucked, and people finally stopped telling me that. But now, since last month, I've been aching to hear it again. Just once more from someone."

There was a long pause, and she looked away.

"You are made in the image of Christ," he said. "You are and always will be."

She picked up her purse and snapped it open, without taking her eyes off him for a second, and took out another cigarette and lit it. The window was open to the snow, the clear evening.

"I went after some rats that had got in behind the shed. They musta smelled something, and look what they were using as their nest."

She tossed him the bag in the greyish darkness that always seemed to be a part of houses like this. It landed on the couch next to him. He gave a slight movement sideways when it landed. It was one of the *secrets*.

Michael opened it. There were a pair of pants, sneakers, and a scarf. He held the scarf in his hand. He could smell it and he could see the heavy splashes of blood everywhere upon it. There was a death imprint visible where she had clutched it. It was as if he could hear her last feeble cry.

"I always wondered where that scarf was," Madonna said matter-of-factly. "I had to hunt all last fall without it."

Michael looked over at her. His lips were thin, and his hair moved slightly in the breeze from the window.

Here her gaze shifted again as if she were embarrassed by him, with a deep unforgivable embarrassment of their time together.

Then she took the final drag of her cigarette and flicked it out the open window so that it twirled in the granite-coloured air, end over end into nothing.

"And now you're getting married – and you don't even know how much I loved you –" She turned, looked at him suddenly, smiled, almost timidly, and was gone.

He hadn't anything to say. In fact, the bag of clothes said it all.

Michael sat with his head in his hands.

"My God, Tom. I'm sorry, I'm sorry, I'm sorry." Yet he had to think. On the one side there was Tom, on the other Laura – both were haunting him. To protect one, he would have to give up the other. There were no other options. If he gave himself up, Laura and his own father would be seen involved in a coverup of drugs and murder to protect a fiancé and a son. And Michael would face the one thing he was afraid of, and the one thing he had heaped upon others – ridicule. But if he remained calm – if Becker could keep quiet – if Everette got away, then Tom would remain in jail, and no doubt be murdered sooner or later.

Yet either way, Karrie was silent now. Now, when he wanted her to say something to him, there was only silence from her grave – a place he had not yet visited.

He could smell Karrie as he grabbed the bag of clothes.

He wondered about her body, remembered it, thought if it, and got sick.

He stood and looked about, wiped his mouth.

He shoved the scarf down into the bag, and turned to leave, snapping out the light.

In the darkness he stopped.

The dump, he thought.

And he made his way towards the shore. He walked along the shore – for he feared being followed if he went any other way.

The shore was dark, a gale wind was up, and he moved with new resolve. Coming off the shore, towards the back path, he slipped and fell. He landed on his back and stared at the sky for a long time.

"Tommie," he thought.

Just then, a voice said, "Are you okay?"

He tried to stand and see who it was. The voice spoke to him again.

"Here, you dropped your bag – let me help you –"

The man put the scarf back into the plastic bag, along with the pants and sneakers, and handed it over.

"Oh, it's you," the voice said. "I just come down here for a minute."

It was Emmett Smith. He moved his false upper plate out, as he smiled slightly, which seemed to make his chin look as rigid as that of a store mannequin's.

"Were you coming to see us?" Emmett said, and he smiled in the same ingratiating way he always had. Michael looked behind him. "I'm glad you're coming to see us. There are things I want to tell you about Karrie – you know, she kept a diary of events – but we can't find it." Emmett said. "How she loved to talk at night about you – and how special you were to her. It would be good to have that in your book. But I have to tell you about our money – I have to tell you – you are the only one to confess this to – Dora doesn't want me to confess – but I have to – Karrie is telling me to from her grave! Tom should not be in jail – I'm thinking – it has to be someone else. Help me find the real murderer!"

"I killed your daughter," Michael whispered, but the wind and darkness made it soundless.

"How she loved you," Emmett continued suddenly, and tears started in his eyes. "And how I loved her – she was my only love. So I don't care – I have to confess about the pumps – that is what Karrie would want me to do. Don't you think Karrie would want us to?"

Michael didn't understand him. He only noticed the tears on the old man's face. The same kind of tears he had seen earlier in the afternoon on Mr. McNair's tired face.

Emmett wore a brand-new winter coat that looked out of place on his old body, a grey shirt and heavy woollen tie. He came down here almost every night while his wife flirted with younger, stronger, more virile men. What she did or did not do he did not know or ask.

The night air moved his hair and in his ruined body was the personification of rudimentary country-business life. Small-mindedness, kindness to his daughter, the disrespect of those younger men towards him, and sickness and misery at the end.

All the things Michael had thought he himself was above. All the things Michael had once felt contempt for. But now Emmett, because of his daughter, was determined to confess.

"I have to go," Michael said.

"Come up to the house – please see Dora," Emmett said. "Please, for my sake, we have to straighten this out." And he smiled once more.

"No," Michael said, "I can't, tonight."

Emmett gave a stiff nod, as if to acknowledge that Michael's business was far above his own, and far more valuable, and grabbed Michael's elbow and shook it.

Michael turned and moved up the bank – the very one Karrie had fallen down five months before.

After a time he reached the dump. But he could not bring himself to do anything. It was now essential that he act. He stood with the bag of clothes in his hands looking at the smouldering perimeter of fires. A girl's ancient bicycle rested against some old car parts on his left, and he decided that this is where he would hide the bag. He breathed the smoke of burning garbage, which was somehow pleasant as he looked at the stars.

By now, the rat with the slick, black face had wandered back into the dump, where it hopped three feet behind him and, nestling under a mat, a cardboard box, and a burlap sack, again found itself in the company of dozens of other rats no more than a foot or two from Michael.

Michael heard them whenever he took a step but paid them no mind. He held on to the bag. Then he turned and started towards the farmhouse again, still with the bag under his new down coat, and the smell of remorse, tears, and Karrie on his hands.

"I will turn them in, and myself as well."

All during this time Everette was trailing him at a distance of about a hundred yards. Everette did not know *what* Michael was doing, but his plan was ingenious. He would kill Michael, which he hoped would relieve him of his burden to Daryll. He would take the tickets, and send the tapes to the police. If they listened to them carefully they would see that Silver had planned everything, from selling bad mescaline to murder. And no one would come looking for *him* any more. He and Madonna would be quite free of everyone. Thinking of this, and pleased with it, he lost Michael near the farm.

SEVEN

The verandah was cold and blue, with the glint and shadow of ice on the window. One might think they had entered a world of constant blue. Michael thought of Spain, of the reservations made for December 29 to fly to Valencia, with its high *apartamentos* lingering under the Spanish sun. Was that still possible now?

The door banged against the wall, and the sailboat chimes started to waver and tinkle.

The snowdrifts were sculpted and high against this side of the house. The barn, where they had spent so much of their time capping mescaline, and hilariously outwitting the police, even once outwitting John Delano, lay solitary in one huge stagnant drift.

Michael came into the living room, shoving the bloodied clothes behind the couch.

"Well, you bolted," a voice said. "Dad said you wanted to see me?"

He turned and caught Laura's smile, a smile that evoked loneliness, hurt, and pain. She was two feet away from the bag of clothes. He didn't know if he loved her but he knew he felt profound sorrow for and responsibility towards her, now, and towards her whole family. And he thought of her dead brother, and his simple unwitting act of heroism. And that heroism seemed to make Lyle an invisible observer over how Michael was treating his sister at this moment.

"We had the party – your taking off didn't spoil it," Laura smiled, her bottom lip trembling. "Neither did Mr. Hutch, who came to be interviewed for a job."

"What job?" Michael said.

"Oh – he said he was going to fuck me," she smiled, her lips still trembling slightly. In her hurt was a feeling of terrible betrayal.

"I will see him," he said.

She waved her hand. "Where can he go?" she said. "They will get him today or tomorrow, and it will be over. Don't worry about it – you might get hurt. John Delano won't let me down."

Michael felt as if a dart had entered his body. He turned and sat down, and looked for a cigarette. After a moment she sat beside him.

"Any light bulbs?" she said, trying a lamp that didn't work.

"I'd rather sit in the dark," he said. A minute or two passed in silence.

Each family is angry in its own way. And the McNairs were distanced from the town and had found no comfort from it. Laura's father had been hooted and howled at as a clumsy inept man. But her brother had brought them out of themselves and had made them part of the community with his dazzling ability to play sports, his high academic standing, and his friends constantly in the house. All of that was gone. As much as his death had caused sorrow, it had also caused Laura outrage.

Her anger came from the lessons she had learned by her family misfortune and her father's chronic failure.

Now she had to pretend that everything was still going on. For her mother, who had small lines in her cheeks, like herring nets in the water, and for her father, who had left his job due to a breakdown after his son died.

"Why is your leg shaking?" Laura said, and she held it, as if to comfort him. "I've just gone for the dress. I need *someone* to marry." She laughed, and tears stood in her eyes. Then she turned to him, and, taking a breath, said very rapidly, as if she had it rehearsed: "I know why you came down here. It's to be close to her memory. I know I can't be Karrie – I know – I can't. I've seen her pictures. She was a beautiful young woman – a child bride. But I put her bastard killer in jail – I can say that to you, Michael – I put her bastard killer in jail. And I will never allow you to forget her as long as you live – neither of us will. I can allow a ghost in my house – I promise." And she rested her head on his shoulder. She then took his hand, and put it on her right breast.

They had not made love before – and she had had no relations with men before. That was her secret.

She looked up at Michael, and tried to open her blouse clumsily.

"Here," she whispered. But her eyes were wide in fear that he would reject her body once he saw it, although she was far more beautiful than she herself suspected.

He felt no emotion, only a grave feeling that he had profoundly tricked her, as he had tricked Karrie and hadn't even known it. For his part he could only smell Karrie's body – the splashes of blood.

She fumbled with her hand against him and tried to arouse him. But it would be no use now. And perhaps never again, he thought.

He stood suddenly and walked away. There was another long silence, then she said: "I want to tell you that John Delano is still trying to figure things out about last summer – about bad drugs – that made people sick – schoolkids –"

"Bad drugs?" Michael said. "When?"

"I'm not really sure – but he's brought certain things to me – he's never come right out with it. But he was at the house the other night after Hutch ran away."

It was as if she had decided the import of this knowledge was graver because Michael had not gone to the party.

He turned.

"Bad drugs – where? I never heard of any bad drugs anywhere." He was angry. He had never given any bad drugs to anyone. And yet now, it *all* seemed logical. Of course.

He turned and looked directly at her mouth as she spoke, as if he were a deaf-mute. In fact, he heard her as one might hear a muffled shot in a drum or the voice of a companion on a descending airplane.

"It was all laced with chemical dust, dirt, insecticide and manure – from a barn floor – that's what they used to give their caps the volume. John Delano is still on the case – he has samples taken from someplace at Thanksgiving, but he won't get the lab results back until after Christmas. Things are slow. Delano is not very respected right now. But I'm almost certain we will sooner or later come to lay charges. He said it must have been Everette and Daryll Hutch."

Laura moved her hands, in the dark, so he could see her thin fingers and the diamond whisk by. She stared at him very strangely. Suddenly he realized she was telling him this to make him excited about the possibilities of doing another investigative work, with her. When he stared at her naive smile he realized this. She had no knowledge at all that it was *he* that John Delano was now most likely investigating. And this made it even more horrible than if she had.

"Cowards," Laura said offhandedly. The voice didn't sound at all like hers. "And my brother dies – that's God for you!"

"Oh," he said. He could say nothing else. So she grabbed his arm.

"You and I could solve it," she said. "That would be *our* investigative book. I could research the legal side –" Again she made a plea, like an adolescent girl: "Oh look, my blouse is still unbuttoned. Look, I'm all exposed."

He stared at her. She wanted so badly to belong to him – to who she thought he was. Perhaps this came because of fear as well. She moved and exposed her breast completely. She smiled tenderly. What was so poignant was that she believed she had no idea how to make love.

He turned and walked across the living room. He tightened the bulb in the lamp and turned it on. Across in the corner sat the bag of clothes. The chimes began to tinkle.

"Now we can see," she said, leaving her blouse open. "The light is like the light you sometimes see in pictures by Rembrandt – in Rembrandt the light means hidden depth of feeling and character."

He took out a cigarette, lit it, blew the smoke up in the air quickly.

"Everyone goes to the wrong people," Laura blurted suddenly. "I have spent my life going to the wrong people. It took me a long time to figure it out. First that boy at law school – who turned out to be gay – and then I too quickly cast away John Delano, who was nice to me after Lyle died – so that now –"

He could still see her left breast. She left her blouse unbuttoned a moment longer, and then, with terrible justice and certainty, buttoned it again, watching him as she did so. "You're white as a ghost," she said, shivering in her mauve pantsuit.

He wanted to speak, to ask forgiveness, but suddenly her eyes turned directly towards him – and these eyes seemed to say, in one small pulse-beat: *For my mother's sake! It's her last year.*

"I'm so sorry," Michael said. "I betrayed you." He did not mean with other women, but the expression in her eyes made him realize this is what she thought.

"Aah," she said, waving her hand in the air. "I don't expect men to be completely faithful anyway – wild oats or something before marriage at any rate – what does any of it mean? There are shadows and mystery on your face too." She smiled.

Her own face was strikingly pale. She seemed to stare right at the bag of clothes, her eyes startled and bright, but did not notice them.

"I don't know what will happen – if in any way – Why is your nose bleeding?"

Michael lifted his finger quickly and rubbed his nose. Some bright, fresh blood streaked his hand.

"Ahh," he said, "this used to happen to me in school." He looked at her. "When I first went there – my nerves – I've not had a nosebleed for eleven years –"

"You must have hated them all," she said. "The principal, all those other boys, the drama teacher –"

"No – never hated them," he answered.

"But you hurt them when it all came out –"

"But I – didn't – mean to –" He whispered. "I just wanted to tell the story – but I can't take it back."

"And Mr. Love is facing charges – I don't blame you – a pedophile tried to hang himself."

"But really he wasn't – not really. He was just a sorry old man – I – don't know –"

"Oh, but you got them all –"

He now waved his hand feebly, as if to plead with her to stop. So she stopped speaking. It scalded him when he remembered how vindictive her prosecutorial skills were against Tom. For one second he felt an urge to grab the bag of clothes and toss it to her, and smile and laugh in the cynical fashion that was so a part of him, that once had so frightened Karrie. But he felt his hands grow numb at that moment, and he couldn't do this. He felt too sorry for her.

There was a long silence. The sky was black over the bay, and the stars had started to come out, webbed together in many ways. The chimes started to tinkle slightly, for no apparent reason.

Finally Laura said, hesitantly and then with more boldness: "Look – listen to me – we could make love now instead of next week – what's a week? I could get pregnant besides," she said, with an insightful if not clinical attitude. "When we got to Valencia, it wouldn't hurt – I'd be used to it – have me whenever you wanted." And she smiled suddenly and wantonly at him. He looked at her, again with deep sorrow, at her innocent shamelessness, so she blushed and felt humiliated.

"No," he said. "I can't – now – I do love you – I only want you to forgive me."

"Ha," she laughed at this impossible moment. "That's exactly what I said to John – after he invited me out for the fourth time!" She paused, cleared her throat. "But you don't love me. You bought two tickets to go to British Columbia," she said urgently. Her eyes darted towards him and then fastened upon the wall behind him. There was a dreadful blue stillness, and her face looked composed by her profound knowledge of his deceit.

Then her thoughts drifted off, and she became muted by a sense of injured merit, and jabbed with her finger at some ice on the window ledge beside the couch.

She waited a moment for Michael to look at her. But he didn't. He only stared into the corner with his head down, his lips half-open, as if frozen in mid-sentence.

"Fine," she said, the dignity of her life coming from her

throat, and a strange desperate grin appeared on her face. "I had some access to some of those pictures you took of Madonna – we had them as part of the investigation. Oh, she was going to get a spread in a magazine – fuckin tramp. Oh, that was pleasant stuff – just like your investigative report, let me tell you. Is that who you're going to B.C. with, a woman who lies in the sun with her legs opened?"

Then she grinned selfishly, which is always painful to see in a person you admire. It was the way she said, "Oh, that was pleasant stuff – just like your investigative report," that grilled him with a kind of small-town fury, and showed she was able to change her views about him, and join everyone else in a second. And once she did, he would be truly alone.

It was in her grin where all the hurt of her family, the sad and pitiless death of her younger brother, took form. And he understood why she was so brilliant and aggressive in court. Took form in the shadows, like Rembrandt, on her face. Of course they never used the word *brilliant* here. *Cute* or *clever* or *some sharp* he had heard about her often enough – even from Everette Hutch.

Then, not knowing what else to do, and Michael hearing only the rustle of her coat, she ran from the house. He couldn't move. He could see her running away, felt the embarrassment of her parents, her sad father, the silence and innuendo of others. The suspicion others would have *about* her. He wanted to stop her from going. But he couldn't.

Laura drove and drove and found herself on the back road. Here she took her diamond off. With tears streaming down her face she flung it out the window, over the old bridge, at Arron Brook. It took some time for it to land, bounce slightly into a small crevice, and settle hidden between a dark boulder and a fallen log, near Vincent Donnerel's pipe.

If Laura McNair had not visited him when she had, Michael Skid would have been killed. During her visit Everette Hutch had moved towards the farm, conscious that he would not leave Michael Skid alive.

It wasn't Laura who stopped his plan, of course. It was Constable John Delano, who had followed her and was sitting in a squad car a hundred yards from the barn. It gave Hutch pause, and he turned and slunk away.

EIGHT

Michael sat in the room in the dark clutching the bag of clothes, and rocking back and forth as if he had terrible pains in the stomach.

"Karrie," he whispered, once, twice, thrice.

He put the bag back under the couch and left the house. He felt himself running towards the church. He came out on the road near the graveyard and waited, almost exactly at the spot where he had waited to see Tom Donnerel all those months before. Perhaps he did not realize that he was five feet from Karrie's grave.

From inside the church, beyond the glowing windows, he could hear the priest's tired voice. And in a few moments parishioners started to file out the door into the golden-coloured night.

"It will snow tomorrow," Michael thought. "It will snow all the days of my youth."

He waited for Madonna. When she came down the steps, she turned and made her way along the path Karrie had taken that final night, her body huddled into the dark. Her entire life

Madonna had fended off men, and really had given herself to very few people, and in her face was the absolute dignity of that struggle, born in poverty and violence and faded skirts and thin blouses.

This is what he suddenly realized, and he made his way through the dark to speak with her. To kneel before her. She had loved Tom, perhaps, and she had loved him.

"Madonna," he said.

He came out from the trees on one side of her, and she looked up, startled.

"You scared me half to death," she said.

They were in that clump of muted winter trees. Here the stars dazzled, and there was a whisper from heaven that all life would of necessity be born again.

"Where did Silver get the bad mescaline?"

"Daryll brought it to us, told us to cap and sell it," she said. "But we didn't know – *we didn't know* it was really bad until after we sold it." She looked past him. "It was done to try to get you out of a scrape after you threw the good mescaline overboard. We sold it the night of Karrie's birthday –"

She said all of this straightforwardly.

"What kids got sick?"

"On the Island – Silver wanted to go back over. To sell it – so Everette wouldn't take the sailboat on you. Silver couldn't think of anything else to do. Daryll gave us the bag and we capped it in the barn – I don't know what in hell was in it, but they say it was poison. They've linked it back to us – or they will. And one of the kids had epileptic seizures – his father will want to kill us – you."

Michael couldn't think of anything to say.

"Because of us, look what happened to Karrie and Tom," she said simply. "Because of us."

He stared at her, at the top of her head, and suddenly he realized how indebted he was to her, and how much she had hidden from him. And how much he himself had used her and Silver. That in a perverted way, Silver had murdered for him.

"I'm sorry," he said. "But we'll find a way out – it doesn't have to go any further."

She said nothing.

"Look, Tom will be paroled in two years – I'll write about it in the paper every day – I'll see to it."

She said nothing.

"Well," he said, a little exasperated, "do you want your own brother to go to jail?"

"He's in hell now – jail would be a blessing – you must decide what to do – I can't decide for you – I mean, I don't want to. The truth is the great investigation book will be turned on us."

She smiled at him, with sympathy and pity and tenderly touched his face, as if no matter how he was used, treated later on, this touch was a reminder of her universal love. He had not realized how tender her touch could be, how it was alight with power and goodness.

"I'm sorry," she said. "I am sorry for *all* I've done. I'm sorry there is no way out – I've tried to find a way out for all of us for months. I am sorry I was Everette's partner in the robbery of that poor man – but there is nothing I can do."

He took her hand and kissed it, and smiled. But there were tears in his eyes.

NINE

"There will be no truce until this is over," Silver thought, sitting upstairs and looking across the room at the model of the *Bismarck*. Suddenly, looking in the tilted mirror and raising his eyes, he realized what had been created over the last thirteen months.

He left the house at 8:30 and went to the shed to get the long screwdriver. He would have to kill Everette. Then, he felt, he would be free with the money. But he hoped he wouldn't have to kill Gail and her boy.

When he went to the shed, he saw that the boards had been pulled back, and the clothes were missing.

Christ, I have to do this now. I have no choice, he thought, shoving the screwdriver into the shed's paper-thin wall. There was only a wisp of wind, some dry rat-droppings, and the body of one thin and hairless baby rat.

He set out, wearing his heavy coat and a pair of white mukluks. He made his way around the back of his house, crossing on dry powdered snow towards the small drain, under the soft moonlight. He had taken nine bennies during the course of the afternoon to stay awake, and they had been taking effect for a while. His mind drifted and raced, like a dory's small motor. His eyes were tracking off lights, which made violent, fantastic rainbows for hundreds of yards.

"The money is at the end of the rainbow." He laughed.

He carried the large screwdriver in his pocket, and he touched the handle every few seconds.

"It's good it's there –" he kept saying.

The air was icy and filled with winter smoke. From the gas bar, lights twinkled, small and obscure, and a Santa with a cigarette smiled. The sky was wide with brilliant stars, firing the heavens for as far as his eyes could see. If he had to kill, he would kill the boy first, so Brian would not have to watch his mother die. That was the best he could give them.

His shadow moved along his left side in the snow. And he passed Bobby and Joyce Taylor's house. He could see them near their tree, and heard music.

After twenty minutes he saw the cold, obscure shack. It was now nearing nine o'clock on December 19, 1974.

The boy, Brian Hutch had had his birthday party, and had been staring at the floor for a long time in a kind of stupor, trying to keep warm. Now and then he would yawn and smile at something, or fold his hands deeper under his armpits. Once he nodded off completely. And then he awoke – because of the wind – and looked at the floor once more. It was as if the flat wind, as Gail called it, suddenly prodded him, making him conscious of what some force of life was trying to explain to him, a voice in his ear.

"Mom –" he said, finally, "look – something must have went across our floor – from under the bed."

Gail, sitting in the chair, herself almost asleep, looked over at the small tiny markings that came from the hole beside a board under the bed, and seemed to cross the room at an angle and run against the wall. Something keeping close to a wall meant only one kind of animal.

"A damn rat," she said.

"It musta gone behind the stove," the boy said. But when he jumped down to check there was no rat near the stove, or in the other room.

Gail said, "Maybe it's gone. But you stand on the bed – with the shovel – and try to hit it when I take up this board. That's what we get living close to the dump."

The boy grabbed the small shovel and waited. Gail tried to lift the board but it was nailed.

"Everette nailed that board," Brian said.

"When?" she asked.

"That day when you was at the funeral – I forgot about it."

So she went to Everette's toolbox and got a tire iron. She came back into the room and pulled and pried until the board came up. It was a brand-new nail.

There was no rat. It had gone.

No rat, but she stared for the longest time at the thousands of dollars. And then, taking them up, as you would remove an old earthen jar from soil, and seeing blood over dozens upon dozens of bills, she said something that was to change the course of everyone's life.

"We have to go to the police."

"The police," the boy said, in disbelief.

She looked at her son, sat with this money in her lap, and considered. The money was wrapped in elastic, and marked just as Dora said it would be, and covered in plastic. But there would be someone coming for this money – her brother or Daryll Hutch

– and she knew she and her son were in danger. For the blood told her. She did not know that danger was already on its way, was now walking towards them.

"This is terrible," she said. "Brian, don't you ever touch this money. You become a good citizen of the world. We are not going to obey Everette any more – ever again!"

She replaced the board as best she could, closed the damper on the fire, put on her old coat, and put the inhaler in her pocket. She waited a moment at the door and listened. Every sound now seemed to be amplified a hundredfold.

"We must cross the road, and take the ditch," she whispered.

And she made her way out into the night air, taking the boy by the hand, rushing across the road to the far ditch so as not to meet anyone. There they hid for a moment and she listened.

"There is someone coming," she whispered, "on the other side of the road – look – shhhh." Then, grabbing the boy by the hand again, she moved away and turned towards the next house on the road.

Silver went to the shack. He drew his screwdriver and kicked the door open. When he entered, he yelled to scare them. But they were gone. The money – which was supposed to be under the board – was missing. The place was still warm, and there was still a pot on the small Coleman stove.

He searched the shack in rage, spending this rage on kicks and screams. Then he fell to the floor, and jabbed his screwdriver at nothing.

Finally he went outside, looked at the sky, stopped in his tracks, wondering in terror what in the world he should do.

He went back along the road, hearing in the distance the music that spoke of angels. He passed Bobby and Joyce Taylor's house, and again saw the lights celebrating Christmas. Gail and her boy were already sitting in their living room, with all the money, and all those streaks of blood. Silver had missed meeting them by twenty-eight seconds exactly.

One second for every year of Vincent Donnerel's life.

~

After a while, the whole town followed these events – riveted to them like tin to a roof. They gathered by the radio, and listened to the appeals from the police, the mayor's statement to the press, and turned on their television sets to see themselves on the national news.

PART FIVE

ONE

After twenty years the events were brought into focus again, by the custodian at the amalgamated school, Bobby Taylor. Sitting in his small closeted office on a cool June afternoon, he thought back to that time.

He could see Silver, after all these years, in his mind's eye.

He took a drag on the cigarette and held it in his lungs, then blew it out the open window into the sunlight, the smell of fresh paint on the window sill, and the warm scent of tilled earth for the flower bed that grew along the brick wall.

On December 19, 1974, at 8:52 in the evening, he and Joyce had been decorating the tree and had drunk a full pitcher of eggnog and white rum. The air was sweet, the fire going with lovely sticks of birch, and outside, above their back porch, the stars illuminated the heavens and seemed to toss off sparkles on the snow, which blanketed their property to the trees.

It was their first wedding anniversary and they were reminiscing about what had gone on over the year. Karrie had been Joyce Taylor's bridesmaid. Tom had been one of the ushers.

"It was as if that was Karrie's wedding too," Joyce said, hesitantly, as good people who sometimes mix deep thought and sentimentality are hesitant to expose this mismatch.

A gloom descended upon their private party and Bobby looked at the nutmeg in his eggnog and was silent. For in truth he had been more than mildly fond of Karrie.

"You know," Joyce said, "it's Brian Hutch's birthday today. He was like Karrie's little boy. She brought him presents last year, remember? I wish we could do something for them – something to help them start all over. Karrie would have wanted that."

"Of course," he said, "but I don't know what we'd ever be able to do – with Everette Hutch as her brother and his uncle. He would either steal it, break it, or threaten them." Then he added, "I pray that someone shoots him soon – but it won't be until Everette kills someone first."

So Bobby said what people always say when someone dangerous is about.

Joyce nodded at him. "Well, something good will happen sooner or later," she said.

Just then the door opened and little Brian Hutch came in, followed by his mother.

To Bobby it seemed the strangest coincidence.

He drove them to the police station, where they handed the money over. Gail felt great fear in going to the police, for she had been conditioned from childhood to hate and fear them. Every one of her relatives had hated and feared them. By now even Brian did. But she hoped that this fear would pass, and knew that her life and the life of her son must change forever.

"I'm going to make them supper – so bring them back if you can," Joyce said.

"Be home by ten o'clock," Bobby said, wondering why in the world that statement sounded familiar.

∼

John Delano took over the case that night of December 19, at ten o'clock, as instructed by Sergeant Fine, who now accepted the notion of spots of blood and a darker, more sinister summer, and made no more derisive comments about Delano's personal motivation of infatuation, or about Tom Donnerel getting what he deserved when he was stabbed.

Delano had no sooner gotten back from downriver when Gail and Brian arrived, with Bobby Taylor. The bills were placed in front of him.

"Whose money is this?" Delano asked.

Gail told him it had to be Dora Smith's – part of the money that had been stolen. And it was hidden in her house.

"And who stole it and hid it at your house – Vincent and Tom?" John asked.

Little Gail Hutch laughed and laughed, and then squirted her inhaler.

"Vincent and Tom never entered our door – it was Everette –" she said.

"You sure?" John asked.

There was silence. And then Brian spoke, his voice clear and calm.

"He hammered the nail," he said, "where the money was hidden – he told me he had to hammer the nail."

John Delano handed the little boy a cup of hot chocolate and patted his head. The little boy gave a crinkly smile.

"It's his birthday," Bobby Taylor whispered.

So John Delano telephoned a person who could find a birthday cake and candles at such an hour. And party hats if she could.

A person who made no judgement, who worked for the police with the homeless and bereaved. A person John Delano admired.

This person was Nora Battersoil.

Rumours began. The river was taking on that agonized, dazzling feeling that a crisis was in the cold December air. And the murder of Karrie Smith was being refitted, retraced. Now Vincent and Tom had both resurfaced out of the din of death and speculation as heroic. Tom again thought of as heroic as he once was by that young woman willing to invest her time in him. And now, because of this exoneration, Emmett Smith wanted to confess, saying he'd known of their innocence all along. Dora caught him telephoning the police station and stopped him. Such was the state of affairs at the Smith house at eleven o'clock that night.

John Delano drove about the small town, and waited for morning. Then at seven o'clock, without an ounce of sleep, he phoned Deborah Matchett.

"You think it's *him* too," he said cautiously and sorrowfully.

"I don't know – I hope not, for Laura's sake."

There was a pause.

"Come over – I want to show you something – something I kept pretending did not matter," Delano said.

He lit a cigarette and lay on the couch in the early-morning dark. Then he once again went over his notes.

The youths who had been treated in hospital in Charlottetown for poisoning had said that the bad mescaline they bought for their beach party had came from a sailboat. (These were the same teenagers Karrie had spoken to from the deck the night of her birthday.) Their statements, each eleven pages long, were given two months ago, the Monday after Thanksgiving.

That was how long John Delano, connecting these events, was certain Karrie had been murdered by someone else.

The pictures of Karrie's discarded body, bruised and naked with a swollen face, were being looked at by John Delano.

He sat with Deborah Matchett at the table in his trailer, at eight o'clock, with a pot of coffee warming. He sat back while she looked down at these photos. She too was now engaged to be married. And it seemed to him that she, too, for one or two moments the previous fall had believed, as others did, that he was stalking Laura. That he had used this murder as a way to stay involved with her. Delano felt Deborah's thinking was a way people sometimes had to make others slaves of their own good conscience.

Now that she no longer felt this way, John took no delight in her change of heart. Other questions were predominant. He had no time to reflect on how slightly he had been treated. But there were one or two moments when she looked at him in whimsical apology.

"I have treated women badly," he mumbled for no apparent reason, as he stared at the picture. He was in a way apologizing to Deborah Matchett, to all women because of this. He looked at her quickly, "I mean in school – and I'm sorry about it now – some of the things I said – did."

"Oh, John – we've all treated people badly – we all have – so –" She stopped short. He nodded pensively and shook his head. Then looked at the picture again.

There was blood on the victim's left breast and nipple. He showed Deborah the picture of Karrie's left buttock, where there was a bloodstain in the shape of what could have been a bill. He showed her the picture of the drip of blood on the path thirty yards away from the murder, in the opposite direction of the Donnerels'.

But there was something else. Delano had something to show her on a photograph taken at the barn the morning Karrie was found, something he had disregarded at the time.

"Look."

"I am looking," Deborah said.

"And what do you see?"

"I see a picture of the victim taken in the barn on September 10, 1974."

"And what do you see?"

(Pause)

"And what do you see?"

(Pause)

"And what do you see!"

"Goddammit, John Delano, will you fuckin shut up – and let me look?"

"Well, come on, Debby," John said peevishly, "what do you see?"

"I don't know," Deborah said finally.

And John pointed. He didn't point to the clot of blood on the head, the swollen face. He pointed down, to the bottom of the picture, on the right calf. "What's that?" he asked.

"I don't know – a birthmark?"

"Let me tell you what that is," John said. "I will tell you what that is, and then I will make a gambler's bet about this whole case. That's a burn from the exhaust of a Harley-Davidson. And it's Hutch's Harley-Davidson."

"Well, why wasn't it mentioned in the autopsy report?"

"I don't know – I don't know why it wasn't mentioned in the autopsy – okay – but that's what it is. That's what the bike tracks on the shore were."

"Well, so what? She went for a ride on a Harley, big deal. Nothing can be proven by that." She smiled indulgently at him, sat back, and lit a cigarette.

He stood and walked to the window. There was a peevishness about him when he knew he was right, and the room was silent and filled with the deadness of cold air. He had not wanted to go against the grain. But not only the grain, of course. He had tried to convince himself that Laura was right about the case, and he felt that if he had pursued what he knew with more vigour, she would not now be engaged to Michael Skid.

The new polished streetlights at the end of the lane had not yet gone off, the traffic continually ground over flat windswept ice.

Delano turned and lit a cigarette.

"I know. For the last few months I thought the same thing. So what? It's just a drive on a bike. It was the grey area, but it fits. It fits since I first met Michael Skid in the hospital last summer. Something bothered me about him. About his rebelliousness. The idea of freedom for Karrie Smith, who never had any. And Hutch posturing as a good man, and Michael replacing his friend, Tom, with his new friend, Hutch, and finally posturing as a bad man. But you see he was not a bad man. That's what was behind all this – not Vincent or Tom – it had nothing to do with them."

Constable Matchett continued to glance through the pictures of the body, and of the barn, now destroyed. Here she lifted her gaze and cleared her throat.

"Oh, I know I'm moralizing about Michael – but moral responsibility in the hands of the frivolous is the real case," Delano said. "Michael traded upon it – I think he traded Karrie's life for it, and by now I think he probably knows this. That's what the pictures at the farmhouse always said to me and I didn't understand why. But Karrie is the only one in those pictures that never belongs – she is always the country girl dressed to go to the city – killed because she knew something. That's what the burn from the exhaust pipe really says. It says this: *Everette had the whole group of them hook, line, and sinker.*"

"Where would Karrie get the money?"

There was silence for a moment, and then John nodded.

"Every cent came from the Smiths. We'll take it downriver and set it in front of them. They didn't admit to losing it, so it had to be stolen money – or a tax ripoff or something."

Constable Matchett said nothing.

"Every cent came from the Smiths – somehow – and if they had told us this back in September, Tom might not be in jail, or Vincent dead."

He looked out the grimy window again, smiled slightly, but only for a second or two. He began to ponder why it was they hadn't reported this money as being stolen.

Two

Dora Smith had Karrie's upstairs room locked, for she could not stand to go into it. And she would not let Emmett near it. His mourning and his remorse burdened her. Sometimes she would go up to him and clap her hands in front of his face.

"Snap out of it – shape up!"

She had sent Gail Hutch into that room to clean it out just after the funeral. The woman had gone in, scared to meet the ghost of her friend, and did what she could, but left a few things where they were, out of respect.

When Constable Matchett came down with Constable Delano at ten o'clock on the morning of December 20, Dora Smith was sitting in the back porch, alone, staring out at the empty bird feeder (the bird feeder Karrie used to fill in the winter for grosbeaks, as soon as she got home from school, and in the summer for sparrows and chickadees) Emmett took the constables in to see her, and stood a little back from them.

Delano asked if she would take them to see Karrie's room. (Deborah Matchett felt that this is where they would be the most vulnerable. And to her it was simply good police work.)

"I have the room locked," Dora told them. "I can't stand to go in and see it. Either can Emmett – can'cha, Emmett."

"No, no," Emmett said, shaking his head. "I can't."

Delano nodded, and asked again if he might see the room.

"If we might just see her room," Matchett said.

Finally Dora said it was okay with her and she picked up a handful of cashew nuts from a dish beside her, and stood, glancing at her husband, popping nuts into her mouth as she went behind them. Emmett followed.

"Soon there'll be a book on poor Karrie," she said. "The whole world is waiting for it – it'll sell."

They went up the carpeted stairs, the stairwell burdened by dark-stained wood, and a picture of a young man in a small fedora, standing proudly by a Ford car circa 1935. This was Emmett Smith at age eighteen, and the ground he was standing upon was where his house and business now stood.

There was a whiff of perfume as Dora passed them on the stairs and moved on her flipflops along the hallway, illuminated by a rectangle of soapy December light from the bathroom. This light seemed discomforting.

"Sometimes at night I hear her in here," Dora said. "I hear her crying. Wanting to come back home, from the path. Goddamn Vincent. Now the room is bare – but I didn't sell her things – did I, Emmett? – I give most of them," she turned the lock, "away."

And with the word *away* she leaned against the door and it opened, with a solemn squeak.

The bed was stripped, and the far window was curtainless. The dresser sat with its drawers open and empty. The small collections of dolls and miniature suitcases were gone as well. And no one would ever know what they had meant to her.

Dora remained in the hallway, with her husband, craning her

neck and smiling at them glumly when they glanced at her. Emmett seemed to be going through what he desperately considered reasonable motions, and in these motions he found sanctuary. This was evident by his wife's cautionary and scolding look every few seconds.

"What is it yas are lookin for? Somethin for the book? I give all the pictures over to her aunt –"

Delano opened the closet, and it opened hard as if the wood had swelled. The air inside was trapped and musty. A coathanger and one shoe lay on the floor.

"Her clothes are gone?"

"Yes, they was all given away – well, most of them were, weren't they, Emmett?" Dora said, patting the edges of her hairnet. "Poor Karrie," she said as an afterthought. And then cleared her throat in the musty stillness.

Constable Matchett went to the window and looked out, at the top of the shingled and snowy porch, looking out at the road, and far away, at what was left of Tom Donnerel's farm. That desolate burned farm gave her a strange sense of foreboding. Below them the two inspectors from Esso that John had called at nine o'clock were opening the gauges on the pumps to check the calibration, and Emmett, who had come to the window, noticed this, at first in perplexity, and then as someone astounded.

"Here we go," Delano said from inside the closet.

Searching the shelf, he brought down from behind the faded pullover and old woollen blanket the mauve jewellery box. It had been hidden there since the night of the murder. The last person to have touched it was Karrie. It brought the feeling of immediacy back – as if she was now in the room scurrying about.

Dora now heard the pumps being turned on. It was like a small rumble. She cocked her head and, listening, looked towards her husband. "Is someone at our pumps?"

No one answered, not even Emmett. Delano brought the jew-ellery box over to the bed and looked at it. Then he took a small wire from his pocket and picked the lock. It opened, not unlike a tomb. Karrie's serious and crisply new passport pictures lay on top of her diary, three hearts engraved upon its cover and locked by a snap. The passport pictures had been done on August 31, and her forms had been filled out, and placed neatly under the diary. There was, under these forms, a small black-and-white photo of her and Vincent at the picnic. And another tiny picture of Maxwell, the dog, beside his tin dish. This picture was dated the winter of '74. There was a locket which held a picture of her mother, and a lock of her mother's hair.

This was what was left of Karrie's memory and her own hidden life. And it made Delano impetuously angry. He could not help glancing about and staring first at Dora and then at Emmett. Dora gave a slight start and Emmett lowered his head and seemed to sink, so that he looked small and frail beside Constable Matchett.

"Who's out at our pumps?" Dora asked. "Tell them to stop running the pumps –" Then she cleared her throat and, looking at John Delano, said: "What is it yas got there?"

John took the money from an evidence bag in his pocket, and threw it on the bed at the same time as he upset the jewellery box. At first there was no sound. And then a kind of squeal accompanied a rushing of flipflops into the room.

"My, my," Dora said, her face beet-red, and looking at them. "My money – look – the little bitch stole my money."

Emmett turned and walked over the stripped bed, his legs wobbly, and put his arms on her.

"How can you say that about her?" he yelled, coming alive suddenly after fourteen years of marriage. "How can you say that about my girl! – I know you – I know who you are *now*!"

But Dora tore loose, angry, and pleased at her anger. Then

Emmett put his hands on her again, and Dora grabbed at his fingers.

"Karrie didn't steal that money – at least not all of it," John said. "Only the money that has blood on it. Why, why in God's name didn't you tell us? If you had, an innocent man might never have gone to jail –"

"Yes, yes – an innocent man, so what?" Dora said, holding the money in her hands, and then glaring. "You see – I knew it! It's the money –"

She looked around at all of them, her head slightly cocked. All of a sudden there was quiet in the room. Dora had been talking very loudly so as to be heard over the pumps, yet the pumps had suddenly been shut off so "the money" sounded loud and brazen. There was a pause, and she stared in silence at her tired husband in his high-waisted, wrinkled suitpants. Emmett had not given them away, she had.

"Our *pumps* – so you think it's us. I didn't kill Karrie."

No one spoke.

"So you think it was my idea – it was Emmett –"

She stopped speaking and closed her eyes. She began to weave back and forth just slightly. Emmett raised his hand, but dropped it and sank upon the bed.

Deborah put her hands on Dora's shoulders to stop her from falling. "Yes – I'm sure of it," she said, over Dora Smith's shoulders. But she was speaking not about Dora. Dora or the money or Emmett didn't matter to her at all.

She was speaking to John Delano – for the first time in three months – about the innocence of Vincent and Tommie Donnerel.

"Silver?" John whispered.

And he looked with pity at the jewellery box and very gently closed its lid.

～

The remnants of the story were vague in Bobby Taylor's memory now. But it must have been quite simple and therefore terrible.

By December 20, people were no longer gathering at the gas bar, but going down to the little store owned by Wholsun Breau – the place where Tommie went to buy his plug the August before. It was a small yellow store with a bit of holly over the door, and a large cardboard cutout of an Oh Henry! bar in the window that winked with soft, forlorn Christmas lights. It was in effect a very different part of the road, though only a mile and a half away. It was a store that had held on to its traditions and had been usurped by the gas bar eight years before.

Each person had a story to tell, standing by the old pot-bellied stove in the store that day, and Bobby realized he had had a story as well, and was somewhat the centre of attention because of little Gail Hutch. Bobby remembered himself and remembered Joyce looking at him in forgiveness.

But most of the talk was about Silver and the various, almost forgotten incidents in his and Madonna Brassaurd's life. And old Mr. Jessop re-informed them, reminded them about this life, as he sat there smoking his pipe.

How they arrived on the road with their father when they were five and six, came from the remotest corner of the woods, and took over the old homestead. How they were an odd mix in the community. How, one night, they were beaten with sticks and left outside after their father took a water hose to them.

All the warmth of the community, the decorations for Christmas, made Silver's life seem particularly sad and cold then. And sadly, a rage began to turn against Michael Skid. He was looked upon now in all his conceit, his money, his smile, which now seemed to annoy them. Four or five people, fathers who worried about their daughters and sons, remembering how their own piety and traditions were laughed at and dismissed over the course of the summer, and remembering the effect

Michael's presence had upon the little community of pleasant farms and tiny houses, said they would kill him.

"He's not even from here – what in hell did he come down here for?" they said.

"Drugs," Dora Smith was reported to have said, "I knew it – he couldn't fool me, I always knew it. If we had men about here who weren't spineless and gutless, they'd take care of people like that."

But no one at that moment was listening to her.

By noon these men were certain nothing could have happened if it hadn't been for Michael, and they set out towards the farmhouse.

"We have to get there before them," Mr. Jessop said suddenly to Bobby Taylor. "That or they will kill him."

They went along the shore road, hoping to reach the farmhouse before the rest.

Michael was sitting in the kitchen when they got there.

"Others are on their way," Mr. Jessop said quietly. "We must go before they get here."

"Oh, I see – what has happened?" Michael said. "Where are Silver and Madonna? Are they okay?"

Sitting on the table in front of him was the bundle of bloodied clothes.

Silver Brassaurd had wandered the road half the night, trying to figure a way out, to keep clear of Everette Hutch. He came down to Breau's store at two the next afternoon, and bought a pint of milk.

"Oh," Mrs. Breau told him, "did you hear? The police was wanting to talk to you – they just put out a bulletin – I just heard it on the radio – wanted to talk to Everette Hutch and Silver Brassaurd. I wonder what that is about?"

He looked at her and said, "Ya, that's about Mr. Jessop's prize pig –"

"Oh," she said.

"Ya – that's what that's about – someone wanted to steal her – we was just foolin."

But he was shaking, and when people again started to arrive and look at him over their shoulders, he went outside and stood in the parking lot with his hands in his pockets, muttering to himself.

Finally he asked the milkman to give him a drive down to the top of the church lane. He stood in the same spot in the white truck as Tom had stood in July, as the milkman, his face solemn and ashen, drove him. But when the milkman made a stop, Silver jumped out and ran into the woods, on the other side of the Jessops' corn field.

He walked deep into the woods, and later police were able to discover that he had cut up some boughs, improvising a lean-to.

As it got later in the day, people passed each other and stopped their cars to talk. Old enemies became enthusiastic pitchmen for each other. Each rumour caused the one before to disappear or to reappear with new traces and lines.

It was reported that Silver was seen at the airport in Chatham and the restaurant in Loggieville, that he had killed an old woman in Neguac, and that he was in Fredericton already in custody.

But no one, in fact, saw him for most of the day.

At five o'clock he appeared at the church and spoke to someone, no one remembered who, asking if they had seen Madonna. He asked if he could go in and pray to the Virgin Mary because he wanted to say something to her, give her a piece of his mind.

But the church was locked. Snow was falling heavily and blurred the shoreline, and the trees lay solid and still, all the way back the church lane.

"That is what the church does – oh yes – it locks me out," he said. "It only picks certain people and it would never pick me!"

"You can pray at any time, anywhere," he was told.

Everyone who saw him that day had in retrospect a kind of grave sympathy for him. They remembered his upbringing, his time in Centrecare. They only asked him, as a favour to himself, to go to the police.

When it got dark he found himself at Arron Brook. He made his way towards the back of his house, came in through the clothesline window, and decided to pack and go away.

Madonna was not home. He looked in her room, and saw that her small blue suitcase had been packed but was still lying open on her bed. The pen she had won for shorthand was on her dresser.

Downstairs the tree had been decorated, its lights glowing softly, and a Christmas present for him sat on the chair near the window. In the distance he thought he heard a shotgun blast.

He sat down, and stared glumly ahead of him. The bennies finally wearing down, his head nodded and he drifted off in anxious sleep. He woke with the lights of a police car in his yard and two constables getting out with their pistols drawn.

"She told," he thought, and jumping up ran to the clothesline window and made it around the side of his house. He hadn't had time to bring his coat, and was wearing an old pair of leather slippers instead of boots.

He crossed the field towards the Donnerel property, every now and then stumbling, putting his leather slippers back on, tears flooding his face.

The trees were gloomy and dark by Arron Brook. And he turned and saw in the distance Constable Matchett shining her light on his tracks.

"He's gone up towards the brook," Constable Matchett said.

He made his way past Guillaume Brassaurd's grave, slipping and sliding over the ice-covered boulders. His hands were raw, his face in torment, while snow lashed his eyes.

"He's following the brook!" he heard one of them yell.

He came up to the bridge.

He climbed under the wooden structure and hid for a moment before his legs gave way and he fell, flat on his back.

"Billy goat gruff," he said, remembering a story from his childhood.

Then he moved onto the road and ran towards the Jessops' corn field. He decided to go back to his camp and hide for the night.

The thing about this, as Bobby Taylor remembered, on June 19, 1994, was that Constable Matchett and Constable Foley were not talking about or chasing Silver Brassaurd.

They were talking about and chasing Everette Hutch, whom they had spied pointing Madonna's shotgun, against the side window of the house, at Silver Brassaurd's head.

They had drawn their guns to protect him.

That night of December 19, Everette had waited for his money, thinking of how well he had planned his life. But nothing happened at all. So, never minding Madonna's ultimatum, he first went down to see Michael, who wasn't there. He turned and went into the woods. Then he visited Gail's shack at midnight. The money was gone. The shack was empty and still.

He thought that Madonna had betrayed him by telling Silver to bring the money to her. For a while he did not want to think this, but vicious paranoia took hold of him.

"We'll see – that bitch," he said. He could feel both his eyes and his body turn to lead. And it excited him.

He was the swirling centre, the black hole where all the debris, the planets and moons, like Madonna and Silver and Michael Skid, teetered and wobbled in their orbits, and were being sucked into. And this is exactly what all of them had sensed from the moment they had met him thirteen months before.

He went and woke Madonna in the early morning, hauling

her by the hair down the stairs, so that her head hit all the steps, and he dragged her into the kitchen where she lay prostrate in front of his thick boots.

"Where is he?" he asked.

Madonna said she didn't know.

He grimly smiled and slapped her face.

"You won't get away with this – either of you."

Then looking into the closet he took her shotgun. He loaded it and put it against her head.

"This is for them," he said. "Michael and Silver. And then I'll come back for you, you tight quiff."

"Don't kill anyone," she smiled, as sweetly as a child. "Don't kill them," she whispered, giggling slightly and touching his face. Then her eyes turned to captivate him in a glance and she lay back seductively, as she pulled at his zipper. Her eyes were as warm as the sun upon him, and she whispered, "Come inside me – get me pregnant and we will go away."

And she hauled her pyjamas down for him and took his hand to fondle her. He was mesmerized by the beauty of her body, her breasts, the hair between her legs. For her, it was so easy.

Afterwards he left the house.

He grinned selfishly, which is always hard to look upon.

"I ripped off a good piece of cunt," he said. He took the shotgun.

"Neither of them will be alive tomorrow," he said. "And, if you want to live, you meet me at Donnerel's farm by six o'clock tonight."

Madonna sat up on a kitchen chair, her hands between her knees, and couldn't bear to look at him again. Everette never understood the meaning of a difference between good and evil.

For two or three hours she stared at the telephone. Twice in that time she picked up the phone, to call Laura McNair and tell everything, and twice she put it down again.

Finally, in the afternoon, the snow fell. And Madonna's tears started. They flowed hotly down her cheeks, from those desperate beautiful eyes, because she had suddenly seen a vision of her own human triumph and despair.

"Jesus, please forgive me," she said.

She fell on her knees and blessed herself. She said a Hail Mary.

She looked at the house, the wallpaper she had started to put up, the new skirt she had bought for her course, still sitting on the chair in the living room. She smelled bread, and heard the ticking clock.

She went upstairs and got the decorations for the tree, brought them down from the attic, and standing on a chair put on the lights, icicles, the small bulbs. Finally finding the star she managed to place it high above her.

She smiled, kissed her rosary, and left it dangling on a branch.

She knew that Everette would kill Silver and Michael Skid with her shotgun. She knew and she had prayed, and had finally given herself to him so he would not.

Now, it had happened and she had lost power over him.

She went out into the dark and the bitter snow.

THREE

Bobby Taylor looked at the June day, the trees in lime-green bloom, and children walking in shorts to the playground. In formation they walked as clean and wonderful as children should be, in hope and love, with no boots or water hoses or beaten heads.

Bobby Taylor was thinking of these events, because information had come this morning about the other person in the case. So he supposed the case was closed, and that everyone now – even Laura McNair – could find some peace or reconciliation.

For that was the only thing anyone ever wanted.

He had a letter to write, for he had promised, and he sat down to write it.

He thought of Madonna, and his throat filled, after all these twenty years, because of her grace and beauty, and tears came to his eyes.

∾

Madonna had gone out on December 20, 1974, in the snow, used the path, and crossed low on Arron Brook. She came up behind Everette in the dark, and set herself upon him.

At that spot on the map ensued the fight between an unarmed girl of twenty and the vicious thug, Everette Hutch. That was verbatim how the provincial paper described the event, which shocked and sickened the entire community, and made people grow in one universal moment kind toward each other, and to those other poor dark-faced children from the swamp road.

For Madonna, this was the only gift she could give back to the Virgin she believed, in simplicity and goodness she had defiled. She managed in fact to hurt him fairly badly, so that he yelled out in fear. But finally his kicks brought her to the ground. He dragged her by her bloodied hair as he spoke about how he would kill her. Her eyes stared at the oak tree and she whispered something.

Her body was thrust against two fallen barn rafters. Her face, quiet and unworried, her eyes opened peacefully to the snow, her chest half blown away.

When the constables spotted him at the Brassaurds' house fifteen minutes later, Everette threw away the murder weapon. He ran to the brook, but not in the same direction as Silver. And his few tapes, so important to a man like him, fell into the deep, placid snow.

Everette Hutch ran to one place for shelter. Michael's farm. He believed Michael Skid was there, with the train tickets in his pocket. But no one was there, the porch door open and the summer chairs half-filled with grey-blue ice.

Michael Skid in fact had been taken into custody an hour earlier – not by the police, but by Bobby Taylor and Mr. Jessop, who came to get him for his own protection. They had led him out from the farmhouse, with a coat over his head, and a dozen people hurling insults at him and his suddenly disgraced family.

He sat in Bobby's car, with the coat still over his head, as they drove away.

Outside the farm the crowd that had gathered was still there as Everette ran past them, and everyone started chasing him.

Everette kept running towards the middle of the inlet before he was stopped by a shot to the leg from the service revolver of Deborah Matchett. Everyone cheered in amazement. A man they had feared so much, that had terrorized their community so totally, was so easily brought down by a 115-pound woman who knew how to fire a pistol. It turned out to be the only time in her career she was to fire her pistol on duty.

It got later and colder that night of December 20, 1974. The snow stopped, the frozen trees tapped, and Silver walked along the fringe of the corn field. He circled back towards his house and heard a group of men shouting about Madonna being dead and Everette being shot, and Michael Skid in custody, and that men were going down to burn the shack.

He went back towards the corn field again to go to his lean-to. He stood in the snow, and waited. Far in the distance he could see the smoke rising from the shack, and then a billow of huge flame when the moonshine was lighted.

Then, after a time hiding, and a time crying, Silver realized that he had slipped away. No one would follow him this night.

He thought of all possible ways out. And he wondered what to do. He looked up at the stars, and breathed the salt in the air. He lit a cigarette and smoked it down. He went into the corn field and stumbled towards the trees. On his way he tripped on the length of cord Tommie Donnerel had thrown away last August, tangled up by the frozen ghostly stalks. He tore it from the stalks and brought it with him.

He took his slippers and socks off, and walked barefoot in the snow.

He made sure the noose was tied and garrotted with the screwdriver so it was certain to break his neck. He blessed himself.

He faced north into a thick row of trees, just beyond the corn field, his hands at his side.

There were thirty-five dollars in his pocket and an address where he could buy a second-hand bicycle for Madonna.

At least that is what those people who found his frozen body maintained.

After that, all the hurrying was over. By 11:15 Michael sat in the police station giving his statement. The bag of clothes was tagged as evidence. The bag of mescaline was also, and so was the money, and by the next afternoon so were Everette Hutch's tapes.

Constable Delano kept his head down, staring at certain notes as Michael spoke.

Michael said that, although it was Everette's idea to sell the mescaline, he had gone along with it. That he had capped it in his barn. That, once, he'd had to convince both Silver and Madonna to go through with it. That though he didn't know bad mescaline was sold, it was sold from his sailboat to make up for a debt. That he had dragged Karrie into the very group that was ultimately responsible for her death. And that the bloody clothes, proof of Tom's innocence, were something he would have been willing to hide to protect both himself and Laura McNair. That he was ashamed of all of this and would regret it for the rest of his life.

Finally he said, "I think we should inform Laura."

"Constable Matchett has done that, I think," Delano said. "But let me check."

And he stood and left the room for a moment, as casually as if he were checking to see if someone had phoned for a taxi. Then he came in and nodded.

"Yes," he said. "Ms. McNair has been informed –" As subtle as it was, he had used *Ms.*, instead of *Miss*, as a sign of respect for Michael.

There was a deep silence as Michael sensed this, and then he felt himself smile slightly.

Now he wanted to be close to this man, and to have John Delano like him. Delano looked up from his typewriter and glanced at him in humility. He took a drag on his cigarette and offered Michael one. He stood and lit the cigarette for Michael and, looking at his lighter, spoke kindly.

"Things look bad," Delano advised, "But look to the future – think of what positive things you wanted to do in your life. Think of the respect people still have for you. I still have respect for you. What Silver did was a terrible act that he might not have been entirely responsible for, but neither are you entirely responsible for Silver. Make sure you get a good lawyer – and then – well, things have a way of working themselves out – and time will pass – you look very remorseful – *remorse* will lessen. You will look upon things more – philosophically. And you will be able in some way at some time to atone – mark my words. Anyone can start a brand-new life, not dependent on a previous life. If you knew me five years ago, you would know I am living proof of that." He smiled.

Michael held the cigarette in his mouth and breathed the smoke into his lungs.

They informed him they would take him to the jail overnight, and handcuffed him in order to facilitate the transfer.

FOUR

The prosecutor's office, feeling that they had been duped the first time, charged Michael with criminal negligence and conspiracy to traffic in illegal drugs.

The prosecutor spoke of how Madonna had fought Everette to the death while Michael ostensibly ran away.

"And how much did she weigh?" the prosecutor said. "One hundred and five pounds? – yes – so get Madonna."

And this made a tremendous impact on everyone.

"Put him away," someone shouted.

Michael had cut his hair, wore the suit he had loaned Tommie Donnerel for his parents' funeral, and sat in the dock near his lawyer. His father had taken a leave of absence.

Laura McNair didn't handle the case for the prosecution. She was under review. But once during the examination of Constable Matchett she came into the courtroom to deliver Karrie's diary to the prosecutor. Her hair was longer – her face looked a little thinner.

At that moment Everette's tapes were being played, the

mescaline shown, and a picture of *The Renegade* was up on the bulletin board, with a picture of Karrie standing on the bow.

Laura glanced over at Michael. Their eyes met for a few seconds only. Then she looked at his lawyer, Philip McSweeney, and smiled, as if at Michael's expense. She turned and quickly left the courtroom, with a movement of her skirt. It was the last time Michael would ever see her.

Professor Becker testified that he was surprised at Michael's appearance that afternoon he and Silver had visited him in Fredericton, and felt that Michael had fallen in with bad company, but because of his sense of duty tried to straighten Michael around.

Yet it was Karrie's diary which was the most damning. It was as if an investigative report had been done on him, conjured up for the papers. Her whimsical writing was matched only by the meaning of her words, which she herself did not understand.

"Michael could fly above us – but he has decided to lower hisself into the pit, just like the pit at the dump. Why? Well I think it's to pretend he has his bad side. But real men never have to do this. Only the sad cruel men he has taken up with. So I will help him get away from them – you see that's my secret summer job."

Michael came to hate that diary, and long for his own destruction.

When he stood to be sentenced he couldn't help trembling. He tried not to. His lawyer pleaded his youth, his brilliance, his potential to vindicate himself someday through good works. That is, all the usual things were said. But his journalistic talents were never mentioned.

"He forgot that a source of self-recrimination always comes tomorrow morning," the judge said.

Dora and Emmett Smith were present for the sentencing. So was old Mr. Jessop, the only kindly face in the court.

Laura McNair was not present. She couldn't stand to be. For she loved him deeply.

He received five years.

"Only five years," people whispered.

From prison he heard that Laura had lost her virginity to his lawyer, Philip McSweeney, and they were engaged to be married.

In prison he was mocked and tortured every day by the man who had stabbed Tommie Donnerel.

Michael wrote letters from prison, one to his father, and one to Nora Battersoil, asking both for forgiveness.

Nora Battersoil sent him a picture of his son, Owen. The picture had been taken the day after Michael had saved Amy and the boy's life. (This was something Nora would not know until twenty years later.)

The picture she sent him had been taken at the church picnic.

Nora informed Michael that she had loved him, but for the sake of the child thought it best to leave and hoped he would someday forgive her. "I'm so sorry and feel responsible that all of this has happened."

The picture had one more striking detail. In the background was Silver Brassaurd, who must have just left Michael's house that August afternoon. He was walking straight towards the camera, wearing the clean shirt and pants that Madonna had pressed, his hands thrust into his pockets.

The Smiths were given a fine and ordered to do community service. After this Dora developed chronic angina, so the gas bar was sold, and the little profit they had made was spent, and Emmett and she moved to an apartment in town, where Emmett took care of his invalid wife, began to drink to forget, and Dora turned very bitter towards Gail Hutch and all other people on the road.

Everette went to prison and, after seven years, his health failed. In time he became a hypochondriac, worrying the guards about his aches and pains, complained about the omission of true friendship, turned feeble, had a local writer write his life story, and forever needed to see a doctor.

Tommie Donnerel was released on December 29, 1974. His neighbours wanted to throw him a party, offered to rebuild his house, and waited for him until well after New Year's Eve, but he never arrived. He moved to Saint John instead and became apprenticed to a mason, working in mortar and brick, and for some years looked at Saint John, from the south end to the new waterfront, as a place that he himself helped design. He received fifteen thousand dollars as compensation.

He grew strong and read much and took night courses at the university and began to write. Never, as long as he lived, did he strike another human being.

Each year during the picnic he instructed Bobby Taylor to put flowers on Karrie Smith's lonely, solitary grave.

But no one from downriver would see him at his old home again. Except, of course, for once.

One summer day, four years after the murders, a sailboat was seen at the mouth of the inlet. Off in the distance the gas bar sat empty, ready to be bulldozed away for the new highway the Conservative government had promised.

The sailboat had been refitted: its prow looked majestic, its sails fluttered, the new spinnaker rustled as it took the sea and went towards one of the inland islands.

At the wheel was a man standing barefoot and in shorts, his body muscular and suntanned, a small tattoo on his arm. His eyes blazed. On the north bay all knew him, but near the islands on the south bay he was known only as the man who had gotten out of jail that spring. His family still loved and hoped for him, but were, because of him, outcasts from the town, and he felt he had let his family, his parents, the fragmented aunts and uncles, who had once considered him a darling, down.

The day was blowy and very warm. He had spent the last three months fitting his sailboat out. But then at the roughest point off Fox Island – an island filled with grey dunes and long sharp whip grass – the man scuttled the proud boat, called *The Renegade*, and made his way to shore.

There he sat in the sun on his haunches and waited for night to come. He took from his waterproof bag a picture of his son, Owen. He looked at it, kissed it, and placed it carefully away. He looked for his passport, and the fourteen thousand dollars given over to him from his father's trust.

When night came with stars in the large heaven, and when he could see the lights of Burnt Church in the distance, he looked up at the sky and said: "This is the decision for the rest of my life. If I make it to land I will live, if I drown I drown – either way makes no difference to me now."

And with that Michael Skid entered the sea and swam. He was a very strong swimmer, but it was a dark, salty, cold bay.

Nora Battersoil married.

She met her husband in May of 1980 on bus number 11, travelling from the south end of Saint John to work. She was looking at him through the window, at the bus stop near Queen's Park. When he boarded the bus he pulled out his copy of Robert Frost, and leaning his head back began to read, as a man who knows how to read, and what it is he is reading, will do.

"I'm glad you like the book – I'm glad I sent it to you," she said. He turned quickly about and saw a woman with short black hair sitting with a ten-year-old boy.

The man was Tommie Donnerel.

And that was how their life together started.

They married and lived near Hampton, for many years, where Tom worked on their farm and mended clutch plates for tractors, and Nora taught school.

His adopted son, Owen, would phone the customer and say, "I am to inform you your clutch is fixed."

Tom taught the boy how to fish and hunt, the grand importance of books, the meaninglessness of fame or material wealth. And both loved Nora.

Their corn field overlooked the Kennebecasis River, and behind them deer moved through the apple grove in the wood. Each night Tom would spend an hour alone, working in solitude at the edge of the field where he had a blueberry crop. Twice a month he visited the prison at Dorchester to give words of hope to prisoners.

By the age of forty-four he was grey, but stood erect at five-eleven. Tom Donnerel loved community-centre dances, and playing horseshoes. He suffered from pain in his left lung, and from insomnia. At times a great melancholy would overcome him because of the way his adopted son smiled, or spoke, and he would remember the boy's father, and all the potential of his wasted life.

It was known that people felt Tom strange and aloof. He seemed content, yet had few friends. And at the happiest moments he would look at Nora, and tears would flood his eyes.

Bobby Taylor reflected on all of this as he sat in the janitor's back room of the school and smoked his cigarette. He wanted to write his letter to Tom Donnerel and Nora Battersoil very carefully, and wanted to sound wise. It had been twenty years since he had seen them.

He wrote about his own wife, Joyce, and joked that, though he still loved her, there was more of her to love every year.

"The yield is greater as the years go by, and the poor thing now has more arse than picnic seat."

This led him to talk about the picnic, and how he was taking orders from Gail Hutch, who was organizing it this year.

"Like a little sergeant major – she's got us all toeing the line –"

He wrote of Gail Hutch, who had married Bobby's brother, the farrier, late in 1975, and had three more children. The prettiest and brightest on the road was her daughter Sarah. Brian was now out west working.

He said that the graves of Karrie and Madonna, of Vincent and Silver, were being tended to – and flowers placed on them at regular intervals.

He wrote that there was not a day that went by that he and many others did not think of Karrie. (This was somewhat of a lie.)

He then said he had some important news that Laura McNair, of the firm of McSweeney and McNair, had just delivered to him and his wife through an RCMP officer who now lived in Taylorville – Sergeant John Delano.

It was about a man, somewhere in Colombia, who collected exotic birds and fish and butterflies for the markets in the U.S. and Canada, and who helped relocate abandoned or destitute children to homes in North America.

This man lived by himself as a celibate. Once a week he would walk into the village to buy pipe tobacco at the store, where he was looked upon as a great oddity. Yet a month or so ago he awoke to hear about an argument in the village.

A group of men had come into the community accusing the village of informing on their cocaine trade. They dragged the mayor out of his house, and the mayor's wife and little boy. They made them kneel, by the brook.

The man lived a good mile away, kept to himself in this most dangerous area, and though people maintained he had always thought "a good deal about himself and how clever he was – and loved to argue about the world, when he drank – he was in no danger whatsoever, as long as he stayed to himself."

But told what was happening, by a small girl who helped clean for him, he said, "Those sons of bitches, never again."

He grabbed a machete and went down to stop it. Always, they said there was this hot and ruthless side to his nature tempered by his idea of justice.

He was dressed in a ragged white shirt, and his beard was long and greying. When he came along the road he saw that some of the horses had been killed. He looked up at the sun, and took a run at the well-armed men.

But he forgot how old he had grown. They took his machete in a second.

He spoke as well as he could. He appealed to them to leave the village alone. He was a great debater. Everyone thought he had convinced them.

But then they laughed, and finding out he was without a woman, put *la barra de labios* on him – I guess it is lipstick. They then put some – *la lenceria* – on him to wear – I guess it is like girl's underwear. They paraded him about like this. So the towns-people could laugh at him. He was given a trial with all of them laughing at him, and some of the townspeople joining in – for often those whom you try to protect are those who betray you. They went and got a rat to act as judge.

The leader of the men who'd invaded the town looked bored and upset, and kept swatting flies with his hand. As all men of power he mimicked power, swinging a knotted stick in his hand.

"I thought it would end in a much better place." Michael smiled. "I was going to go back home, tomorrow."

Then at the end he proudly yelled out the name of Madonna, which surprised people because he had always argued against the blackmail of religious dogma.

He was shot, in the back of the head, just as the mayor's family had been, and left to die, for the villagers were too frightened to offer help.

He fell face down in the stream – called "Ah-ron" by the locals. His body was set afire to destroy the evidence. The rat, as judge, was shot, as well.

But one piece of identification remained. Someone rifling through his shack found under the floorboards a picture of his son, the date, and the name of the country.

The ambassador was informed in May. A computer search was undertaken. His parents were both dead. He had no living relatives – except a son out of wedlock. External Affairs in Ottawa wrote to the Department of Vital Statistics in Fredericton. His name was discovered.

Laura McNair was informed of this by her chronically unfaithful husband. This information struck her very hard. For she thought the man had already been dead for fifteen years.

"His name was Michael Skid. Those townspeople who stole his wallet and rings, rifled through and burned his shack, were never brought to justice –"

It struck Tom Donnerel and Nora Battersoil hard as well. It took them a week to tell Owen what had happened. At first he seemed unconcerned about it: "I'm sorry. It is terrible – but I didn't know him –"

But as time went on he became solemn, whenever it was spoken about, and on more than one occasion was seen in the den looking for old pictures.

"He has died," he said one night, when he found a picture of Michael Skid from the summer of 1974. "He is gone."

There was a few months of red tape before the remains of Michael Skid were brought back home.

The funeral was attended by Bobby and Joyce Taylor, by Gail (Hutch) Taylor, her children, by Laura McNair, Sergeant John

Delano, Amy (Battersoil) Holstein, Tom Donnerel and Nora Battersoil and their son, Owen, who was now doing his master's in history at UNB.

Owen found himself attracted to Gail Hutch's oldest girl – Sarah – now eighteen, starting her first year of university. While the older people were at the grave they managed only to think of life, and walked along the August path, talking about what courses she should take, Owen saying that he would help her when she arrived in the city at the end of the month.

They walked down to the shore and Owen was happy and talkative. But suddenly at the rocky red cliff near the path, where Michael had once liked to come to read, Owen heard an echo, felt in his heart a deep overwhelming presence in the sunlight, and in grief began to cry.

"They murdered him –" he said.

"Here," Sarah Taylor said, holding him as a mother does a child. "Have no fear – and I'll give you a hug." And she reached up, in the promise of young womanhood, and bravely – quite bravely – kissed his startled eyes.

The body of Mr. Skid was laid to rest very close to the grave of Madonna Brassaurd.

BOOKS BY DAVID ADAMS RICHARDS

FICTION

The Coming of Winter 1974
Blood Ties 1976
Dancers at Night (short stories) 1978
Lives of Short Duration 1981
Road to the Stilt House 1985
Nights Below Station Street 1988
Evening Snow Will Bring Such Peace 1990
For Those Who Hunt the Wounded Down 1993
Hope in the Desperate Hour 1996
The Bay of Love and Sorrows 1998

NON-FICTION

A Lad from Brantford, & Other Essays 1994
Hockey Dreams: Memories of a Man Who Couldn't Play 1996
Lines on the Water: A Fisherman's Life on the Miramichi 1998